Secrets and Spells
Witches of Crescent Cape
Book 1

L. Danvers

Cover Design by Melody Simmons

Copyright

This is a work of fiction. Similarities to real people, places, or events are entirely coincidental.

SECRETS AND SPELLS

First edition. February 12, 2021.

Copyright © 2021 L. Danvers.

Written by L. Danvers.

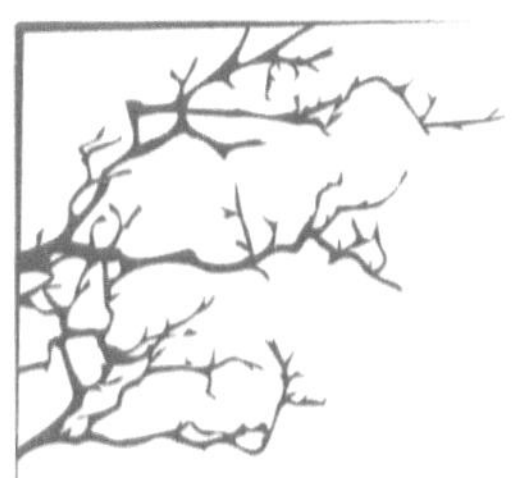

Grace

A breeze swept past as I fired off a text to my twin brother, making wisps of blonde curls slap against my stinging cheeks. "Come on," Xander called out, tearing me from my thoughts. My lips pressed into a hard line as I lifted my chin and waited for my eyes to adjust. We were blanketed by a velvet sky, and were it not for the hazy yellow glow of the porchlight up ahead, I doubt I would have spotted him. Finding our surroundings particularly eerie, I took in a sharp breath. The crisp October air filled my lungs, carrying with it the scents of wet earth and pine. Scents that I would have found comforting and reminiscent of better days were it not for what we were about to do.

Realizing Xander was already paces ahead, I stuffed my phone in my pocket and zipped up my black biker jacket. I hurried along the sidewalk, the heels of my boots clicking on the cobblestones as I caught up to him.

As I approached, I felt a slight quiver in the pit of my stomach. My gaze flitted about. We were miles away from the nearest city, somewhere in upstate New York. I couldn't shake the feeling that something was very wrong here. "This doesn't look right," I muttered as we neared the faded green Victorian house. "Why didn't you just let me do a tracking spell?"

"Pshhh," Xander quipped with a flourish of his hand. "Who needs a tracking spell when you have an address?" Picking up on my unease, he added, "Relax, Grace. I did my research. Isla was married to a faerie once. If anyone has access to faerie dust, it's her."

I hugged my arms tighter around myself. I hoped he was right. Xander and I had been searching for faerie dust for four years. All the faeries had left this realm ages ago, so it was a hard item to come by. But Xander believed this latest lead could be the answer to *everything*. I wanted to believe him, but I had learned not to get my hopes up.

So here we were, showing up unannounced at a witch's doorstep. What could go wrong?

Between Xander being a vampire and me being a witch myself, we had no reason to be scared. We were more than capable of taking care of ourselves. But still, something felt off here...

As we climbed the brick steps, I rested my hands on one of the columns that punctuated the wraparound porch. But I quickly pulled it away as a spider skirted across it. After a couple of shakes, my hand settled on the back of my neck. I rubbed it mindlessly as I focused on the peach-colored door. *This feeling is nothing*, I told myself. *You just don't want to get your hopes up. That's all.*

"Are you going to ring, or what?" Exasperated, Xander brushed past me and pressed the doorbell. But it didn't do anything. The house was old. I figured it must have been broken. So, coming to the same conclusion as I had, he gave the brass knocker a couple of raps. His ears perked as he used his heightened hearing to eavesdrop on what was going on inside.

"I don't think anyone's home," I said plainly as I came up to stand beside him.

In an instant, he turned to me and pressed his finger against my lips, silencing me.

I swatted his hand away. "You have boundary issues, you know that?"

He offered me a smirk.

"Isla!" he called out. He cupped his hands around his mouth, making his voice thunder as his back arched. A flash of lightning split the sky, and by the time he'd finished calling out her name, thunder cracked overhead. Rain pummeled from the sky, the heavy drops drumming on the cover above. I rubbed my hands together as a shiver rushed through me. But Xander wasn't fazed. "You have company!" he continued. "Be a nice witch and open the door, won't you?"

There was no answer.

"Maybe she's waiting for you to say please," I offered sarcastically.

Ignoring me, Xander tried the knob. Surprisingly, it was unlocked. He glanced over at me, a mischievous grin dancing on his lips. Unfortunately, though, the handle was stuck. So, with a powerful thrust from his shoulder, he forced the door open. I had to admit—there were perks to being friends with a vampire. "Showoff," I teased.

"Jealous, much?" He winked at me.

"Of you? Never."

"Are you ready for this?"

I nodded. "Let's do this thing."

Xander led the way into the dark, wallpapered entryway. The place smelled of just-blown-out matches and old books.

Brushing his dark hair away from his face, Xander strode forward searching for the switch. But then he stopped short.

"What are you doing?" I huffed as I bumped into his muscular back. I rubbed my forehead, which was now throbbing. It was easy to forget how strong vampires were until you slammed into one.

The yellow overhead lights flickered on, making the dust particles in the air shimmer and upping the creepiness factor by a thousand. When the lights finally stayed on, the broken porcelain vase shattered across the floor came into view. As I scanned the room, my expression sobered. There were overturned bookshelves, a dining chair strewn across the floor and a half-eaten slice of pizza still sitting on the table. And yet, no one was home.

A muscle in Xander's jaw tensed. "Looks like someone else got to her first."

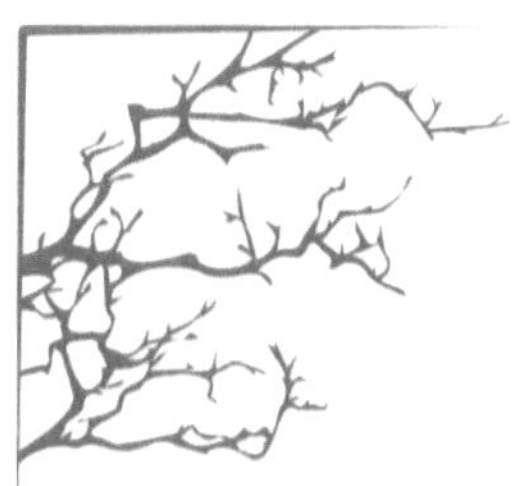

Grace

Xander stepped over the vase and edged toward the staircase. He rested his palm on the wooden banister and stilled.

"Do you smell any blood?" I asked, lowering my voice to a near whisper.

Nostrils flaring, he inhaled deeply. "No."

"And you're sure we're at the right house?"

"Yes," he said, eyes tightening. "Believe it or not, Grace, I'm perfectly capable of reading a map."

I tilted my head and shook it. With a knowing raise of my eyebrows, I pointed out, "You used your phone's GPS, hotshot."

He shrugged. "Same thing."

Despite the worry gnawing at my insides, I followed Xander up the creaky stairs. Thunder rattled so hard it made the entire house shake, only adding to my unease. And by the time we reached the top of the stairwell, tingles were racing along my skin. It wasn't just my mind playing tricks on me, though. I could *feel* the residue of magical energy. What on earth had happened here?

Xander pushed a bedroom door open, and I craned my neck to peer inside. Unlike the rest of the house, the room was pristine—with the exception of the crocheted blanket casually draped across the corner of the bed. While I closed the door behind us, Xander stalked the perimeter of the mauve bedroom, picking up photographs and trinkets along the way. The place was perfectly ordinary—aside, perhaps, from the ungodly amount of perfume bottles lined up neatly on the makeup vanity.

There were no magical objects in sight. And, more importantly, I didn't see—or sense—any sign of faerie dust.

I could feel tears beginning to collect in my eyes, and I hurried toward the window, not wanting Xander to see me upset. I blinked them away as I folded my arms across my chest, thinking of how we ended up here.

You see, when the boundaries to the veiled kingdoms across the globe fell, the existence of vampires, werewolves and witches were revealed to the world. War broke out between humans and supernaturals. And after Xander's older brother, Julian, was exposed, he and my best friend, Danielle, fled to Oasis, a realm created by the faerie Aurora. His sister, Charlotte, had gone with them.

The only problem? As part of the deal with Aurora, the portal was sealed behind them. Which meant we couldn't get in—and they couldn't get out.

But now that the war was over, Xander and I were determined to find a way to *unseal* it.

We'd hit one dead-end after another. But Xander had finally tracked down a witch who had been rumored to have been married to faerie a long time ago. It was a long shot, but it was our best chance at getting our hands on faerie dust—the key ingredient we needed for me to perform the spell to get that portal open.

But there was no faerie dust here—and Isla was long gone. I wondered what had happened here...

Finally, Xander came up behind me. Handing a framed photograph to me, he said, "How about you do tracking spell on Isla?"

Something had clearly happened here earlier. If I had to guess, Isla had been taken. Tracking her was the logical—and right—thing to do. Maybe we could help her. And if we did, maybe she could help us in return. Even if she didn't have faerie dust, perhaps she knew where we could get our hands on some.

I took the picture and placed my palm on top of it. Closing my eyes, I uttered the spell that had become second-nature to me now.

But nothing happened.

Forcing down the lump in my throat, I handed it back to him, shaking my head.

"She's dead?" he asked knowingly. "She *can't* be dead." He looked around in shock before curling his arms over his head. "She can't be," he whispered to himself.

Suddenly, he began to pace, giving off a manic sort of energy.

"Xander," I said in as steady of a voice as possible, hoping I could calm him. But he wasn't listening.

Desperate, Xander tore the room apart, searching for any sign of faerie dust the witch might have had tucked away. I did my best to help, but it was clear that if there *had* been any faerie dust here, it was long gone now. I would have felt its energy. And anyway, faeries were intoxicating to vampires. And faerie dust was made of the remains of faeries—well, the remains of their magic left behind after they passed. If there was faerie dust here, he would have been drawn to it. But now wasn't the time to point that out to him. I knew him better than that.

Xander and I had a long history together. I'd hated him once—despised him, actually. He could be cocky and downright arrogant, and over the centuries, he'd learned his rather charming looks could help him get away with just about anything—a trait which I found infuriating. But despite his faults and our extremely rocky start, over time we'd learned we made a good team. And with Danielle gone, he was my closest friend. Well, him and his sort-of uncle, Ben. But Ben was much older and had become more of a father-figure as of late.

As for me and Xander, we bickered constantly. Four years of working together hadn't changed that. But when push came to shove, we always had each other's backs.

Plus, we *had* to work together if we had any chance of getting our loved ones back.

I knew that's what this was about. It wasn't about Isla or the faerie dust. It was about hitting yet *another* dead end.

Growling in frustration, Xander picked up the bench to the makeup vanity set and heaved it across the room, making the furniture shatter.

I flinched instinctively, protecting my face with my arms. I knew he was upset. I was, too. But succumbing to our emotions wouldn't do us any good. We needed to keep ourselves in check if we had any hope of getting that portal open one day.

"Xander, it's okay," I said, trying to assure him. "We'll find another way."

"*Another way?*" he snapped. I stepped back, not liking this side of him. "Grace, it's been *years*. We've been looking for people with connections to faeries for *years*. Isla was our last option. And she's dead. Which means I'm never getting my brother and sister back. And you're never going to see Danielle again. We might as well accept that."

Growing agitated, I planted my hands on my hips. "I don't get it. There's plenty of time to get them back." I shook my head in disgust. "So, what? You're going to give up? Isn't four years just a blink of an eye to you? You're *immortal*."

"You're not," he reminded me, his gaze burning with such intensity that I felt my pulse quicken.

"I don't care if it takes fifty years," I said, steeling my resolve. "I'm going to figure out a way to get that portal open."

"At what cost?"

I shrugged ambivalently, which only seemed to upset him more.

He dragged his hands through his dark hair. "You're missing out on your life, Grace. Danielle doesn't want you wasting your life trying to save hers. What are you trying to prove?"

My jaw set.

He knew he'd gone too far.

He squeezed his eyes shut, and I could see the muscles in his face relax. Closing the distance between us, he peered down at me, his deep brown eyes tormented by emotions I was struggling to decipher. "Can't we take a break? For a few months? That's all I'm asking. All we've done is chase lead after lead, and they've all led to nowhere. You've almost been killed twice. And I'm getting tired of the never-ending disappointment. Aren't you?"

He offered me his hand, but I refused to take it. "You're being selfish," I hissed.

"You deserve more than this out of life," he said sincerely.

Eyes narrowed, I lifted my chin. "I am not giving up on them. Don't you want your family back?" I was so mad I was shaking. I was just as frustrated as he was. But that frustration only firmed my resolve. I couldn't believe he was suggesting that we take a break. The more time we wasted, the more time my best friend and two of his siblings spent trapped in another realm. *What was wrong with him?* "I know this is your thing, Xander," I said, practically shouting now. But I didn't care. Flames of anger shot through me, and I couldn't bite my tongue. "I know you run away when things get tough. So, is that what this is about? Is that what's happening now? Are you just going to give up and leave me to finish the job myself?"

"Quiet," he said abruptly.

"*Excuse me?*" My pulse was slamming in my neck now—not ideal when you're alone with a vampire. But I knew he wouldn't hurt me.

I was about to tell him off, but in a flash, he was behind me, cupping my mouth with his hand.

"No," he whispered, his breath tickling my ear. "I mean we're not alone."

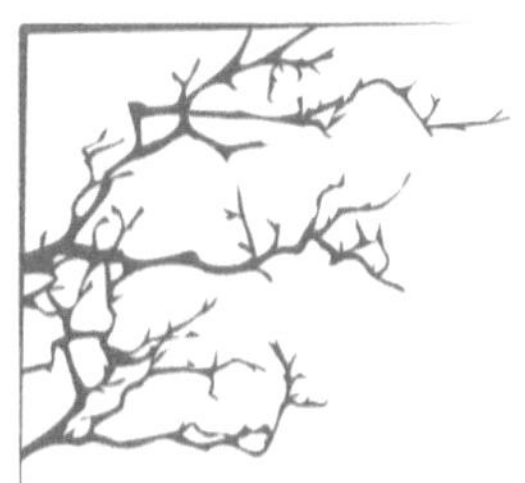

Grace

Xander released me from his hold, and we exchanged knowing glances. My chest tightened as I listened to the sounds below. He was right. Hurried footsteps could be heard clomping around, growing louder by the second. Someone was coming upstairs.

Maybe we'd be lucky and it'd be a neighbor or someone checking on Isla. Xander could compel them to go home and forget they were ever here. Easy.

I'd almost started to believe my wishful theory, but then the door burst open, and a petite yet terrifyingly fearsome woman appeared in the doorway. Her long, dark hair was pulled into a tight ponytail, revealing scars on her neck. My eyes flicked toward Xander. Those were bite marks.

With a satisfied smirk, her eyebrow lifted. "Grace and Xander, I presume?" The iciness in her tone sent chills down my spine. How did she know who we were? We were hours away from Quarter Square, and even there, we'd kept a low profile...

Not waiting to find out, Xander lunged toward the stranger, but she held up her hand and tightened her fist. She advanced toward him, her hips swishing in a confident stride. She muttered a spell, using her powers to strangle him. Xander let out a sharp gasp, and his hands clawed at his throat. His knees gave out, and he buckled to the floor.

Memories of the last time I'd seen that spell used on him flooded back to me, bringing up a time in my life I'd do anything to forget. "Stop it!" I shouted, trying to draw the mysterious witch's attention to me. But she only chuckled.

I was *not* about to let her hurt Xander. We may have been in the middle of a fight, but that's what friends did—they fought and made up. The truth was, he was one of the few people left in this world keeping me grounded.

Gathering my strength, I widened my stance. My arms were outstretched to my sides. Magic pulsed through me, and I could feel its energy dancing along my fingertips. Staring the witch dead-on, I recited a spell, too. I didn't want to kill her. I wanted *answers*. And it was hard to get answers from a dead woman.

My gaze flicked to the window. At my command, violent winds rushed inside the bedroom. The lights flickered overhead as a rush of soggy leaves swirled around us. Perfume bottles, photographs and pillows spun up around the room. And between the rattling of objects and the crackling thunder outside, it was hard to hear myself think.

Using the distraction to his advantage, Xander wrestled free from the witch's magical hold. He spun on his heel, and he uncorked his rage. The objects swirling around the room came to a sudden halt and clanged to the floor. Not taking his eyes off his target, Xander's chest swelled. With a curl of his lip, he revealed his sharp fangs. He wouldn't drink from her. Witch's blood made vampires violently ill. But he had enough time to rip her throat out before the symptoms set in.

With a sinister gleam in his eye, he lunged toward her. He was mid-air, arms outstretched to grasp her, when she recited a spell that made him freeze in place. The woman tilted her head back and laughed in amusement. Then she swiftly snapped his neck. He collapsed onto the fraying carpet.

Horrified, a primal scream escaped from my lungs, echoing out into the night. I took a step back, mind reeling as I worked out a plan. Xander was incapacitated—and if she could do that to *him,* who knew what she was capable of doing to me? I wanted to run to his side. To hug him and tell him I was sorry for arguing with him earlier. To tell him that he was one of my closest friends and that I knew that in his own way, he had only been trying to look out for me. But I didn't dare move. My heartbeat was thrashing in my ears, and all I could think about was one burning question: *why*? "Why did you do that?" I asked, voice trembling. "Who are you?"

The woman's eyes sparkled with amusement as her mouth curved into a satisfied smile. Ignoring my question, she snapped her fingers, and two men entered the bedroom. "You sure we can't just kill him, Sofia?" the burlier of the two asked.

Disinterested, she smoothed down her lacy black top and plucked a leaf out of her hair. "No, he has plans for the Blood Heir, remember?"

"Who does?" I asked. I tried my best to sound assertive, but my voice came out shaky and uncertain. It didn't matter. I might as well have been talking to myself. No one bothered to respond.

Following Sofia's orders, the men flung Xander's arms over their shoulders and carried him out into the hall. The tips of Xander's shoes scraped across the carpet behind him, then *thump thump thumped* as the men dragged him down the stairs.

"What are you doing with him?" I demanded. Xander and I had run into our fair share of trouble in recent years, but nothing *this* bad. Had these people been following us? And if so, what did they want?

The witch's green eyes narrowed, and she stalked toward me. She held her chin high as she gave me the once over, sizing me up. "That's none of your concern, little witch."

Everything in me wanted to fight, but this Sofia woman had just taken out a Blood Heir—one of the world's original vampires. How could I ever hope to take her on myself?

I wished there was someone I could call for help. The police were out of the question. After the war, it became illegal to openly use magic. And yet, there was only so much the authorities could do about it. If anything, I'd only be putting them at risk.

I could call Ben, maybe? He was Xander's uncle... or descendent, technically. He would *want* to help, but he was a human. He had his magical objects, but I wasn't sure they'd be enough to take Sofia down. And anyway, he was back in Maine. I needed help *now*.

And then there was Xander's brother, Aiden. He was a former vampire (long story). *He* had to have some supernatural connections. Maybe he knew someone in New York who could get here quickly...

Despite knowing it was futile, I reached for my pocket. But Sofia shot me daggers with a look.

Heart pounding, I swallowed. "Are you going to kill me?"

"No, Grace." Sofia's mouth twisted in amusement. She placed her strong hand against my cheek, making me recoil. "You're far too important for that."

"Important to whom?" I demanded.

"You have a vital role to play in the plan. But not yet." Not offering any further explanation, the witch retrieved a vial from her back pocket. Before I had the chance to ask her what it was, she dumped its contents—some sort of white powder—in her hand and blew it in my face.

I coughed uncontrollably at first, fanning away the gritty substance. But when the dust settled, I felt fine. Not just fine. *Relaxed.* "What's going on?" I blinked.

"Vampires aren't the only ones who can alter people's memories," she said matter-of-factly.

What was she talking about? "That's impossible." Could that powder alter my mind? Now that she mentioned it, my head did feel a little fuzzy.

She gripped my jaw between her long fingers and jerked my head, forcing me to look her in the eye. I tried to pull away, but Sofia was strong. Not just magically, but physically, too.

"Grace?" she asked. And for some reason, I couldn't help but nod in response. She flashed a wicked smile. "Grace, you are going to forget that you are a witch. You are going to forget everything you know about the supernatural world. You are not going to look into your past. You are going to live a quiet life in Amber Falls. You're a perfectly mediocre human. And that's all you need to know." She studied me for a bit, curious as to whether the mind-altering powder had worked. "Now, tell me who you are."

"My name is Grace Addington," I said, pretending to be in an altered state just to mess with her. As soon as I saw that glimmer of satisfaction, I spat in her face. Whatever the consequences would be for that, they'd be worth it after what she'd done to Xander. "And your stupid powder didn't work."

My cheek was promptly met with a strike from the back of her hand.

Face burning, I stretched out my jaw. No longer caring about getting answers, I decided to fight back. I wasn't as powerful as Sofia—I'd only come into my powers four years ago, and I was self-taught. But I was stronger than most. If I was going to go down, you'd better believe I was going to go down fighting.

I lifted my head and started casting another spell, but Sofia forcefully grabbed my face again. "One vial didn't take." She cocked her head to the side, examining me like I was some sort of lab rat in a twisted science experiment. "Interesting."

Before I had the chance to finish my spell, she blew another handful of powder in my face.

This time, I felt different. Like I'd taken a few too many antihistamines and chased them down with a bottle of gin. Everything went woozy like I was floating in a dream. Something clawed at my mind, and I tried to remember what it was. But then, the thought was gone as quickly as it had come.

Sofia went over the whole spiel again. I tried to block out her instructions, but I wasn't strong enough. And her voice seemed so soothing now. I wondered if she might be part siren...

Entranced by the rhythm of her voice, I hung on every word, nodding along as she went over her instructions.

I blinked.

Where am I? And who is this woman in front of me?

"Now," the enigmatic woman said in an authoritative tone, "tell me who you are."

Grace:
Weeks Later

"Would you like a glass of milk with that, too?" I asked, scribbling down the sweet old woman's order. The question was more of a formality. She was one of the regulars at the Sunny Side Grille, and in addition to her coffee, she always asked for a glass of milk so she could take her morning pills.

The corner of the widow's eyes crinkled, deepening her wrinkles. They were the lovely sort of wrinkles you got from a life well-lived—one filled with joy and laughter. "Yes, dear," she answered in her usual gentle tone as she fished through her light pink purse for her pill organizer. "That would be lovely."

"Sure thing, Mrs. Johnson." I headed toward the kitchen to pass along her order, smiling to myself. There was something strangely comforting about seeing her every morning. She showed up for breakfast promptly at 7:00 a.m. every day without fail. In fact, she was the first customer I ever waited on when I first landed this job. Honestly, she was the most consistent person in my life.

I handed the order off to Madison, who promptly passed it along to someone else. More interested in chitchatting than working, Madison adjusted her pink 50s-style waitress uniform. "Ugh, these things are so lame." She wasn't wrong.

Aside from being comically hideous, the material was itchy and bothered my skin. Madison propped an elbow on the counter and mindlessly curled her highlighted hair around her finger, her mind somewhere else. Finally, with a sigh, she said, "I can't wait to get all dressed up tonight."

"Uh," I started, not quite onboard for the plans Madison had in store, "about that..."

She held up a hand to silence me. "Don't even start with me, Grace Addington. Tonight is your twenty-first birthday, and we are *going* to celebrate." Her voice was getting shriller by the second. She may not have taken her job all that seriously, but you'd better believe Madison Kent took partying seriously. "We're going to find a nice bar, take way too many shots and flirt with strangers. Then we'll go dancing. And then... who knows?" She winked with her thick, spider-like lashes. "Got it?"

I pressed my lips and nodded, knowing trying to talk my way out of this was useless. Shortly after I'd started working here, Madison had invited me to go as her plus-one to one of her friend's birthday celebrations. I'd seen her in action, so I knew what to expect. I'd tried telling Madison I never made a big deal out of my birthday—I couldn't even remember doing anything for the last several of them. But when Madison made her mind up about something, there was no arguing with her. And in her head, birthdays were of the utmost importance. I didn't even like dancing, but I didn't bother objecting any further. It wasn't like I had any other plans.

Resigning myself to an evening of Madison's version of how a birthday should be celebrated, I brought Mrs. Johnson's coffee and milk out to her. By the time I did, her order was up. So, I brought her strawberry and whipped cream-topped pancakes out, too.

"So, what are you wearing tonight?" Madison called out.

Cheeks reddening, I shushed her as I headed back behind the counter.

"What's the problem? Everyone knows it's your birthday."

"And how does everyone know?"

She gave a playful shrug. "I told them, of course." Eyeing me, Madison frowned. "How do you not even care that it's your birthday? Most people are counting down the days until they turn twenty-one. It's like, the biggest, most important birthday ever."

Mrs. Johnson chuckled to herself and offered a sympathetic grin.

Playfully rolling my eyes, I shook my head and headed back behind the counter. Honestly, though, I didn't know how to answer Madison's question. I just... hadn't felt like myself lately. Weeks ago, I woke up in my apartment. My memories from the previous who-knew-how-many years were all a blur. The most recent memory I had was being with my family back in Portland. My first thought when I woke up that morning was to call my mom, but when I checked my phone, there were no contacts in it whatsoever. I must have gotten a new phone and forgotten to transfer over my contacts. Aside from the ID in my wallet—which, according to the date, had been renewed the day before—I felt like I didn't know anything about myself. After taking a very short tour of my studio apartment, I'd found a pale pink waitress uniform laid out on my couch with a name tag and *Sunny Side Grille* embroidered in the upper corner. So, I showed up for work that morning. And I'd been here ever since.

Sometimes, I thought about looking into my past. But for whatever reason, I always decided against it. Perhaps it was best not to know. I didn't know what had brought me to Amber Falls, but I'd ended up here for a reason. Even if that reason was getting up before dawn each morning and serving up pancakes to sweet old ladies.

"Well?" Madison pressed, her penciled-in eyebrows raising in expectation.

"I don't know," I said ambivalently. "There's not much worth celebrating." It was harsh but true. My life was incredibly boring. I'd been on this earth for twenty-one years, and what did I have to show for it? A boring job. An apartment that smelled like an old casserole. Not exactly celebration-worthy in my book.

Some of our other coworkers asked about the plans for the night—they were going to meet us later at a local nightclub. I forced a smile as they talked about how much they were looking forward to blowing off some steam tonight. It was what normal twenty-somethings did—go out and party after a long week of work. But that sort of thing just wasn't my scene.

Desperate for an excuse to remove myself from the conversation, I checked on some of our other patrons. Then, realizing Mrs. Johnson had finished her meal, I brought out her bill. She was ready for me, waiting with her purse in her lap. She promptly handed over a wad of bills. I was headed for the register when I realized she'd accidentally handed me *a hundred and fifty bucks*. She was usually good about paying the right amount. I worried that maybe her mind was taking a turn for the worse. It broke my heart that she didn't have anyone looking out for her...

I brought back her change—all one hundred and thirty-eight dollars and fifty-two cents. Mrs. Johnson looked mortified and grateful all at once.

When I came back later to clean up her table, I realized she'd left a generous tip, along with a sweet birthday message for me that she'd scribbled on a napkin. I smiled, making a mental note to thank her tomorrow.

I was busy scooping up her dishes when Madison came up behind me, startling me so much that I nearly dropped the ceramic mug. "Most people would have just pocketed it," she observed, referring to Mrs. Johnson's overpayment.

"I'm not going to steal from an old lady," I said, eyeing her as I tried to determine if *she* would have.

Madison shrugged carelessly. "Anyway, I'll pick you up around 8:00, okay?"

"Sounds good."

"Oh, and Grace? I promise you—we're going to make this a birthday to *remember*."

I FELT LIKE A BARBIE doll. Madison wasn't confident in my abilities to put together a proper birthday outfit, so when she dropped by my apartment to pick me up, she came prepared—with a suitcase in tow. I rummaged through the pieces of clothing, trying to find the tamest outfit I could put together—and believe me, that was not easy. I finally settled on a sequined skirt and black tank top. I hated that the tank top showed the tattoo on my shoulder, though, so I covered it up with my leather jacket. It wasn't so much that I was against tattoos. But I had no idea where it had come from. And every time I started thinking about what could have compelled me to get a tattoo, I was overcome with the urge to stop thinking about it. So, that's exactly what I did.

It was 8:45 by the time we reached Shaken & Stirred. It was the newest bar in Amber Falls, and Madison's older brother was a part-owner of the place. "So, what should I try first?" I pointed to the liquor bottles of varying colors stacked up in neat rows. They were tiered against the arched mirror, which reflected the glittering yellow tones of the chandeliers behind us.

"Actually," Madison said, half paying attention as she scanned the massive room, "I need to run to the restroom first. Go check out the drink menu, and we'll order something when I get back."

Off she went, so I found an empty seat at the bar. The place smelled of leather and beer, but that was to be expected. Feeling profoundly out of place, I fiddled with the hem of my skirt for a bit. I couldn't shake the feeling that I was being watched. Maybe I just wasn't one of those people who could confidently sit *alone*.

Looking for a distraction, I began flipping through the tabletop cocktail menu when a man slid into the seat beside me. He lifted a sausage-like finger to get the bartender's attention.

"Back for more?" the bartender asked.

"Another Budweiser," the guy answered with a nod. I caught him sliding his gaze toward me.

I flipped through the pages, trying to make myself look busy. But something about the guy's crooked smile was giving me the heebie-jeebies. *Ignore him, and he'll leave you alone. Madison will be back any minute.*

I could feel the creep giving me the once over, so I turned slightly away from him. I purposefully adjusted my top to make sure it wasn't dipping too low, not wanting to give him a show. I wished Madison would hurry up.

"Hey, blue eyes," the guy finally said, craning his head toward me and giving me a cheesy tip of his yellowed baseball cap.

I swallowed. I chose to ignore him, pretending to still be flipping through the menu.

"Are you f-f-from around here?"

Seriously? What did I need to do? Put a "not interested" stamp on my forehead?

I quickly scanned the area to see if there was another seat I could find, but they were all taken. That's what I got for coming to the most popular bar in the city. Whatever. It'd be fine. Madison would be out in a second, and then we could find some other place to go. I was sure her brother would understand.

"What's wrong?" the guy said, sliding closer toward me, even going so far as to put his hand on top of mine. He reeked of alcohol, and I was betting this wasn't his second—or even third—drink tonight. "Don't you want to talk to me?"

I snatched my hand out from under his. "No. I don't," I spat. "Leave me alone."

"Do we have a problem over here?" another man said in a raspy voice, coming up behind me. Startled by the much-appreciated interruption, I turned around. The man was looking past me, his focus solely on the creep. His striking hazel eyes were narrowed, his jaw set. Waiting for a response, he leaned his head back a bit as he stuffed his hands in the pockets of his brown leather jacket, which hugged his impressive frame. The fabric of his gray button-down lay flat against his broad chest. His shirt was tucked neatly into dark jeans. *Please tell me this isn't Madison's brother.*

"N-n-no, man," the guy said, slurring his words now. He began to sway, even though he was still sitting down. "There's no problem. This pretty little thing and I were just talking." He offered a toothy smile.

"I believe this *woman* asked you to leave her alone."

"Oh yeah?" the drunk guy said, standing up now, puffing out his chest. I noticed then that other patrons were staring at us. Great. *Totally not embarrassing.* I pressed my fingers to my brow, cheeks reddening, wishing I could turn invisible.

My rescuer lifted his chin, unblinking. His shoulders were squared, his posture strong. "Yeah."

The drunk guy shoved him. "And who do you think *you* are?"

The stranger steadied himself and smiled broadly. "Bellamy Mortimer," he said with an easy confidence about him. "One of the owners. It's time for you to leave."

The man glared at him, then looked at me with disgust. Deciding it wasn't worth the fight, he allowed Bellamy to drag him toward the security guard posted out front. I found myself releasing a huge breath, glad to be rid of that guy.

I cocked my head, watching with curiosity as Bellamy whispered something in the guard's ear. The guard nodded and took out his phone. I realized Bellamy had asked him to call the guy a cab.

Moments later, Bellamy strode back toward me, brushing his fingers through his curly brown hair as he approached. "I'm sorry about that," he said sincerely when he finally reached me. "Are you okay?"

"Yeah," I nodded—a little too eagerly. I felt like some silly schoolgirl making googly eyes at the crazy-popular jock. *Don't make it weird, Grace.* I breathed in, trying to compose myself. "I'm fine."

Just then, Madison came up to join us. She pursed her lips, her eyes sparkling with mischief.

Upon seeing her, Bellamy placed his hand on Madison's head and teasingly mussed up her hair. "Hey, kiddo."

She swatted him away. "You're three years older than me, loser," she said before pulling out her compact mirror and assessing the damage.

"Wait," I asked, "is this your brother?"

Madison cringed, letting out a laugh of relief. "Ew. No." She glanced around the room, a line forming in her brow as she realized she had no idea where her brother was.

"Nathaniel's in the back helping out." Bellamy gestured toward the double doors to the side of the bar with his thumb. "We've been slammed since we opened. Which is great, but a couple of our kitchen staff members are out sick with the flu."

"That sucks," Madison said plainly. "So," she said, swiveling in her chair as she turned her attention toward me, "I see the two of you met already..."

I tucked my hair behind my ear. "Yeah. He just saved me from some jerk."

The corners of Bellamy's hazel eyes crinkled. "It was nothing."

"Well, that's good," Madison said. "We wouldn't want anything to ruin Grace's big night."

"Big night, huh?" Bellamy's left eyebrow lifted. "What's the occasion?"

"We're celebrating Grace's twenty-first birthday. And I bet she'd just *love* it if you bought her a drink."

He smiled one of those full-face smiles, boyish and innocent for his age. Then he glanced at me for approval. I could tell that he didn't want to come across as being too forward, seeing as that he had just saved me from another guy chatting me up.

Cheeks flushing, I nodded to signal that I was okay with it. Quite frankly, I could use a drink about now.

"Well, then, birthday girl. What'll it be?"

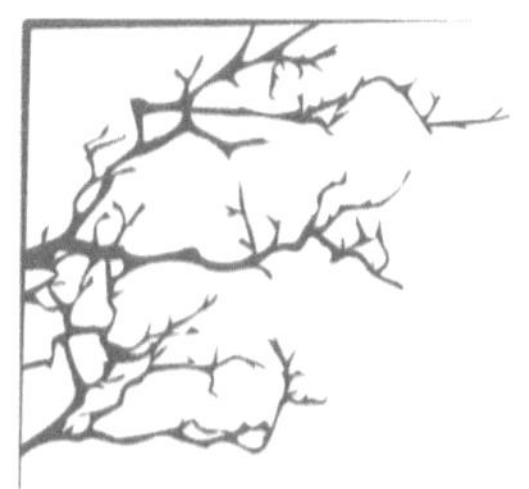

Xander

My head pounded like a jackhammer. Brows furrowed, I opened my eyes. Even *that* took an extraordinary amount of energy. My breaths were shallow and heavy. I was weak. Which didn't make any sense, seeing as that I was a vampire.

Unnerved, I tried to sit up. But I quickly discovered that my bare chest was constrained by musty leather straps. I tried to break through them. I *should* have been able to break through them easily. But I couldn't.

This wasn't good.

Letting out a grunt, I fell back against the bed. The stark white room was fairly small—and really cold. I noticed that my right hand was trembling, and I realized then that my arm was covered in tubes that hooked up to a machine behind me.

How had I ended up here? *Think, Xander. Think.*

But my memories were a fog.

With my brain not functioning on all cylinders, I decided to go over what I *did* know. I was strapped into a hospital bed hooked up to more tubes than I could count. The reason for my current state became apparent when I spotted the blood bag, which was nearly full of *my* blood. Which meant someone had captured me.

But what did they want with me? And who were they?

A chill flooded through my veins. When the supernaturals were first outed to the world, my older brother Julian had feared the humans might one day experiment on us. After all, our blood could heal wounds. Was that what was happening?

I heard a beep, and the metal door opened. A woman entered the room. She was devastatingly beautiful—olive skin, emerald eyes and a killer body. And by killer body, I meant that she looked strong enough to strangle a man with her bare hands.

She glared at me with contempt before calling for someone named Evangeline. A redhead rushed into the room behind her, eyes widening upon seeing me.

"He's awake," *the body*, as I decided to refer to her, announced.

Evangeline pushed her glasses up the bridge of her nose. "I'm sorry. I didn't think he'd be strong enough to—"

The body held up a hand to silence her. "Stay here while I have a little chat with him, won't you?"

"Of course, Sofia."

Sofia. The name triggered a rush of memories to return.

Grace and I had been in upstate New York looking for faerie dust when Sofia and her lackies attacked us...

My stomach dropped.

Grace! Where was Grace?

Beads of sweat formed on my brow, and I clutched the mattress, attempting to use it as leverage to push against as I tried forcing myself free. I had hoped I could use the sudden adrenaline rush to my advantage. But my body betrayed me. I fell back against the bed, trembling in a cold sweat. Moaning, I muttered, "Where is she? What did you do with her?"

Sofia shook her head mockingly. "Tsk, tsk, tsk. So many questions, Xander Dumont. But you're asking the wrong ones."

My lip curled. "What questions should I be asking?"

"Why you're here would be a good one to start with," Sofia said casually. She folded her arms across her chest, kicking her hip out while she waited for me to take the bait. I wasn't going to give her the satisfaction, though. So, I waited her out.

After a few moments, she grew bored. Examining her deep purple fingernail polish in disinterest, she said, "You have a very important role to play in the plan. Consider yourself lucky. Because if it had been up to me, I would have driven a stake through your heart."

Good. She didn't know I couldn't be killed by traditional means. At least that was something. "So," I said, voice cracking, "you're not the decision-maker? Who are you taking orders from?" Her mouth twisted into a devious smile. Now I knew why it infuriated people so much when I gave them that same look. "Who are you, anyway?"

She straightened at that. "You really don't know, do you?" She seemed mildly offended.

"Should I?"

Sofia drew nearer, shaking her head. "My name is Sofia Albright."

Oh. That wasn't good.

My siblings and I had a long history with the Albright witches. Their ancestor, Claudia Albright, was the one who had inflicted the supernatural curses upon us. While humans could be turned into vampires by dying with vampire blood in their systems, we had been *made*.

You see, my mother had been desperate for true blood heirs to the throne. My older brother Julian was adopted, and she couldn't stomach the thought of the kingdom being turned over to him. So, she'd summoned Claudia to the castle and cut a deal with her. Claudia agreed to ensure that my mother carried four blood heirs—Aiden, Charlotte, Natalie and myself. But on our twentieth birthdays, Claudia's curse took hold. The four of us were turned into vampires. The *Blood Heirs*, as we were now known. And that same night, Julian shifted into a werewolf.

The werewolf curse had been Claudia's failsafe. For centuries, we'd believed that Julian's bite would kill us. And it did, in a way.

Now, Natalie was dead. Thanks to Julian, Aiden's vampirism curse had lifted. He was now settled down with Victoria, living a perfectly ordinary life as a human many miles away from here. And Julian and Charlotte were trapped in the portal that Grace and I were trying to unseal. Grace's best friend Danielle was there, too, along with Keo and some other allies.

But Claudia's curse wasn't the only reason for the rift between us and the Albrights. In fact, for many years, Albright witches had held up the boundary between Crescent Cape and the human world. The boundary prevented humans from accidentally stumbling into our kingdom—but it allowed us to go out and hunt as needed. And to bring in blood slaves when we needed to restock our supply.

But two of their witches had died on our watch in recent years: Freya and Evanna. We suspected Freya had been killed by the rival Carlisle coven. As for Evanna—that was my fault. Kind of.

Look, in my defense, Reed Carlisle had cursed me to do his bidding. So, technically, the Carlisle coven was behind that one, too.

I still couldn't believe that Grace was that mad-man's *daughter*. She was lucky to have grown up without him in her life. And as far as I was concerned, it was a good thing he was dead.

Thinking about Reed, Evanna and Freya made me think about the boundary spells that had been dropped when supernaturals were outed. It was a known fact that in order to perform a counterspell, a witch needed a Silverleaf sapling. Phoebe Mather, a witch from the Kingdom of the Silver Seas, had helped with that. The catch, though, was that only a witch from the same bloodline as the witch who cast the *original* spell could perform the counterspell. Grace and I had wondered how Reed had managed to drop the boundary to Crescent Cape, given that he was a Carlisle. I had a feeling now that the answer was right in front of me.

Sofia was towering over me, brushing my dark hair away from my eyes. Examining me. I was sweating bullets. She flicked the residue off her fingers with contempt.

"What are you doing to me?" I asked.

"Draining you of your blood. Isn't that obvious?"

She was *harsh*. "But why?"

"Your kind has brought enough harm to this world. With your help, we're going to put a stop to that."

"I don't understand."

She smirked at that. "Oh, you have *no* idea."

Swallowing hard, succumbing to the pain and fatigue that were taking over, I managed to ask, "Where is Grace?"

"Don't pretend for one second that you care about that little witch. How many witches, how many humans, have died because of you? You're a monster. Selfish. Incapable of caring about *anyone* other than yourself."

I ignored the thick feeling in my throat. Using every ounce of energy I could muster, I forced my fangs to emerge from my gums, trying to look as threatening as I could despite my current state. I had to find a way out of here. If they had so much laid a finger on Grace, I was going to rip every one of their throats out.

Muscles cording in my neck, I lifted my head. *"Where is she?!"*

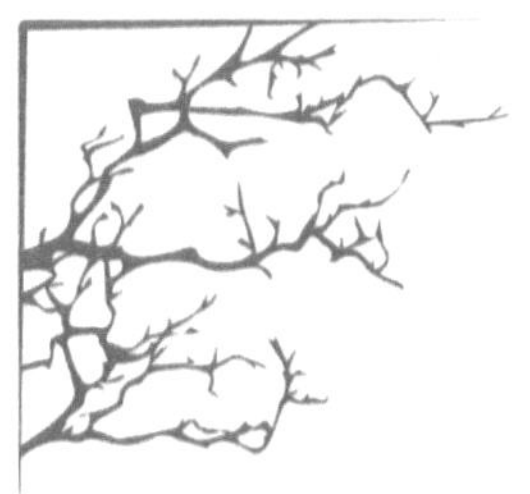

Xander

It didn't matter whether my eyes were open or closed. All I saw was a dizzying explosion of stars. I groaned as a harsh light flicked on overhead. I wondered why they hadn't just killed me already. How much of my blood could they possibly need?

A lot, apparently.

Sofia and her witchy minions still hadn't explained what they were using it for. I highly doubted they were donating it to local hospitals. Were they planning a larger attack and storing my blood so that they could heal themselves if they were injured? Were they trying to figure out exactly vampirism worked? I honestly had no idea. Whatever it was, it wasn't good.

I didn't care anymore.

I'd lost track of how many days I'd been here. I kept a mental tally at first, but I gave up after a while. The witches were providing me with enough blood to stay alive, but nothing more. I was painfully weak—even my breaths felt heavy.

The only thing keeping me going was knowing that Grace was depending on me. The Albright and Carlisle covens were rivals. And being that Grace was the daughter of one of the most infamous Carlisle witches to ever roam the earth, I shuddered at the thought of the various ways the Albright witches might be tormenting her right now.

I twisted my head to the side, staring at the wall in despair. I felt like I was failing her. She could be *right there*, and yet, I couldn't protect her.

It was strange how far Grace and I had come. When I'd first met her, she was a blood slave in Crescent Cape—the kingdom once ruled over by my brother Aiden before Grace's dad dropped the boundary. According to Grace, I'd fed on her. But I didn't remember that. At the time, she had merely been food. Harsh, but true.

When she and the others had first been summoned to the castle as part of Julian's "master plan" to arrange a marriage for Aiden, I had to admit she'd caught my eye. All dolled up thanks to the maidservants, she looked like a bombshell. And it turned out she had the personality of a firecracker. She hated my siblings and everything we stood for. I couldn't blame her, but I also didn't particularly care. It wasn't until Aiden had gone off the artificial blood and left a trail of bodies from the hidden kingdom of Crescent Cape to the neighboring town of Quarter Square that we really got to know each other. And it took longer still for us to tolerate each other. The corner of my lip tugged into a faint grin as I thought about our history.

Up until we were attacked, we'd spent nearly every day over the last four years together. Honestly, I was starting to think Uncle Ben (*technically,* my very human descendent) liked her more than he liked me. Which I guess wasn't saying much. But still. He was always inviting her over for family dinners—when we weren't on the hunt for faerie dust, that is.

I wondered if Uncle Ben had realized something had gone wrong. I was starting to regret my last words to him being, "Don't wait up for us." I'd been being sarcastic. I hoped he realized that... Not that there was anything *he* could do.

As much as I wanted to give up, I had to find it in me to hold on. Because if Grace *freaking* Addington hadn't figured out a way to get us out of this, she was in serious trouble. And I wasn't about to let these witches win.

The security system beeped, and Evangeline walked into the room. I let out a sigh of relief. Sofia was a walking nightmare, but Evangeline at least had a sliver of a heart. "Time for your daily allowance," she said coldly. She untwisted the cap of a bottle, dipped a syringe dispenser into the red liquid and squeezed some into my mouth. Artificial blood. It was thick like syrup and had a tangy aftertaste. My brother Aiden used to drink this stuff back when he was a vampire, before, you know, slaughtering a whole village. But before that, to keep himself in check, he had witches spell up artificial blood for him. I'd only had it a handful of times myself—personally, I found it revolting. And I had far more control than he did when it came to feeding, so I didn't need it. But now, the daily allotment of artificial blood Evangeline provided me was all that was keeping me alive.

"Evangeline," I said in the most charming tone I could muster, "be honest with me, will you? Why am I here?" Maybe if I could figure out what they wanted I could make some sort of deal with them. Or come up with a plan. It was a long shot, but it didn't hurt to try.

"You know why," she said, her voice void of inflection—and empathy. "Now, open up."

I opened my mouth and gulped down my second and final dose for the day. "I know you need my blood. But you haven't told me *why*."

Her jaw twitched, and she pressed her lips into a hard line.

"Come on. What does it hurt to tell me? It's not like I can do anything to stop you anyway."

The corners of her eyes crinkled, and for a second, I thought I had her. But then she abruptly shook her head. "I'm sorry. I can't."

Her hand happened to be within reaching distance of mine, so I grabbed hold of it—not to scare her, but to get her attention. Her hand was soft and delicate—typical of witches. They didn't like to get their hands dirty. In the literal sense, at least. "Please. I can tell you're not like the others," I said, hoping to charm her. I'd tried compelling her days ago. But it didn't work. She wasn't stupid enough to hold my gaze, and my arms were strapped to my side, so I couldn't force her. "You don't think this is right, do you?"

She snatched her hand out of my hold. "You have no idea what I think. You don't know anything about me."

Relaxing my head against the makeshift hospital bed, I sighed. "You're right. Enlighten me, won't you?"

Evangeline scowled. "Evanna was my best friend."

Oh. That was all the explanation I needed. She had no idea I was the one who had killed Evanna, but it had happened while Evanna was at the castle helping us keep up the boundary that surrounded Crescent Cape. She'd died while under our care. And that was enough of a reason for Evangeline to hate me. "I'm sorry about what happened to your friend," I said sincerely.

She shook her head. "Don't lie to me. You and your siblings made it abundantly clear over the years that the only lives that matter to you are your own. Everyone else is expendable."

"That's not true."

"It is," she hissed, clearly wondering why she was even wasting time having this conversation with me.

"Evanna believed she was doing the right thing by helping us. And she was. Look what happened to the world after the boundary fell. *War*. You want to talk about treating lives as being expendable? Tell it to Reed Carlisle's ashes. He's the reason that happened, not me." She shook her head, indicating that she was done with the conversation. But I wasn't. "You may not trust me, but you say Evanna was your best friend. She trusted us. Maybe you should trust her judgment."

"Her lack of judgment got her killed."

"Get me more blood," I pleaded.

"You've had your allotment for the day." She started to get up and walk away.

"No—give me enough to get my strength back," I begged. I didn't care how it looked—me, a Blood Heir, begging from a witch. I was desperate to get out of here. Desperate to save Grace. "I'll break out of here. You can come with me. I'll protect you. All you have to do is slip me more blood. They'll never know you betrayed them. I swear. I'll break free, make it look like I kidnapped you, get Grace out of here and you can start over somewhere far away from here."

Her brow wrinkled at that. Was she considering my offer? She paused for a moment, studying me. Then, she lifted her chin. "They didn't tell you?"

"Tell me what?"

"About your friend... Sofia really didn't tell you?"

I was growing agitated with the vague questions. "Tell me what? What did they do to her?"

"She's fine," she said flatly.

"Where is she? I want to speak with her."

"You can't," she explained. "Grace isn't here."

"*What?!*" She had to be lying. This whole time, I thought Grace was here being tortured. But now, Evangeline was telling me Grace wasn't even here? Where was she, then?

Despite my knee-jerk reaction, I felt a glimmer of hope. Had Grace escaped? Had she defended herself?

But if she wasn't here, and she was fine, why hadn't she come to rescue me? She knew they had taken me, didn't she? She was there when Sofia snapped my neck... It didn't make any sense. Grace didn't just abandon people she cared about.

Sofia disposed of the syringe dispenser and washed her hands in the sink at the other end of the room. "You're wasting your time worrying about her," she said, looking at me through the reflection in the mirror.

Despite the fresh dose of artificial blood, the room was spinning. Why would worrying about Grace be a waste of my time? What had they done to her? "What are you saying?"

She dried her hands off with the towel and headed for the door, not bothering to have the decency to look at me while she spoke. She pulled the door open and paused, her gaze still focused ahead. "I'm saying Grace isn't here, and she isn't coming back for you. Sofia made sure of that." And then she walked out, letting the door slam shut behind her.

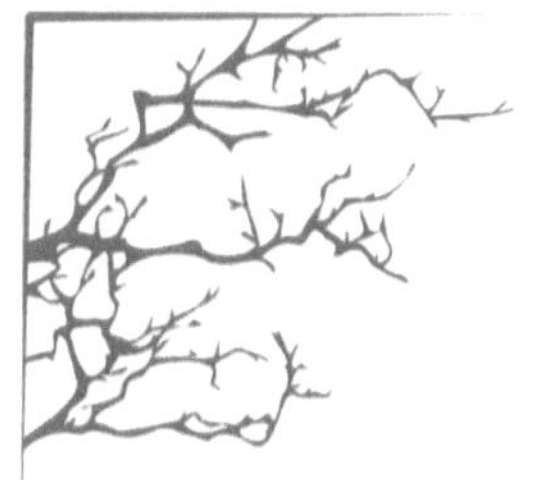

Grace

Startled, I bolted upright. I'd had the same nightmare running on repeat for as long as I could remember. I was standing in a strange room with three other people mumbling in some other language—Latin, maybe? The more I spoke, the more one of the men screamed. He was clawing at his skin, which was melting right off his bones. His lips had tugged into a smile right before he died, which was weird, even for a dream.

I'd run a Google search a while back to see if I could figure out what it might mean. According to one site, dreaming about a stranger dying could mean that you felt disconnected from the changes in your life. Maybe so, but it still didn't explain why my subconscious was so *dark*.

And as for the site's interpretation, I *did* feel detached as of late, but there hadn't been any major changes of note. Every day was the same. Wake up early. Work. Chat with Mrs. Johnson and the other regulars. Listen to Madison rattle off her latest gossip. Come home. Go to sleep. Have nightmares. You know—normal stuff.

I headed to the kitchen and popped some ibuprofen to dull the headache, wishing there was a pill I could pop to erase the memories of that nightmare from my head. When I was finished chugging my glass of water, I set my cup down on the pale blue Formica countertop. Chewing my fingernail, my cheeks flushed as I thought of everything that had happened last night.

Nightmare aside, my birthday *had* been fun. Thanks to Madison's prodding, Bellamy bought us a couple of rounds of drinks. We talked for at least an hour about everything from our childhoods to our favorite types of music. I could have talked to him all night, but he had to get back to work. I'd hoped he would ask for my number, but he never did. And I was too nervous to offer it. I hadn't dated anyone since high school—and that hardly counted as *really* dating.

Even though I was bummed that he didn't ask me out, after a few drinks, I was much more amenable to Madison's vision for how a birthday should be celebrated. And I had to admit, partying was a good distraction from thinking about Bellamy. We'd hopped from bar to bar around downtown, and eventually, we found our way to a club. Some of our co-workers from the Sunny Side Grille showed up to celebrate with us. We'd stayed out way too late dancing, and I'd only gotten about four hours of sleep. And thanks to my recurring dream, those four hours hadn't been restful. Still, it was worth it.

After a quick shower, I stood in front of the mirror as I blow-dried my hair. Was that... a piercing? I tucked my hair behind my ear to get a better look. You'd think I'd remember getting piercings. Sure enough, small crescent moons dangling from golden hoops hung from each of my earlobes. I shrugged. At least drunk-me had picked something cute.

I finished drying my hair, tied it into a messy bun and put on some concealer to cover up the bags under my eyes. Then I added a little blush, too, because—who was I kidding? If there was ever a reason to use makeup, it was when you'd only gotten four hours of sleep the night before. Once I looked semi-human again, I threw on my uniform and sneakers and headed out the door.

It was 6:35 a.m. by the time I made it to the Sunny Side Grille—five minutes past when I was *supposed* to be there. The manager, Harriett, gave me the stink-eye, but she didn't say anything. This was my first time being late, and she'd undoubtedly picked up on my shame as I walked in the door, apologizing profusely.

I busied myself with the daily morning tasks, and before I knew it, it was time to open. Mrs. Johnson was there, waiting by the door. As soon as we spotted her, I unlocked the door and held it open for her. She told me she wanted her usual order, so I gave the kitchen a head's up and started pouring her a cup of coffee.

The front door chimed, and when I instinctively glanced up, I froze. I don't know how long I stood there gaping like an idiot, but as soon as I realized what I was doing, I abruptly spun around, managing to splash the scalding cup of coffee all over the front of my uniform.

"Grace?" that familiar, husky voice called out.

Closing my eyes, I chewed down on my lower lip, trying to think of a way out of this. I'd give anything to be invisible right about now...

His footsteps were getting closer. And it wasn't like he hadn't *seen* me. It was time to face reality.

I spun around to find Bellamy standing there—his button-down doing little to hide his broad shoulders. Why couldn't he have shown up in sweats or something?

Deciding it was better to make the best of it than wallow in my embarrassment, I smiled, trying to play it cool. "Oh, hey. What are you doing here?"

His face crinkled into that full-face smile again. Glancing back over his shoulder before speaking to me, he said, "I was in the neighborhood and thought I'd swing by for a cup of coffee. But, uh," he started, noticing the massive stain on my top, "orange juice would be good, too."

Madison came up behind me and whispered that she'd take over Mrs. Johnson's table. So, I poured Bellamy a cup of juice to go. "In the neighborhood, huh?" I asked as I fitted the lid onto his drink.

"Alright, you caught me," he answered with a charming grin. "I might have remembered that you worked here."

"Oh." I nodded a little too emphatically.

He took a step closer toward the counter and propped his elbows on top of it, leaning in to speak to me. "I just wanted an excuse to see you again."

"Yeah?" I swallowed, trying to push down the sensation of heat that was rising in my chest.

He looked like he wanted to say something, but shook his head. His cheeks started to flush, but he instantly composed himself. "Would you like to go to a Halloween party with me tomorrow? I know it's last minute, but it should be fun. They're throwing a big bash in Crescent Cape near that old vampire castle that burned down. They'll have a band, and there's this big costume contest. It's a whole thing," he said with a flourish of his hand.

"Of course," I said in an awkwardly high-pitched tone. I vaguely remembered hearing about what had happened at

Crescent Cape, but the thought quickly evaporated from my mind. I cleared my throat. "Yeah, that'd be great."

He chuckled. "Great."

Unable to contain my smile, I scribbled my phone number on the back of a napkin and slid it to him.

He folded it neatly and tucked into his pocket before sliding me a five-dollar bill and taking his juice. "I'll see you tomorrow, Grace," he said with a flirtatious wink.

"See you tomorrow, Bellamy."

I cocked my head to the side, enjoying the view of him walking away.

After the door shut behind him, Madison and the rest of the employees mockingly yelled in a high-pitched voice, "*See you tomorrow, Bellamy.*"

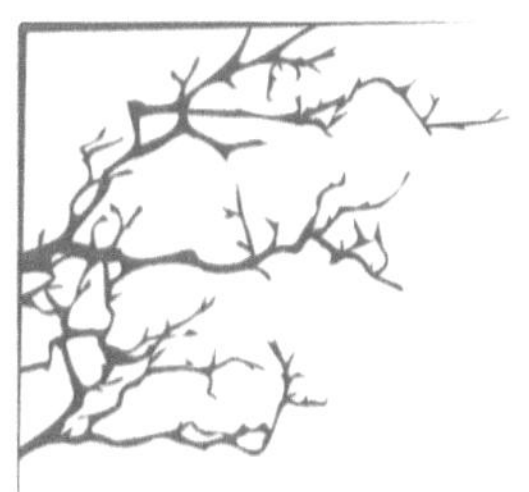

Ben

Fangs hopped into my lap. Despite her name, Fangs was anything but threatening. She was a cream-colored Goldendoodle. She was massive in size, but she had no idea she was a big dog now. In her head, she was still a puppy.

I scratched the top of her head, and she nuzzled against my shoulder. She was the world's cuddliest dog. I'd gotten her a couple of years ago in an effort to have some sense of normalcy in my life. I'd managed to go three decades with minimal interaction with my supernatural ancestors, the vampire Blood Heirs and their werewolf brother, Julian. But ever since Julian concocted his hair-brained Choosing Ceremony scheme, I'd found myself tangled in their drama.

It wasn't like I hadn't been prepared for the chaos that always seemed to follow them. I was the last of the family line, and for centuries my human ancestors had kept tabs on the siblings.

Some generations had minimal interaction with them. Others, like me, weren't so lucky.

Yet, part of me didn't mind. Like it or not, they were my family. And they were the only family I had. Besides Fangs, that is.

And I'd managed to get myself even further involved in the supernatural world. Now, in addition to being a travel blogger (working a 9 to 5 didn't exactly mesh well with dealing with vampire and werewolf drama), I was a *Collector*. I traveled the world collecting magical objects. Sometimes to understand them. Sometimes to prevent them from getting into a supernatural's hands. I stored most of them in my attic, which I'd had Grace protect with a spell. But I kept some of the more benign pieces around the house—upstairs, mostly. She'd put up protective wards around those rooms, too, just to be safe.

I stared at my phone as I'd been doing every night since Xander and Grace left on that trip. I hadn't heard from either one of them since.

Part of me thought I shouldn't worry. Xander had told me not to wait up for him. He had a history of disappearing for long stretches of time—sometimes for decades. But Grace was different. She'd become like family in recent years, and I couldn't imagine her running off with Xander and not bothering to reach out. I'd texted and called them both. But I hadn't heard any response. I could see Xander ignoring me. He usually only thought of himself anyway. But Grace... it was just so unlike her. Perhaps after finding the faerie dust, they'd gone off to follow another lead. But you'd think they would have had the courtesy to give me a heads up.

Reaching for the phone again, I decided it was time to try something new. I couldn't remember the last time I'd spoken with Aiden. Ever since his vampire curse had been lifted and he'd become human again, I'd tried keeping contact to a minimum. He and his new bride, Victoria, deserved some time to themselves. They deserved to build a happy life together, away from all of this chaos.

And yet, I could no longer ignore the heavy feeling in the pit of my stomach. I needed to get his opinion. To see whether this sounded like typical Xander behavior or something more. I couldn't fathom what could have happened to them. Xander was a Blood Heir and Grace was a powerful young witch. I couldn't imagine any situation they couldn't handle. But I still couldn't wrap my head around why neither one of them had bothered checking in.

After a couple of rings, Aiden answered. "Uncle Ben," he said, the surprise in his tone evident. "How's it going?"

"Things are going well," I said, purposefully not dumping my worries on him right away. "Just wanted to check in with you and see how you and Victoria are doing. Is she there with you? Please tell her hello for me."

"She's at the grocery store," he answered. "But I'll pass your message along."

I shook my head. I got up from my La-Z-Boy chair and began to head upstairs as we chatted. "How very *normal* of her."

"Groceries. Cooking. Chores. Sinus infections. Living the dream."

"I take it being a human isn't all it's cracked up to be?" He didn't answer, and I had to check the phone to make sure the call hadn't ended. "Aiden?" I'd always wondered how Aiden would adjust to being a human. He had ruled over Crescent Cape as its vampire prince for centuries. In the blink of an eye—or, rather, the bite of a wolf—his entire identity had been stripped away. Yes, he was madly in love with Victoria. But was that enough to keep him happy? He had gone from being one of the most fearsome vampires in the world to a nobody. That couldn't be easy.

"Yeah, I'm here. Sorry." He cleared his throat. "Anyway, I'm guessing you didn't call just to ask about how my day-to-day life is going."

"No, actually." By now I had wandered into one of the many rooms which housed the various objects and artifacts my family had collected over the years. My hand trailed along the edge of the shelf, past the siphoning tool, the shapeshifting ring, the dragon claw—I still wasn't convinced the dragon claw did anything, but hey—who didn't want a *dragon claw*? "I was calling to see if you've heard from Xander or Grace lately."

"No. Why?"

"They went to New York weeks ago, and I haven't heard from them since. I was hoping they might have checked in with you."

"Afraid not. But Xander's not one to reach out. And Grace hates me."

"She doesn't hate you, Aiden. At least, not anymore."

"Either way," he said, "she's never called or texted, so nothing out of the usual there. Did you try reaching out to Nick?"

Nick was Grace's twin brother. The one she didn't even know she'd had until Danielle had figured it out after going through old Carlisle coven records back at the castle, back before the castle was burned to the ground. Grace and Nick had connected, but their relationship had been rocky ever since the incident at the hotel—the incident which we were under strict orders from Grace to never speak of again. From what I understood, though, she and her brother were on speaking terms again. She checked in with him every so often—sometimes to give him a heads up if she found a new lead, sometimes to pick his brain for ideas. But Nick had moved away and left his coven. I didn't have a way to track him down even if I wanted to. And I wasn't stupid enough to try to ask someone in the coven where he was. Not after what Grace and Xander had done... "I don't have his number," I explained. "And I don't know anyone other than Grace who would have a way to reach out to him."

"Honestly," Aiden said, trying to calm my nerves, "I wouldn't worry too much. You know how Xander feels about Grace. He probably told her how he felt, and they're off riding into the sunset together."

"Yes, because your brother is totally the *riding off into the sunset* type. Not to mention, that would require Xander being honest with himself about how he really feels about her."

"Fair enough."

"And while I wouldn't be surprised if Xander gave up on trying to open that portal, Grace would *never* do that. Once Grace puts her mind to something, there's no stopping her."

Aiden thought on that for a moment. "You're really worried about them?"

"I am."

"Have you tried tracking them?"

I laughed at that. "You want me to get the police involved?" The number one rule when dealing with supernaturals was to keep the police out of it. They only complicated things. Plus, they were human. Which meant involving them in supernatural matters could cost them their lives. I'd never put them in that position. And the police seemed to prefer it that way anyway. After the dust settled after the war, supernaturals agreed to keep to the shadows. If they left the humans alone, the humans would leave them alone. And for the most part, both sides complied. There were outliers, of course—bloodthirsty vampires and crazed hunters. But they were few and far between. The fact that vampires could now buy fake blood over the counter had cut way back on the needless deaths. And anyway, supernaturals had existed for thousands of years without humans being any the wiser. They knew how to keep a low profile.

"Of course not," Aiden replied. "I'm asking if you've had a *witch* try to track them."

"The only witch I trust is Grace." To be fair, she was also the only witch I knew.

Aiden was quiet for a few moments more. I regretted ever calling him. He was trying to start over. I should have respected that. "I'm sorry. I shouldn't have bothered you with this. You're right. It's probably nothing."

"No," he answered firmly. "If your gut is telling you something is wrong, we should listen to it. Worst case, we find them and see that everything's fine. Right? I know of a witch who will help. I'll get her to do a tracking spell, and we'll find them."

"Thanks. I'll keep trying to get ahold of them. I'll let you know if I find anything."

"Oh—and Uncle Ben?"

"Yes?"

"If the worst happened... if the wrong person discovered just *who* and *what* they are..."

"Yeah?"

"I guess what I'm trying to say is that you need to be careful."

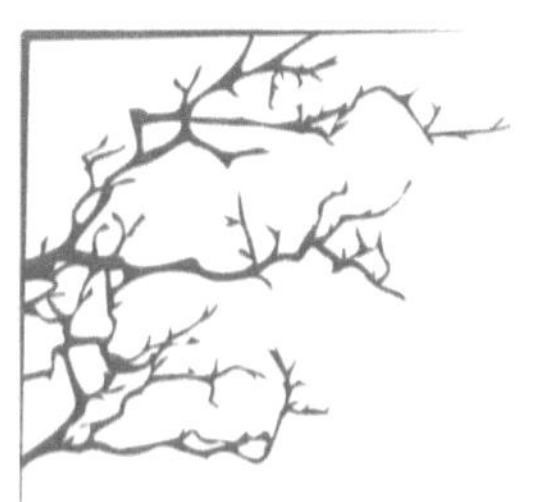

Grace

I had just finished applying my lip gloss when I heard a knock at the door. Despite the concealer, my eyes still had dark circles under them. The nightmares had been getting worse. Not so much that they were different. Just more vivid. More real.

I gave myself one last glance in the mirror, checking out how I looked in my witch costume. I doubted I'd win the costume contest as it wasn't all that unique, but that was okay. Satisfied, I tousled my hair, checked my teeth and rushed to answer the door. I wiped my palms against my robe before opening it. "Hey, Bellamy," I said, breathlessly. And then I covered my smile with my hand, giggling at the coincidence. We hadn't even discussed our costumes—mainly because I was scrambling at the last minute to find one and just went with the first thing that fit. What were the chances that we'd dress alike?

He flashed a smile. "You look amazing."

"Thanks." I flushed.

"Are you ready to head out?"

"Yep." I locked the door behind me and hooked my arm around his. Placing my palm on his robe-covered bicep as we walked down the hall, I asked, "What, no broomstick?"

"It's being repaired, I'm afraid. You'll have to settle for my truck tonight."

We took our time heading downstairs but picked up our pace when we stepped outside the building. There was a sharp chill outside. The wind whistled as it passed, and I wondered if I should have grabbed a coat. But Bellamy assured me there would be plenty of heaters at the party. I'd assumed we'd be partying *inside* the remains of the castle, but apparently it served as more of a photo op.

We crossed the parking lot, passing under the flickering yellow light from one of the streetlamps. Bellamy led me to his 1978 blue and white GMC Sierra and opened up the passenger door, and I slid inside. His truck was surprisingly clean and carried the lingering traces of the rich, musky cologne he wore.

"Want to pick out some music?" Bellamy asked as he climbed inside and clicked his seatbelt. He gestured toward his phone, which was sitting on the bench seat between us. "I have some playlists on there if you're interested. Or you can pick out whatever you want."

I wasn't a big music person myself. At least, I wasn't interested in anything current. I probably couldn't even name one of the top ten artists right now. But, curious about what sort of songs my date listened to, I tapped on the icon on his phone and began perusing. He'd mentioned liking country the other night. I found an album cover of a dude with a cowboy hat. I figured I couldn't go wrong with that—after all, he'd put together the playlist.

"So, have you been to Crescent Cape before?" he asked.

Scalp prickling, I shook my head. "Isn't that the place where the vampires lived?" I'd heard bits and pieces about it. According to what I'd overheard from my coworkers, Crescent Cape—and other vampire kingdoms—had been magically veiled from the human world. But years ago, the boundaries fell, exposing the supernatural world. I wasn't sure if I bought into all of that supernatural stuff. Maybe it was because my memories were still foggy from that period of my life. But, even so, you'd think I'd remember being told *vampires* existed.

"The vampires don't live there anymore," he quickly pointed out. "It's perfectly safe."

I studied him quizzically, thinking. Cocking my head to the side, I asked, "Is this where you take all of your dates? There really is a party, right? You're not secretly a *vampire*, are you?" I narrowed my eyes, but I was unable to hold back my laughter. Madison was coming tonight, too, with her own date, so I knew the party was legit.

"I promise I don't bite," he winked. "And I came to the Halloween party last year—with Nathaniel, if you were wondering."

"So, you and Madison's brother have known each other for a while then?"

"Ever since Kindergarten," he said. "And when my parents died, the Kents took me in. Madison's like a sister to me. A very annoying sister," he said jokingly.

"I'm sorry about your parents."

"You mentioned you were adopted?"

I nodded. "I don't know anything about my birth parents. My mom and dad—the Addingtons, I mean—adopted me as a baby." A line formed between my brows as I thought of them, wondering when I'd last spoken to them. But the thought quickly vanished. Starting to shiver, I hugged my arms around myself. Bellamy must have noticed because he promptly cranked the heat up. "Thanks." Curious to learn more about my date, I asked, "So, what made you decide to open a bar?"

Bellamy shrugged. "It was Nathaniel's dream. I majored in business, and he majored in—well, partying, mostly." He laughed. "But in all seriousness, we make a good team."

"That's nice that you get to work with your best friend."

"Yeah, it is."

"What about you? How long have you been working at the Sunny Side Grille?"

I thought about that for a moment. Weirdly, I didn't know the exact answer to that. "Not long."

"You and Madison seem to have hit it off," he said.

"Yeah, she's kind of taken me under her wing," I answered. "I'm still not sure if that's a good thing or a bad thing." I laughed. Just then, my phone rang. "Speaking of Madison," I said to him, holding my phone so that he could read Madison's name on the screen. I answered it. "Hey, what's up?"

"Where are you guys?" Madison shouted over the noise in the background. The music was blaring so loud that I had to turn down the volume on my phone before I answered. "I keep texting you, but you haven't been texting me back."

I glanced at my phone again and realized that I had, in fact, missed a few messages from her. Oops. "We're on our way," I answered. "I don't think it'll be that much longer. I'll text you when we get there."

"Good. Because my date's already plastered, and I caught him sticking his tongue down Daenerys's throat."

"Who?"

She huffed. "Grace, I swear. Sometimes it's like you're from another planet. Just get here as fast as you can, okay?"

She hung up before I could answer. Bellamy chuckled to himself. "Boy drama?"

"You heard…"

"Typical Madison." He shook his head. "Ah," he said, pointing ahead, "there's the turn." He took a sharp right, leading us up the mountainside. I felt a slight shiver along my spine as we drove along the winding stretch of road, passing a sign that said: NOW CROSSING THE BOUNDARY INTO CRESCENT CAPE. It wasn't one of those official blue or green signs. This one had been made by hand—by a talented artist, to be fair. The top right corner of the sign looked like a chunk had been bitten out of it, and the whole sign was splattered with red paint that looked like blood. I frowned, suddenly filled with unease.

"What did you think when you first heard about all this?" Bellamy asked, gesturing vaguely with his right hand.

I didn't remember anything from the time of the raids. Or anything about the supernatural war. I still questioned sometimes whether Madison had been messing with me. I don't know why it hadn't occurred to me to look into it more myself… But rather than going into the whole memory gap thing, I told him exactly what I felt when I overheard Madison and some of our co-workers talking about vampires for the first time. "After the initial shock, I was revolted by all the vampire books I read as a teen. You know, romanticizing the leading men as heroes instead of fearing them. It's a weird phenomenon, isn't it? The whole vampire craze."

Bellamy pursed his lips in amusement. With an arch of his left eyebrow, he said, "Don't tell me you were a fan of—"

I lifted a hand to silence him. "Don't even start," I said with a laugh.

He just shook his head.

Soon, we reached the top of the mountain. I let out a little gasp as we began our descent. Ahead, I spotted the remains of the castle—from what I'd gathered, there had been a massive fire on the night of the first raid, the night this place was first discovered, yet no deaths had been reported. The impressive structure still stood, though, and I marveled at the sight of it. If I didn't know better, I'd think I was on some abandoned-castle tour in Europe, not here on the coast of Maine. It was both beautiful and terrifying.

It was hard to wrap my head around the whole thing. What had become of the supernaturals who lived there? Where were they now?

Wild grass and weeds overtook the vast lands surrounding the castle. Though, by the looks of it, a large portion had been mowed down for tonight's event. Seemingly endless rows of cars were parked in the grass. But the cleared land beside it had been transformed into what I could only describe as a faerie wonderland. Hundreds of garlands of lights had been strung around the perimeter of the sectioned-off plot, and massive bonfires illuminated the scene like torches against the night. My mouth fell open.

"Crazy, isn't it?" Bellamy said, glancing over at me briefly.

"That's an understatement. I had no idea this Halloween party was such a big thing."

"Oh, you have *no* idea," he assured me. "It's epic."

After spending what seemed like forever waiting in the car line to find a parking spot, we were finally there. Even from the truck, I could feel the vibrations of the speakers blasting music up ahead. Bellamy hopped out of the truck and came over the passenger side. He opened the door for me and offered me his hand, and I eagerly took it. His hand was strong, his skin rough.

Together, we hurried through the maze of cars. While the wind had died down, it was still quite cold. And when Bellamy wrapped his arm around my waist, I eagerly nuzzled against him as we walked, appreciating his warmth.

The place smelled of booze and burning wood. I lifted my gaze as I drew in a long breath, and when I did, I noticed a trail of lanterns along a stone bridge leading up to the entrance of the castle. I thought the party was outside, but I could make out several silhouettes in front of the grand, gothic structure. Craning my neck to get a better view, I asked, "Wait—can people go *inside*?"

"Of course," he said, and he squeezed his arm around me a little tighter. "Let's go check it out."

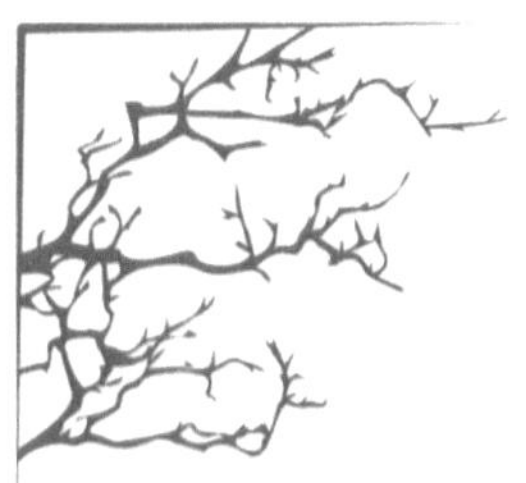

Grace

A couple dressed as a vampire and his bride were perched on the stone steps leading up to the castle. The guy puffed some smoke out in our direction before handing his cigarette to the girl beside him. As we reached the top step, I lifted my chin. A shudder rushed through me as I gaped at the massive stained-glass window on the exterior of the castle, towering overhead. I scrunched my eyebrows together. Some of the glass had shattered, but you could make out a splash of red. A wave, maybe? "What's that supposed to be?"

Bellamy shook his head. "Some people think it's a cape. I think it represents blood, though."

A lump formed in my throat. "Oh."

"Are you okay?" His tone was thick with concern. "We can leave if you want."

"No, I'd like to see it."

So, we passed through the sizable oak doors and entered. The place had an almost sad hollowness to it. Whatever possessions had once filled the entryway were now gone. My gaze dragged from the scorched floor to the staircase, which was still intact. And I found myself walking upstairs. A group of giggling teenage girls came stumbling downstairs, sloshing their cups as they headed down, their knees bobbing all the while. I stepped aside to let them pass before continuing.

"It's hard to believe vampires lived here," Bellamy observed. "Have you ever seen one?"

"No. At least, I don't think so. From what I understand, they look human." He shivered. "That's what makes them so scary. You expect monsters to, well, *look* like monsters. But they don't. Nathaniel claims to have seen one once. He said he saw one feeding on someone in an alley."

"You don't believe him?"

He shrugged. "I don't know what to believe. He had been drinking that night, and it was dark. For all I know, it could have been two people making out."

"I thought they weren't supposed to feed out in the open anyway."

"They're not. But who says they follow the rules?"

"Good point."

As we went upstairs, I hooked a left. For whatever reason, I found myself drawn to a particular room like it was somehow familiar to me. Though of course, it wasn't. Heart pounding, I pressed the handle and opened the door. Upon entering, I released a pent-up breath. I wasn't sure what I'd been expected to find. It was empty, just as the rest of the castle had been. "You've been here before?" I asked Bellamy. "Inside the castle?"

He nodded. "Yeah. There's a dungeon downstairs if you'd like to see that."

I grimaced. "I don't know about that." I crossed the room and gazed outside the window, past my reflection. Even from here, I could hear the beat of the song the DJ was blasting. It was kind of morbid to host a party here—who knew how many innocent souls the vampires had killed here? But it *was* Halloween.

Past the party on the lawn, past the line of trees, I spotted the water that bordered this land. It was a strangely beautiful sight. I glanced over my shoulder at Bellamy, admiring the way he looked in the blueish glow of the moonlight. He stuffed his hands in his pockets and hung back by the doorway, smiling while I stalked the room's perimeter, trailing my fingers along the wall as I did so. A fluttering sensation danced along my fingertips, and I felt a jolt of energy. I quickly jerked my hand away.

"Grace?"

I shook my head, trying to snap myself out of pondering whatever that was that I'd felt. "Sorry, I thought I felt a spider."

"Maybe we should head back outside. Madison's probably freaking out that we're not there yet."

I hugged my arms around myself. "Yeah, I think that's a good idea," I said, catching up to him. "So, what was the dungeon like?" I asked, making conversation as we headed back downstairs.

"As creepy as you'd imagine," he chuckled.

"Do you think they kept humans down there? Like to feed on?"

"No one knows for sure. Other kingdoms had blood slaves, so it would make sense that the vampires that lived here would have, too. There were some mass graves found not too far from here."

"Geez."

"It's still hard to wrap my head around."

"I know what you mean," I admitted. We were halfway down the stairs now, and while part of me wanted to go catch up with Madison, the other part of me was still fascinated by this place. "Anything else interesting here?"

"Not really. Well, that's not true. There's a tunnel system beneath the castle. Or, there was one. It's sealed off now."

I stopped in my tracks. "Seriously? A tunnel system? Where did it lead?"

"To Quarter Square."

"Quarter Square?" I repeated.

"Yeah, it's the neighboring town. It explains a lot. I mean, there had been a large number of mysterious deaths there over the years." He looked at me, eyebrow raised. "You've heard about all of this before, haven't you?"

What was I supposed to say? I couldn't tell him that I was missing *years* of memories. He'd think I was crazy. So, I stretched the truth. "I try to avoid watching the news."

He laughed at that. "I don't blame you."

Once we were back outside, we hurriedly crossed the stone bridge and headed for the party.

Bellamy pulled aside a portion of the lights that surrounded the sectioned-off area, and I stepped through. There were hundreds of people there, all in costumes. Most of the girls were scantily clad, but I spotted one girl in a taco costume, and I couldn't help but nod at her in appreciation. Plenty of the partygoers were dancing, though some had pulled aside to chat around the perimeter.

Dizzying, colorful lights shone from the stage. The DJ threw his arm up in the air to the beat of the music before grabbing the microphone and shouting, "Who's having a good time tonight?" The crowd roared in response, arms flailing and cups rising in the air.

I glanced back over my shoulder at the castle. I wondered what the vampires who had once lived there would think of humans partying on their lands. What if they were here now—in the crowd? Everyone was in costumes. No one would ever suspect a thing...

I shook my head, pushing those thoughts away. This was a party. I was here to have fun.

"Hey, is that her?" Bellamy asked, pointing ahead.

A girl in a nurse outfit walked by taking a swig from a red cup, and I quickly recognized her. "Madison!" I yelled. But she couldn't hear me. I pulled out my phone and texted her, and Bellamy and I waited in amusement for her to check her phone. Soon, she spun around and spotted us. "Finally!" she said. Then she stopped short. "What are you two *wearing*?" Her face scrunched up into a judgmental scowl.

"Can you believe it?" Bellamy asked, proudly brushing his mop of curly brown hair away from his face. "We didn't even plan it."

Madison blinked her thick lashes and feigned a wide-eyed smile. "Wow. Cool, guys."

"I'm sorry about Tad," I offered, referring to her scumbag of a date.

"It's his loss," she said matter-of-factly. "And anyway, I already found another cute guy. Nathaniel's girlfriend introduced me to her friend Drew. *Super hot*." She fluttered her lashes, fanning herself. "Would it be totally rude of me to go back and chat him up? I was just going to get a refill," she said, dangling her empty cup in front of her.

"Drew didn't offer to refill it for you?" Bellamy asked incredulously.

"Don't be so old fashioned, Bellamy. I'm perfectly capable of refilling my own cup."

Bellamy just shook his head.

"Go on," I said to her. "Have fun."

Bouncing on her heels, she smiled and gave a *toodle-oo* sort of wave before heading in the direction of one of the kegs.

"So," Bellamy said, offering me his hand. I quickly took it, smiling broadly. "Would you care to dance?"

BELLAMY AND I SPENT the next two hours drinking and dancing the night away. Eventually, though, we grew tired of that and decided to set out on a walk. While there was one trail of lanterns leading to the castle, there was another trail that led straight to the water. We decided to go check it out.

I couldn't believe how easy and effortless things were with him. I felt like I'd known him forever.

He chuckled to himself as we strode hand-in-hand.

"What?" I asked.

"I'm still laughing about taco girl."

I smiled. "I have to admit, I never imagined the day I'd see a breakdancing taco. That girl had skills."

"Whoa," Bellamy said, holding his arm out in front of me to protect me. With it being so dark out, I hadn't even noticed the big dip in the trail before me. "Careful."

"How did you even see that?" I asked as we walked around the hole.

"How did you *not*?" he teased.

We continued along the path, the chilly air filled with the earthy scents of the balsam fir and red spruce that surrounded us. I spotted a pair of yellow eyes watching us from one of the trees. "Oh, look. An owl," I pointed out. The owl seemingly hooted in response.

"That's a Great Horned Owl."

I gave him a playful jab with my elbow. "So, what? You're a wildlife expert, too?"

He shook his head. "No. I just enjoy being outdoors. I love hiking and camping."

"Really?"

"Does that surprise you?" He smiled one of those full-faced smiles that made his eyes crinkle.

"Maybe."

"What's something about you that would surprise me?"

I tucked a strand of blonde hair behind my ear. "Nothing, really. I'm afraid I'm perfectly ordinary."

"I assure you, there is nothing ordinary about you, Grace Addington."

I was thankful the night sky kept him from seeing me blush.

"We're here," Bellamy announced. I let out a gasp when I saw it. The reflection of the moon sparkled like diamonds in the water that seemed to stretch out for eternity. The shore was hugged by rocks and boulders, and we carefully climbed on top of one of the larger ones to get a good view. We talked for hours under the velvet sky, which was speckled with what seemed like thousands upon thousands of stars.

Just as our evening together was about to come to an end, Bellamy brushed my hair away from my face. "You're freezing," he observed. He removed his robe and wrapped it around my shoulders. I turned to face him. His hazel eyes locked in on mine, and he lifted my chin with his finger, drawing me closer. A tingly sensation filled my chest. His lips brushed against mine, his kiss somehow delicate and passionate at the same time. And I knew that there was nowhere else I'd rather be than here in Crescent Cape, tangled in Bellamy's embrace.

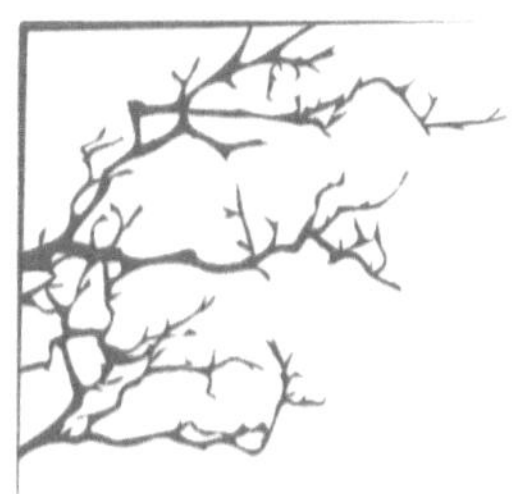

Xander

I blinked. My clouded vision faded in and out. My breaths were slow and shallow. I tried to breathe deeper. I *had* to get it together. I needed to gather whatever strength I could. I had to find a way out of here. I needed to get to Grace.

I hated myself for the way I'd left things with her. I'd never meant to fight with her that night. I wondered what had happened to her... Evangeline never did give me the full story. All she said was that Grace was fine and that she wasn't coming back for me. But that didn't make any sense. Grace wouldn't have abandoned me. Would she?

We'd bickered, but we'd never *fought*. What if I'd gone too far? I'd suggested she walk away from reopening the portal—from getting her best friend back. Even worse, from getting my brother and sister back. I never had been the best sibling. I left Crescent Cape as I pleased, leaving Aiden to rule. I fell off the map completely from time to time, enjoying my freedom. I'd never been one to put others first, which my siblings had no problem pointing out. Maybe that had been the last straw for Grace. She'd seen that I was willing to walk away from something because it was the easier choice. But Grace didn't do easy. She'd get Danielle back or die trying.

Maybe she'd found a lead. Maybe she'd actually managed to get her hands on some faerie dust and was working on a spell to reopen the portal right this minute... I wouldn't put it past her. She was more than capable. And while we made a good team, or so I thought, she certainly didn't *need* my help. She could take care of herself.

Even still, after watching what Sofia had done to me, she would have tried to stop her. Or she at least would have sent someone else to come for me. Though who would she have sent? Aiden was a human now. And Uncle Ben had his magical objects, but could he take on an entire coven? I highly doubted it.

I'd lost track of how many days I'd been here. I wondered if I'd missed Grace's birthday... I felt a deep ache in my chest at the thought. Looked like I had another thing to apologize for—if I ever found a way out of here.

An all-too-familiar beep blasted from beside the metal door, which promptly opened. Letting out a groan of annoyance, I tilted my head to watch as Evangeline strode in. Her hair was tied up into a tight bun, and her glasses were sitting atop her head. Her mouth was pressed into a hard line as she marched around the table and situated herself by my side.

"Rough day?" I asked.

"Not as rough as yours is about to be, I'm afraid." I realized then that she hadn't yet offered me my usual ration of artificial blood. "Now that you're weak enough," she explained, "I'm going to take a peek into your mind."

"You just can't get enough of me, can you?" I said, but it came across more pathetic than I'd meant for it to given the unnatural quivering of my voice. "What are you looking for, anyway? Maybe I'll just tell you what you want to know."

"I want to know your greatest weakness," she said flatly. "Would you care to enlighten me?"

I certainly wasn't about to tell a deranged witch how to kill me. Did she know it took more than a wooden stake to kill a Blood Heir? "Do I look stupid to you?"

She smirked. "I had a feeling you wouldn't be interested in sharing."

"I thought you weren't planning on killing me…" I still wasn't sure what they were doing with all of the blood they were collecting from me. Storing enough to heal themselves in the midst of battle? Creating their own vampires?

Her deep red lips curved into a grin. "Actually, I said we weren't killing you *yet*. And anyway, there are plenty of ways to make someone suffer without actually killing them." She stood above me now, an arrogant gleam in her eye knowing that there was *nothing* I could do to stop her. She pressed her fingertips to my temples and lowered her head, her nose just inches away from mine as she spoke. "This is going to hurt," she warned matter-of-factly.

She recited a spell, and a scream so feral erupted from my lungs that I didn't even recognize the sound as coming from myself. It felt like her nails were scraping against my brain. Jaw clenching, I closed my eyes, trying to fight her off. Whatever it was she wanted to know, I wasn't going to share willingly. Beads of sweat trickled from my temples, and heat flooded my veins. I balled my hands into fists and tried fighting, tried breaking free from my restraints. But it was no use. I wasn't strong enough.

Opening my eyes now, I realized just how closely Evangeline was hovering over me. Her eyes were closed, entranced with her spell. She clawed deeper, scraping my mind for information. But I could tell she wasn't getting whatever it was that she'd wanted.

Seizing the opportunity, I willed my razor-sharp fangs to slice through my gums. And with a swift jerk, I thrust myself toward her throat and sank my teeth into her throat.

Evangeline's eyes flew open, and she shoved me so hard that the back of my head slammed against the hospital bed. Wincing, she covered her neck with her hand, which quickly turned red with blood. "You know what happens to vampires who drink witch's blood," she spat.

Of course I knew. Soon, I'd become violently ill. But it was worth it.

The door beeped again, and a witch I didn't recognize popped his head in the room. "Evangeline? What happened in here?"

"Nothing," she said abruptly, still covering her throat. "What's wrong?"

"It's Sofia. She wants to speak with you."

Nodding in submission, Evangeline shot a nasty glare at me before charging out of the room.

A smile split my lips as I watched the door slam shut, glad that I'd staved her off, at least for now. Then, all at once, I felt that familiar sensation of my insides being shoved into a woodchipper.

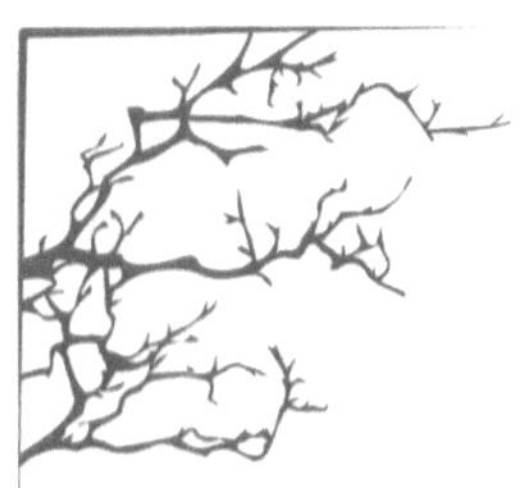

Ben

"**G**lad you could make it," I said, squeezing Aiden's shoulder. He had called me a little while ago and told me that he was in Quarter Square, the small town where I lived. I was both excited and concerned. He was family, and these days, I rarely got to see him. And yet, I couldn't shake the sinking feeling in the pit of my belly.

I'd suggested we meet for breakfast at Magnolia's, a local café. We had a lot to catch up on, and I felt like I was going to need a strong cup of coffee to brace myself for this conversation. Because if Aiden had left Victoria's side to come all the way here and talk to me in person, something was very wrong.

The redhead behind the counter handed over our maple pecan scones and drinks of choice, and we found a table by the window. Magnolia's was packed, but it was so loud that we didn't have to worry about anyone overhearing us.

I took a bite out of my scone and shook my head in appreciation. "Mmm. *Mhmm.*"

"So," Aiden said, leaning across the table and speaking in a hushed tone—ignoring my appreciation of this local delicacy entirely, "I found a witch and got her to perform a tracking spell on Xander."

My eyebrows rose. "She found them?"

"Yes, but..."

"What's wrong? Where are they?"

"The place is somewhere on a dirt road about fifteen miles out of town."

Xander and Grace had been a short drive away this whole time? It didn't make any sense. Why wouldn't they have just come home? Judging by the hardened look in Aiden's eyes, I was guessing they weren't there by choice. I chased down the mouthful of my scone with a long sip of coffee, burning my tongue in the process. "What are we waiting for? Let's go find them."

"It's not that simple," he said, blowing at his drink before sipping from it.

"Not that simple? Your brother has been missing for weeks, and you're telling me he's just outside of town. Let's *go*." I started to get up, but he grabbed me by the wrist, stopping me. Warily, I sank back into my seat. "Okay, then. Why don't you enlighten me as to why we shouldn't go rescue Xander and Grace?"

Aiden dragged his hand through his dark, brownish-red hair. "Do you remember how the witches fled Crescent Cape when the boundary fell?"

I nodded. Of course I remembered. The Carlisles had been long gone—after all, it was Reed, their leader, who had dropped the boundary in the first place. But the Albright witches weren't stupid. So, as soon as they realized the boundary had come down, they got out of there, too.

"Well," Aiden continued, "the location the witch pinpointed is the location of the Albright coven's new compound."

"I don't get it. What would the Albrights want with Xander and Grace?"

Aiden shrugged. "I don't know. But it can't be good. They know Xander is a Blood Heir. They know what happened to Freya and Evanna. Maybe they want revenge. And as for Grace," he said with a sigh, "what if they found out Reed Carlisle was her biological father? The two covens were bitter rivals..."

I rubbed my temples, feeling the beginning of a pounding headache coming on. I suddenly wished I'd opted for booze rather than coffee. I'd had my fears about Xander and Grace, but I never would have imagined that they could have been taken hostage by the Albrights. "Are you sure they aren't there of their own will? You know how Grace is always studying grimoires and learning about magic. Maybe she went to them with questions."

Aiden had to keep himself from laughing. "You're joking, right? Xander and Grace are smarter than that. And why would her going to them for questions lead to them staying there for so long? That doesn't make any sense. Something is definitely wrong. And if we want to get them back, we're going to have to be smart about this."

I straightened in my seat. "Of course," I said, gathering my wits. It wasn't like I was new to the world of supernaturals. I had shelves overflowing with magical objects—some of which I had experience using. Granted, I'd never infiltrated an entire compound full of witches. But if that's what it took to get Xander and Grace back, I'd find a way. "Let's head back to my place," I suggested. "I can show you some of the objects in my collection. If we put our heads together, we can figure out the best ones to bring with us." Aiden's throat bobbed as he swallowed hard. I eyed him, trying to decipher the emotions he was trying so hard to hide. "It's okay," I said, trying to reassure him. "We'll get them back."

"It's not going to be enough."

Perhaps he was right. After all, he was the former vampire. He had more experience with witches than I did. And he did have a point. Could two humans really take on an entire coven? "What if we reach out to the Book Slayers?" I offered. The Book Slayers were a sect of vampire librarians that Xander had turned decades ago. It stood to reason that they would be willing to help us.

"They chose to live peaceful lives. They're not fighters. And they aren't all that strong, even for vampires. Living off the over-the-counter stuff has its downsides."

I nodded, understanding. Since vampires had been outed to the human world, they could now get synthetic blood over the counter. But Aiden knew all too well that when vampires weren't on the *real* stuff, they weren't as strong as they would be otherwise. "What other choice do we have? We have to *try*."

He glanced up at me, the hint of sapphire in his eyes darkening like a summer storm. His jaw twitched as he clenched his teeth with determination. Resigning himself to whatever had been weighing on him, he finally agreed. "You're right. We can't just sit back and do nothing." He took one last sip from his coffee. "We have to get Xander and Grace back. Whatever it takes."

"Whatever it takes," I repeated.

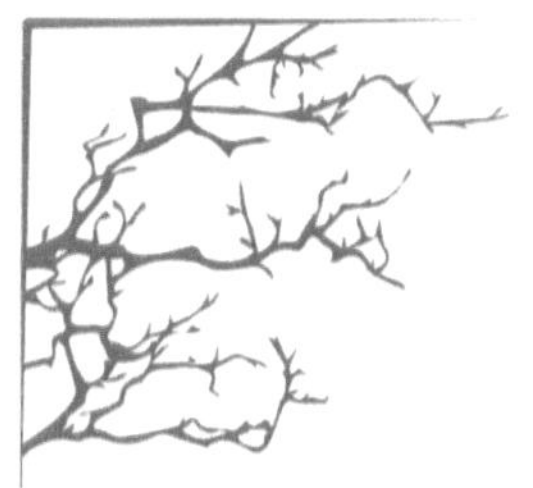

Ben

Needing to speak with the Book Slayers, we headed to Books & Brews, the shop Xander owned here in Quarter Square. To your average customer, Books & Brews was your typical bookstore—well, typical bookstore-slash-bar. But what the humans (other than myself) didn't know was that the Book Slayers lived upstairs in the restricted section. He had recruited them to help us dig up information on how to open the portal. And we hoped they'd be willing to help us now.

The front door chimed as we entered the shop.

"Hi, there!" a male voice called out from the back of the store. "Welcome to Books & Brews. Is there anything I can help you with today?" By the time he reached the front, his deceptively innocent-looking face paled. "Oh. It's you."

I wondered which one of us he was referring to. "Sorry to disappoint you," I offered.

Jasper flipped his ashy brown hair out of his eyes. "No, I'm sorry. I didn't mean it like that." He stuffed his hands in the pockets of his jeans. "This little visit wouldn't happen to be about Xander and Grace, would it? No one's heard from them since—"

I nodded, and his mouth pressed into a hard line as he eagerly awaited what we had to say.

Aiden gestured toward the staircase. "I think it'd be best if we spoke upstairs."

Understanding, Jasper lead us in that direction, weaving between rows upon rows of bookshelves. On the second floor, we found the Book Slayers gathered around the fireplace, open books scattered across the floor. Most didn't even look up to acknowledge us. They weren't being rude, though. They were just busy. They worked tirelessly to help Xander and Grace find someone who might have an idea about how they could get their hands on faerie dust. Though at times it seemed futile, they refused to give up.

Though most weren't looking anyway, I gave a polite wave before Jasper ushered us into his room. "Somebody please tell me what's going on," he said.

"We found Xander and Grace," Aiden explained.

"And?"

"The Albright witches have them."

Jasper's face fell. "You're kidding, right?"

I shook my head. "I'm afraid not. A witch Aiden knows did a tracking spell and found them. We wanted to ask you and the Book Slayers for help," I explained, pausing for a moment to gauge his reaction. But by the way that Jasper lowered his eyes when I said it, I knew he didn't want to fight—even for Xander and Grace. Whoever would have thought there could be a downside to there being a peaceful group of vampires? Clearing my throat, I added, "We have to figure out a way to rescue them."

Jasper's gaze ping-ponged between the two of us, waiting for further explanation.

"Do you think you could speak to the others for us?" I asked. "Maybe someone will be willing to help. If you recall, he's human now," I said, gesturing toward Aiden with my thumb. "He's not any more useful than I am. I mean, we'll try to get him back ourselves if we have to. But it'd be a lot easier if we had vampires on our side."

"You know that we chose to live in peace," Jasper calmly reminded me. With a sigh, he added, "I'll go speak with them. You two wait here. And... don't get your hopes up." With that, he strolled out of the room and closed the door behind him on the way out.

"There is another way," Aiden said in a heavy tone.

I cocked my head to the side. "Do share."

"As you just pointed out, this is only an issue because I'm a human now."

"You aren't suggesting what I think you're suggesting... are you?" I gulped.

Aiden dipped his head. "You heard Jasper. They're not going to help us. What other option do we have?"

"You can't do that!" I said, raising my voice. I didn't care if all of Books & Brews heard me. I wouldn't stand for this. "You just got your life back." Aiden tore his eyes from mine. "What's really going on here? Aren't you happy? You got everything you ever wanted. Why would you give that all up?"

He shook his head. "I don't expect you to understand."

"Try me."

"It's not just Xander I'm at risk of losing. It's Julian and Charlotte, too. Whoever took Xander took Grace, too. And you and I both know we don't stand a chance of reopening that portal without Grace's help. We have to save both of them." He finally looked back at me. "I already lost one sibling. I'm not going to risk losing three more."

My shoulders slumped. "And what would Victoria say?"

He pressed his lips together, thinking. Eventually, he lifted his chin. "She'd tell me to save my family."

"At the risk of you succumbing to madness? I don't need to remind you what you were like as a vampire, do I?"

He shifted in his seat, leaning across the table now to speak to me. "Things are different now. After we rescue them, I can live off of synthetic blood. I lived off the spelled artificial stuff for a decade, didn't I?"

"Yes, but I also remember what happened when you finally gave in to your cravings. Or did you forget about slaughtering the entire blood slave village? Not to mention your killing spree here in Quarter Square." I swore I saw a vein protrude from his forehead for a flicker of a second at the mention of what he'd done.

He shook his head. "It won't be permanent," he asserted. "Once we get Julian back, he can bite me again."

He had a point. It had worked once before. We'd all thought that, being an immortal werewolf, Julian's bite would be the end of his vampire siblings. That's what everyone assumed the witch who had cast the curse upon them meant when she referred to him as being the "failsafe." But as Aiden discovered when he was bitten by his brother, it turned out that Julian's bite *cured* them of their vampirism instead, effectively killing them by giving them a human life that would come to an eventual end.

It was a shame they hadn't figured that out, oh, a thousand years ago...

I dragged my fingers down my unshaven face. "What if it doesn't work again?"

"We already know it'll work. I'm human now, aren't I?" He could tell I was about to bring up more concerns, but he cut me off before I had the chance to start listing them off. "And I'll handle Victoria."

"And if she's not okay with it?"

"She'll be okay with it."

"But if she's not?"

He shook his head, not wanting to even go there. "She will be."

We argued about the prospect of Aiden turning into a vampire for fifteen minutes or more before Jasper finally returned—with another vampire, Naomi, by his side. She was dressed in all white—looking more like an angel than a creature that could tear your throat out—and had her mousy brown hair tied in a braid that hung over her shoulder. Her blue eyes dragged toward Jasper, who was standing with his arms folded across his chest. "Naomi and I are going to help."

"That's it?" Aiden asked, an air of annoyance in his tone. "Just you two?"

"You're lucky we're doing this at all. This goes against everything we stand for."

"But Xander *did* turn us," Naomi added. "And Jasper and I feel like we should at least try to help him."

"And Grace is our friend," he added.

"But even still," Naomi continued, "going up against a coven of Albright witches isn't going to be easy."

"Which is why you should both drink human blood," Aiden pointed out. He rolled up his sleeve and offered his arm to them. "It's the only way this is going to work. It will make you stronger."

"No," Naomi said firmly. "We offered to help you, but we refuse to drink from humans. Even *you*."

Aiden huffed. "Well, I hate to break it to you, but the two of you are not going to be enough to take on a coven."

"We can use my magical objects," I reminded him.

"They took on Xander and Grace and won. Do you seriously think we stand a chance?"

"Then what do you suggest we do?" Jasper asked.

"I'm glad you asked, actually. Because that's where you come in," Aiden added. "If you recall, I'm no longer a vampire."

Jasper nodded. "I'm aware."

"I need you to change that."

Jasper visibly gulped. "You want *me* to turn you?"

"Yes."

"Why me?"

Aiden shrugged. "To be fair, either of you could do it. I know how much you all care about Xander. And you *are* loyal to him, aren't you?"

"...Yes."

"I appreciate you being willing to temporarily set aside this code you choose to live by. And I'll still take you up on your help. But if we're going to take on the Albrights, we better make sure we're prepared. And that means doing whatever it takes. Someone has to rescue him and Grace, right? We need *someone* who can be at full strength. Someone willing to drink human blood. Someone who will be ruthless if needed."

Jasper was looking more uneasy by the second. "Okay..."

"And who better than me?"

The Book Slayer glanced at me, seeking my input. So, I offered it. "Look, I don't like this idea any more than you do. But Aiden has a point. It's our best chance of saving the two of them."

Jasper nodded warily. Pacing, he dug his fingernails into his scalp. "Let me get this straight—you want me to give you my blood and *kill* you?"

"Yes," Aiden said, looking curiously at ease about the prospect of becoming a vampire again.

Jasper stepped back a few paces until he bumped against the edge of his bed, which he promptly plopped down onto. "Like, right now? Here?"

Aiden cocked his head to the side. "You've never turned anyone, have you?"

He shook his head.

"Look, we can make this easy on you. Just give me some of your blood. You don't have to kill me." He glanced at Naomi. "She can do it."

She shook her head. "I will help rescue Xander and Grace, but I am not about to be the person responsible for turning Aiden Dumont back into one of the world's most infamous vampires."

"Fine. Then I hope you enjoy spending the rest of your immortal life knowing that you refused to do the one thing that could help you save your Maker. Oh, wait. You won't be able to. Because we're going to get massacred if we aren't successful. And it will be your fault."

"Alright," she spat. "I'll do it."

"I'm glad to see that you've come to your senses, Naomi." He smiled, his temper quickly vanishing. "Jasper? Your blood, please?"

Reluctantly, Jasper stood. He sank his fangs into his wrist and let Aiden drink.

Once he was finished, Aiden walked over to Naomi. Placing his hands on her shoulders, he said, "Ready to do the honors?"

"Oh," she said coyly. "I think I'm going to enjoy this part." With a quick snap of his neck, Aiden thumped to the floor. Naomi towered over him. Her bright blue eyes—in perfect contrast to her dark hair and porcelain skin—lifted and locked in on mine. "I hope you're ready, Ben. Because when he wakes up, he's going to be *very* hungry."

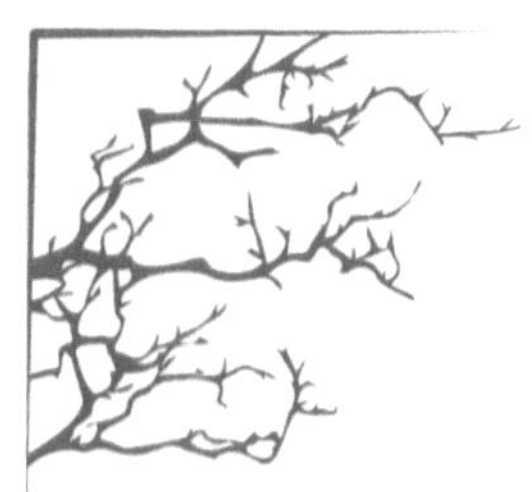

Grace

*F*lesh *crawling, the man began screaming. Fire burst from his veins, melting his skin. He clawed and screamed and pleaded for help. Pleaded for mercy.*

In his last breath, he muttered something. Some futile last attempt to stop us.

Then, strangely, he smiled.

But it was already done.

Clutching my chest, I woke up in a cold sweat. I wiped my brow and reached for the glass of water I kept on my nightstand and drank it in one gulp. The nightmares were getting more vivid. They almost felt... real.

When I checked my phone, I saw that it was 4:00 a.m. I was tired, but I was too afraid to go back to sleep. I knew the nightmares would just return, perhaps stronger than before. So instead, I headed to the bathroom. With the twist of the faucet knob, I allowed cool water to pool in my hands and proceeded to splash my face with it—unfortunately, I did not look like the girls in the face wash commercials when I did so. I looked more like a fish out of water—literally. Though I often felt that way figuratively, too. Things were just... off.

By all accounts, my life was good. I had a job, a friend, a crush... But I also felt strangely detached from it all, perhaps because of the memory gaps. *Something* was missing. I just didn't know what. And every time I thought on it for too long, my thoughts somehow drifted to something else entirely. Which was what was happening now, so I let it go.

Grabbing the blue towel from the counter, I patted my face dry and stared in the mirror. I was still trembling slightly from the nightmare. I remembered bits and pieces. But I also remembered this intense fear—and anger.

I was in what appeared to be a hotel room, though it was hard to tell as the lights were flickering. There were three other people in there with me. They were all men. One was the man who was dying. There was something bone-chilling about the way he had smiled as he died. Like he knew something I didn't. I didn't remember enough from the beginning of the dream to have a guess as to what that might have been, though.

There was another man behind him. He had dark hair and a handsome face that was covered with blood as he hunched over on the floor, coughing and gasping. He was holding his throat like he was struggling to breathe.

And the final person was holding my hand, though he didn't seem to want to. It was more like I was making him.

I couldn't recall any distinct features on any of them. Or who they were supposed to be. Or why I was with them in the first place. But then again, dreams rarely made sense.

Now that I was more awake, the memory of the nightmare was growing hazy.

I stood on my tiptoes and leaned in closer to the mirror to check out the bags under my eyes. I looked like a raccoon. What did women do before concealer? I needed some desperately, but I'd deal with that later. Right now, I needed coffee. So, I tied my hair up into a ponytail and headed into the kitchen.

I turned on the coffee maker waited for my liquid energy to brew. The smell of the freshly brewed coffee filled my lungs, and I could already feel my mood lifting. I retrieved one of my coffee mugs from my dishwasher. But, being too tired to properly function, I dropped it. The ceramic pieces scattered across the floor, and I had to grab a broom to make sure I got all the fragments. With a sigh, I picked up another mug and proceeded to fill it up. But I frowned as I cupped my hand around it. Taking a sip confirmed my suspicions. My coffee maker must have been broken because this wasn't even close to hot. Warm tears collected in my eyes from frustration, and I let out an angry moan. Why was nothing going right today? All I wanted was one hot cup of coffee. Was that too much to ask?

I heard a strange bubbling sound, and I realized my hands were suddenly warm. When I opened my eyes, I saw that the coffee was now simmering, and steam was rising from it. I rubbed my temple, feeling a headache coming on. Was I going crazy? The lack of sleep must have been getting to me.

With my coffee in hand, I headed back to bed and turned on the TV in hopes of trying to find something to keep my mind off of that nightmare. I stumbled upon reruns of some reality show about rich women who argued a lot and settled on that. I needed something mindless and hoped it would be a good distraction. While the drama was entertaining, my mind continued to wander.

I drew a long sip of coffee, savoring the taste as its warmth spread through me. I was reminded of when Bellamy had first walked into the Sunny Side Grille. I'd spilled coffee all over myself, which was mortifying. But it had all worked out in the end. I thought back to our kiss after the Halloween party a couple of nights ago. I wondered if he felt the same way about me that I felt about him. I didn't have much experience with dating—other than one guy back in high school. I wondered what had happened to Ryan…

Anyway, Bellamy and I hadn't talked about being exclusive yet. Honestly, I wasn't sure if we were officially dating. Did one date count as dating? I thought about asking Madison, but I was worried she'd say something to him about it. She had known him practically forever.

I checked my phone, even though there was no reason to. I knew he hadn't texted. I hadn't heard from him since yesterday afternoon. I'd texted him, but he hadn't responded. I tried not to be one of those girls who obsessed over a guy she barely knew, but I couldn't help myself. I thought we'd had such a good time together.

By the time my wake-up alarm buzzed on my phone, I could barely keep my eyes open. But duty called. So, I hurriedly got ready and headed into work.

I was on the sidewalk a few paces away from the door when my phone rang. I thought about ignoring it, figuring it was a scam call. But curiosity got the better of me.

My eyes widened when I realized it was Bellamy. I'd hoped to hear from him, but it seemed strange that he would be calling so early. "Hello?" I said, unable to conceal my smile in spite of myself.

But my smile quickly faded.

"Grace?" It was Bellamy. But his voice sounded more rough than usual. He let out a raspy cough.

"Yeah, it's me. Is everything okay?" I knew it wasn't, though. I couldn't explain it, but he sounded off. Something was wrong. My heart sank into the pit of my stomach. "What's going on?"

"Something happened," he started, pausing before adding, "I'm at Amber Falls General."

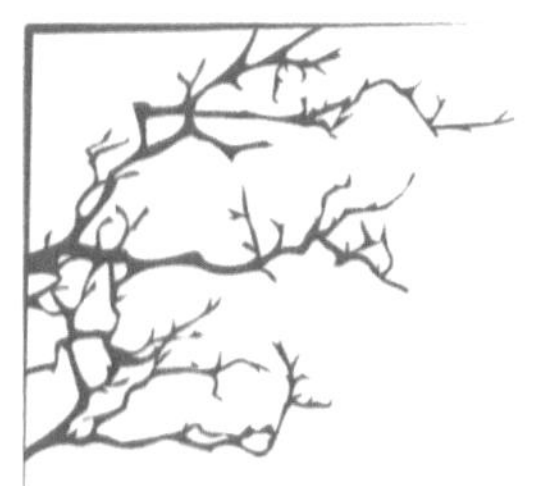

Xander

The door flew open. I didn't even flinch, figuring Evangeline was in a rush today. But then I heard *two* sets of footprints. Curiosity got the best of me. So, naturally, I dragged my gaze toward the door.

My forehead wrinkled, and I scowled, thinking the measly portions of artificial blood I was living off of were starting to affect my brain. This had to be a hallucination.

"I'll check the other rooms," a familiar voice called out while Uncle Ben rushed over to me.

When he reached me, he shook his head, giving me his most sympathetic look. "What did they do to you?" His voice was heavy and sad like I was some pathetic wounded puppy. I couldn't remember the last time someone had *pitied* me. My stomach twisted.

I blinked, still unsure whether it was really him. It wouldn't have been the first time my mind had played tricks on me lately. I couldn't tell you how many times I'd thought Grace had been in this very room. I'd had full-on conversations with her, or what I had hallucinated to be her, only to discover I'd been talking to a broomstick propped against the wall. I swore, the Albrights left the stupid thing there just to mess with me. "Is it really you?" I asked, put off by how measly my voice sounded.

"Yes, it's me."

"How do I know?" I growled, beads of sweat dripping from the creases in my forehead.

Realizing the quickest way to prove himself, Uncle Ben rolled up his sleeve. "Drink," he ordered.

And I gladly did. It was the first taste I'd had of real blood in... How long had it been now? The days and weeks blurred together. But it didn't matter anyway. I was so close to freedom. I could taste it.

I wanted more, needed more, but my arms were still restrained, so he was able to pull away. I let out a groan. "You have no idea how much I needed that," I said, thinking more clearly now as if a fog had lifted from my mind. Now that my senses were back on full alert, I realized just how loud it was in the compound. There was shouting and screaming—and what sounded like furniture being thrown against walls.

Uncle Ben kept stealing anxious glances at the hallway as he hurried to break me out of the restraints. He couldn't get them off. "Where's the key?" he asked.

"I don't know." It wasn't like they told me where they kept it.

He mumbled to himself as he spun around. He frantically began opening drawers and rummaging through their contents.

I didn't know where Evangeline kept hers, but he certainly wasn't going to find a key here. The witches weren't that stupid. "Where are the witches?" I asked. I mean, I knew they were the ones I was hearing in the background. But who was holding them off? Then it hit me. It was obviously Grace. I knew she'd come for me.

"Handled," he answered curtly. "For now."

I nodded in appreciation, thoroughly impressed. Taking out an entire coven—even temporarily—was no easy feat. But, knowing Grace, I shouldn't have been surprised. Sure took her long enough, though.

Now that I was feeling more like myself, I decided it wouldn't hurt to give busting out of here myself another shot. Using every ounce of strength I could muster, a roar escaped my lips as I flexed my muscles, ripping my wrists out from their restraints. They were covered in blood by the time I was done, but the wounds quickly healed.

Uncle Ben rushed to my side and rested his hand on my back, trying to be supportive despite being utterly useless—except for his human blood, that is. I broke free from the ankle restraints, too, and Uncle Ben knowingly offered me his wrist again so that I could gather more strength. "Thank you, by the way," I said when I was done.

"Of course. I'm just sorry we didn't get to you sooner." He patted me on the shoulder.

"Where is Grace, anyway?"

"Isn't she here?"

I scowled. "I thought she was with you." I thought on it for a moment, trying to process this. "If Grace didn't help you bust me out of here... who did?"

Aiden popped his head into the doorway. He entered, giving me a nod of mutual respect. "Xander." Aiden marched over to me and flung his arms around me, drawing me in for a hug. I tried squirming out of it, but his hold was strong. *Very* strong.

My brows stitched as connections started forming in my mind.

When he finally released me, I pulled away. "How did the two of you manage to infiltrate the Albright witches' compound?" I asked.

"Jasper and Naomi came with us. They're handling the witches. Aiden and I were looking for you and Grace."

"Jasper and Naomi?" I said, trying not to laugh. "You broke in here with Jasper and Naomi? What did they do? Read to the witches until they were bored to tears? They're not fighters."

Uncle Ben cleared his throat, and I caught him looking at Aiden as if he was waiting for him to tell me something.

Aiden's gaze flickered, and all at once, the pieces started coming together. Infiltrating the Albright compound. Fighting off witches. His strong hold.

No. No, he couldn't have... Not after everything he'd built with Victoria.

"Aiden?" I pressed.

But his deep blue eyes were locked in on Uncle Ben's bleeding wrist—confirming then and there just how far my brother had gone to save me.

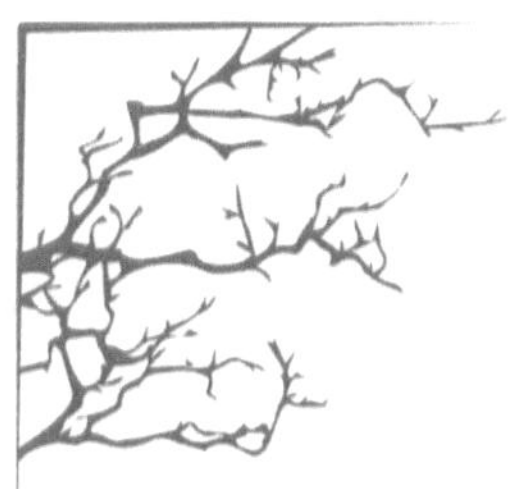

Grace

"You're at the hospital?" My throat suddenly felt dry. I scrambled over to the nearest sidewalk bench and planted myself on it. My arms trembled despite my jacket as my mind immediately jumped to the worst-case scenario. "What happened? Are you alright?"

"I'm fine," he answered, even though he clearly wasn't.

"I'm coming to see you. What's your room number?"

"I'm in Room 256," he said.

"Does Madison know?"

"Yeah," he confessed. "It happened last night."

"What happened?"

"I'll explain when you get here. But yeah, the Kents were with me all night. They just left. Madison called out of work. She didn't get much sleep." I wished she had texted me so that I wouldn't worry, but it made sense that her focus had been on Bellamy, not me.

"Okay," I said, mind reeling. "Try to get some rest. I'll get there as soon as I can."

I ended the call and stood up, looking around frantically for a cab. My apartment wasn't that far from the restaurant, so I had walked to work. But the hospital was miles away, and I needed to get there *fast*. I spun around slowly, pressing my palm to my forehead as I thought. Icy raindrops slid down my cheeks, causing me to shiver.

"Grace?" a familiar, sweet voice called out. "Are you alright, dear?" It was Mrs. Johnson, the widow who frequented the Sunny Side Grille. She stood there with a black umbrella clutching her purse with her other hand. "You look like you've seen a ghost."

I realized then how rapid and shallow my breaths had become. I tried to calm myself. Hugging my arms across my waist, I answered, "I'm fine. It's my friend. I just found out he's in the hospital."

"Do you need a ride, dear?"

I chewed my lip. "Oh, you don't have to give me a ride. I can catch a cab."

Mrs. Johnson dragged her gaze along the street, calling attention to the fact that there were no cabs in sight. "I'm afraid you'll be waiting a while then." She jerked her head in the direction of her car, which was parked in its usual spot in front of the restaurant. "Come on. I'll be happy to take you."

Deciding to accept her help rather than waste time by not wanting to put her out, I eagerly nodded. "Thank you so much."

Mrs. Johnson fished her keys out of her light pink purse and motioned toward the vehicle. I quickly climbed into the passenger seat.

My stomach was in knots the whole way there. And hitting every single red light along the way didn't help. I pressed my head against the window, staring out blankly at the shops and businesses we passed along the way. Thunderclouds rolled across the sky, casting us in their shadows. Seconds later, an onslaught of rain pounded against the car.

"What happened to your friend, if you don't mind me asking?" Mrs. Johnson asked. I think she sensed that my thoughts were spiraling out of control, and she was trying to snap me out of it by making conversation.

"I'm not sure," I confessed. "All he told me was that he was in the hospital and he would explain everything when I got there."

"*He*, huh?" she asked, and when I glanced over my shoulder at her I noticed her mouth had pursed into a knowing smile. "Would this be your boyfriend?"

I shook my head. "No. At least, I don't think so. I don't know what we are exactly." I didn't know why I was so worked up. He was obviously okay—after all, he'd been the one who'd called me. I think, when it came down to it, that with a big chunk of my memories missing, I'd felt so alone in the world. And somehow with Bellamy I felt like I belonged. I wasn't naïve enough to think that whatever was going on between us was serious or something that would last forever. But for a while now, I'd been living my life on autopilot, wanting so badly to piece together the fragments of my past, yet somehow not actually making the effort to do it. It was like I was living someone else's life. But even if what Bellamy and I had wasn't *forever*, it was real. And it made me feel alive.

The thought of that being ripped from me tore me to shreds.

Distracted by our conversation, Mrs. Johnson didn't realize the upcoming light had turned red. And neither had I until it was too late.

She slammed on the breaks, but thanks to the rain, the car began to skid across the intersection. All at once, time around me slowed. A red truck was heading right toward the passenger side of the car. My hands flew out in response. As if by magic, the truck veered around us at the last second, and Mrs. Johnson steered us back into the proper lane unscathed.

She released a breath, and I noticed her lower lip was quivering. She blinked, clearly in shock. "I'm so sorry, dear."

"It's okay," I answered, trying to sound more reassuring than I felt. I took a deep breath, too. "Everything's okay."

We spent the rest of the ride in silence until she pulled up and parked in the circular driveway in front of the hospital.

"Would you like me to come in?" she offered.

"I'll be fine. Thanks for the ride, though."

She dipped her head in acknowledgment, and I shut the door, not wasting a second to watch her drive away. I ran for the door, my sneakers sloshing in the large puddles with each stride. I pushed my drenched hair away from my face as I entered through the automatic doors.

The elevator was out of order, so I had to take the stairs. I was out of breath by the time I reached Room 256—more because of the sheer panic blossoming in my chest than the climb. I took a split-second to compose myself before deciding that trying to do so was utterly useless. My hair was a mess, my pink waitress outfit was soaked to the point of looking like it was painted to my body and I knew without a doubt that I had mascara all over my cheeks.

None of that mattered.

Eager to see Bellamy, to see for myself that he was okay, I opened the door. "Bellamy?" I called out.

Bellamy sat up in his bed, wincing as he adjusted himself. I rushed to his side, holding his face in my hands. Our eyes locked, and I leaned in and kissed him gently. I rested my forehead on his and let out a breath. "I'm so sorry this happened to you," I whispered. I sat on the edge of his bed now and took his strong hand in mine. "Please, tell me everything."

Wincing as he did so, he readjusted himself so that he was sitting higher. He pulled his arm out of his hospital gown, allowing the thin fabric to fall and reveal his chest. Across his abdomen was a massive square of multiple layers of gauze. The gauze was saturated with blood.

I let out a gasp, and my fingers reached toward the injury—though I didn't dare touch it. Lifting my gaze, I locked in on his hazel eyes. "What happened to you?"

He shook his head. "I don't know how to explain it. Last night, Nathaniel and I had closed up the bar and were going to head home—but he was all riled up after a rough night of work and wanted to blow off some steam. He needed to vent, so we decided to walk a couple of laps around the park. And then..." His voice trailed off like he didn't know what to say next.

"Then?"

His throat bobbed as he recalled the events of last night. "We were attacked."

"Attacked? What happened?"

His eyes glossed over like he was lost in a memory. "I don't know exactly. I was talking, and I thought Nathaniel was right there beside me. But when I looked over at where he should have been, I realized he was gone. When I turned around, I saw him face-down on the ground. And the next thing I knew, there was this burning sensation in my side. The back of my head hit the sidewalk, and then I woke up here."

I placed my hand on top of his and squeezed it. "And you don't know who did this to you?"

"I never saw the guy," he said with a tinge of both sadness and anger in his voice. "The police think it was a mugger, but the weird thing was that nothing was taken."

"That's really strange," I said, trying to process this. "So, what did the mugger attack you with?"

"I have no idea. The doctor said it looked like a really deep cut or scratch."

I frowned, not knowing what to say. Eventually, I trailed my thumb along the back of his hand. "I'm glad you're okay," I said. He smiled at that. Wanting to lighten the mood, I added, "I had a great time with you at the party, by the way. Thanks again for taking me."

"I had a great time, too. And I'm sorry I didn't text you back sooner. We were slammed at work, and then..."

I playfully rolled my eyes. "I guess getting attacked is a reasonable excuse."

"You know," he said, brushing his curly brown hair away from his face, "I was worried you wouldn't want to see me."

"Why?"

"I thought maybe you'd thought I'd ignored you and you wouldn't give me a second chance."

"That's silly."

He chuckled, which caused him to wince and reach for his wound. With a sigh, he added, "I'm glad you think so. Because I—" A knock at the door interrupted him. "Come in!" Bellamy called out.

The nurse flew through the door, medicine and a cup of water in tow. "Time for your painkillers," she reminded him. He tossed them back in his throat and chased them down with the water. "Get some rest, okay?"

He nodded and waited to speak until he heard the door click shut behind her. "Anyway," he carried on, "I was trying to say that I like you, Grace."

Heat rushed to my cheeks, and I knew they had turned bright red. "I like you, too."

"I know we haven't known each other that long, but I'd really like to keep getting to know you. And if anything, this," he said, gesturing toward his injury, "was a reminder of how short life is. I hope this doesn't sound too bold of me, but I'd love it if you'd be my girlfriend."

I paused for a moment, processing what he'd just asked. "Are you sure those aren't the painkillers talking?"

He smiled. "I'm sure."

I leaned forward and kissed him. "Good. And for what it's worth, I happen to like *bold*."

He broke away from the kiss and asked, "Is that a yes?"

I covered my mouth with my hand as I laughed. "Yes."

He scooted over to the side of the hospital bed and motioned an invitation for me to lie down beside him on his uninjured side. Carefully, I did as he asked, nuzzling my head against his shoulder. "It's amazing how in less than twelve hours I've managed to have both the worst and best day ever," he said to himself as he drifted off to sleep, smiling.

I rested there beside him delighting in the warm fuzzy feeling of belonging. I may not know who I had been in recent years, but I knew who I was now.

I tried to stay awake, but eventually, the lack of sleep got the better of me. I dozed off—only to startle awake at one of my nightmares. Gasping out of instinct, I clutched my chest as my eyes popped open.

Bellamy jolted awake, too. He moaned as he turned to face me. "What was that about?"

How could I begin to explain that I had recurring dreams about murdering someone? "Nightmares," I answered vaguely as I sat upright, drawing my knees in close.

"Do you get those a lot?"

I chewed my lip and shook my head. "Every single night. The same one over and over, playing on repeat."

"That sucks. What's it about?"

I looked away. "I'd rather not say."

"Keeping secrets, are we?" he chuckled innocently. "Should I be worried?"

"No, no. Definitely not. It's just... sometimes I feel like I'm living someone else's life. And the nightmares feel so real. More like I'm reliving a memory."

His left eyebrow arched. "Well, are you?"

"No way." I rested my chin on my knee. "At least, I hope not."

"Um, wouldn't you know if it was one of your memories?"

I stopped short of being honest with him. I wanted to tell him about the memory gaps, but things were so perfect right now. I didn't want to risk ruining that. "You'd think so, wouldn't you?"

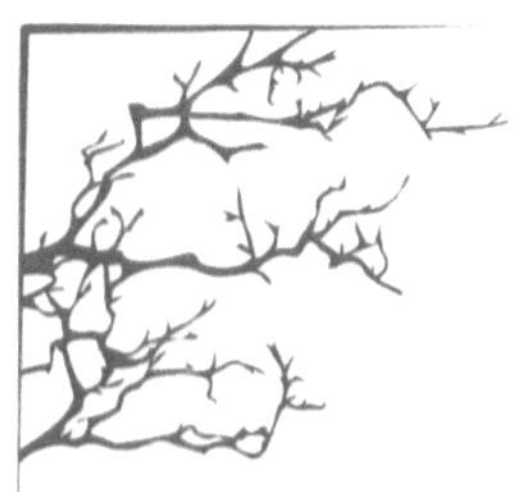

Xander

"What if she never wants to see me again?" I groaned, burying my fingers into my dark hair as I sat hunched over on Uncle Ben's couch. My nails dug into my scalp.

"You had a fight," Uncle Ben pointed out from the kitchen as he mixed a drink for me—as if that would help. "Friends fight. And then they forgive each other."

I shook my head. He didn't understand. This was more than just a fight between friends. It was deeper than that. And now, I feared I'd lost her forever.

I'd never wanted to hurt her.

But I couldn't wrap my head around why she hadn't come back for me. Why she hadn't gone after the Albrights. She'd seen Sofia attack me. She *knew* it was her. And even if I could justify her ditching me completely, why hadn't she returned to Quarter Square?

Uncle Ben offered me a martini—extra dirty—and I downed it in one giant gulp. He towered over me, frowning. "She forgave this guy," he said, gesturing toward Aiden. "She'll forgive you, too."

Aiden nodded along in agreement.

"Part of me wants to track her down," I confessed, "and the other part of me wants to let her walk away. Maybe I was too harsh with her."

"Xander—" Aiden started.

"You weren't there!" I growled, not meaning to take my anger out on him, but unleashing it anyway. I stood, pacing now across the living room. "Someone got to Isla, the witch we were tracking down, first. Which meant our final lead turned out to be a dead end. Which meant..." I let out a breath, knowing they knew the rest.

"Even if you went too far," Uncle Ben said, cautiously stepping closer to me, "it's Grace we're talking about. She would never have abandoned you knowing you were in trouble."

Aiden shifted in his seat. "Did you overhear the witches saying anything about her?"

"No," I barked. Then I thought on it for a moment. I vaguely remembered something Evangeline had said to me... I closed my eyes, thinking, trying to replay the moment like a movie in my mind's eye. "One of the witches said Grace wasn't coming back for me—and that Sofia had seen to that." They exchanged uneasy glances at that. "But she also said Grace was fine."

Uncle Ben crossed his arms, his brow wrinkling. "That doesn't make any sense. What could that mean?"

"It doesn't matter," Aiden said, standing now, too. "The Albrights can't be trusted. We need to find her, and when we do, she can explain everything herself."

I briefly considered objecting. What if Grace had decided to give up on this futile hunt and start over somewhere else—far away from me and my siblings and everything that reminded her of Crescent Cape? And yet... I couldn't let her walk out of my life without knowing *why*.

Why had she given up on me? Why had she abandoned me when I needed her the most?

"I'll get my witch friend to do another tracking spell. This time, we'll need something of Grace's."

I planted my hands on my hips, scanning the room for anything she might have left here. I guessed we'd have to break into her old apartment...

"Would that work?" Uncle Ben asked, gesturing toward me.

Realizing what he was referring to, I glanced down at the bracelet on my wrist and instinctively ran my fingers across it. It was the Bracelet of Wynstar—a woven cord made of dark unicorn hair with a gold pendant in the center. Grace had infused it with her magic when I was under Reed Carlisle's control years ago. Her father had cursed me, forcing me to attack Danielle. And, naturally, Grace wasn't about to let that happen. When she finally got the bracelet on me and said her little enchantment, it rendered me powerless to fulfill the orders I'd been forced to carry out—effectively nullifying Reed's curse. Now that he was dead and Danielle was nowhere to be found, I probably could have taken it off. Well, *I* couldn't. Only another person could remove it. But I'd never thought to ask her to, and she'd never offered. Most of the time, I forgot it was even there.

I stared down at the gold pendant, mindlessly trailing my thumb along the engraving that had appeared when Grace cast the spell—an ancient rune that said *grace*. I still wasn't sure if she'd done that as a joke. She claimed she had no idea that would happen, but I always wondered if part of her just wanted to make me walk around with her name on my wrist for a laugh. We weren't exactly on great terms back then. We'd tolerated each other, at best.

"That's the bracelet she used to—?" Aiden started.

"Yes," I answered, cutting him off.

"So, it has her magic in it," he announced, clapping his hands together. "That's perfect." He retrieved his phone from his pocket and wandered into the hallway to call that witch friend of his.

With Aiden out of the room, I decided to press Uncle Ben about something else that was on my mind. I jerked my head toward the kitchen, and he followed me over there. Not that it would do us much good since Aiden could hear us from all the way over here again. I hoped he would be too preoccupied with the phone call to eavesdrop, though.

"What's up?" Uncle Ben asked, resting his hip against the counter as he folded his arms across his chest.

"You really think this was a good idea?" I asked, glancing over toward my brother.

Uncle Ben sighed. "Absolutely not. Believe me. I tried talking him out of it."

"Don't get me wrong, I'm glad you two rescued me and all. I'm just surprised that he *turned* willingly. I thought he wanted to be a human."

"Maybe he wanted his brother more."

I clenched my teeth so hard it made my jaw twitch. There was more to this, I was sure. But I didn't have time to think about it much longer because Aiden came storming back into the room. "We've got a problem."

Rolling my eyes, I asked, "What now?"

"Starla won't help us. She said she helped once as a favor to me, but that she doesn't want to get caught up in some supernatural showdown with the Albrights."

Great. Just great.

"Well, then," Uncle Ben said, "we can always do this the old-fashioned way." I cocked my head to the side, waiting for him to continue. "We split up. Xander, why don't you check out her hometown—Portland, isn't it? Aiden can go back to where you last saw her in upstate New York. And I can check around neighboring towns. I'll start with Amber Falls."

Considering we had no other ideas, Aiden and I agreed. Was it a great plan? No. But it was a plan. And it would have to be good enough for now.

The three of us gathered our things and then filed out the front door heading in different directions. Aiden had arranged—through compulsion, no doubt—for my car to be brought to Uncle Ben's. Having my brother as a vampire again did have its perks.

I climbed inside the car and turned on the ignition, smiling as it thrummed to life. I mindlessly glanced at my bracelet. *I'm coming for you, Grace,* I thought to myself as I sped in the direction of Portland. *And I'm going to bring you back home where you belong.*

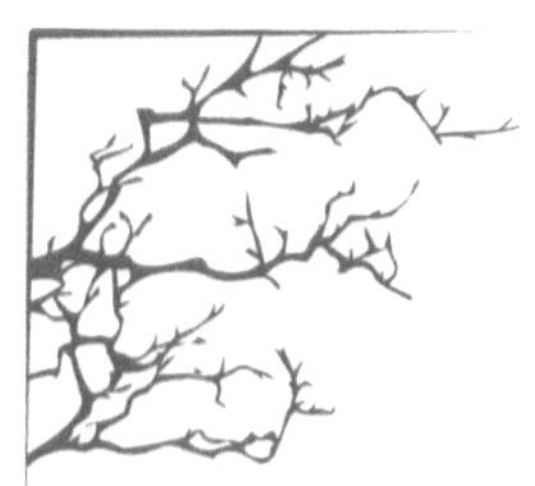

Xander

Once my hunger had been satiated, the redheaded middle-aged woman sat there staring mindlessly at the romantic comedy playing in theater nine. The humans had outlawed vampires feeding on them. But let's be honest, vampires had been feeding on humans for centuries without them being any the wiser. Their laws meant nothing.

I complied for the most part for Grace's sake. I drank the "red drink" most of the time. But it was like eating a carrot to satisfy a craving for a juicy burger fresh off the grill. It was food, but it wasn't the same. And it certainly didn't satisfy you.

So, sometimes it was necessary to drink from the vein. To get the real stuff.

I found that movie theaters made for the perfect spot for feeding. They were dark. Crowded. All you had to do was find a seat in the top row. To anyone who might happen to turn around, it would simply look like I was in the midst of a make-out session.

I compelled the moviegoers I fed on to keep quiet and keep watching the movie. To stay calm. To not feel pain. And then, I drank.

Bars and nightclubs made for great feeding spots, too. But it was the middle of the day, and I was hungry. Plus, I was going to need all the strength I could muster if I was going to track down Grace.

Now that I'd had my fill, I left the movie early, not particularly interested in actually watching a chick flick, and headed for the restaurant situated at the front of the upscale movie theater complex. I needed to take a minute to think through what I was going to say to Grace. *I'm sorry* didn't seem sufficient. I never meant to fight with her. But, being a vampire meant that my emotions were always running on overdrive. The frustration with what was beginning to feel like a futile search and the shock of what we thought was our one hope of finally getting faerie dust slipping away was too much for me. And I lost it. But now, it was time to make things right.

Helping myself to an empty red booth, a waitress promptly greeted me with a menu.

"Good afternoon. Welcome to Mike's Bar and Grille. My name's Skylar, and I'll be your server. What can I start you off with this afternoon?"

"Can I get a coffee? Black?"

"Sure thing." She gave me a flirtatious wink before collecting the payment from the couple at the table behind me.

"It was so great to see you again, Mr. and Mrs. Addington," the waitress said to the people seated behind me. My ears perked up. Curious, I glanced over my shoulder. The middle-aged couple flashed warm smiles at the girl. Mr. Addington dipped his head and replied, "Sure thing, Skylar. Say hi to your parents for us."

"Will do."

I was trying not to stare, but I couldn't help myself. What were the chances that they could be who I thought they were?

Pretending like I was looking for someone, I stole glances at the couple. I tried to memorize everything about them. The wrinkles around Mrs. Addington's eyes. The way Mr. Addington coiffed his graying hair to the left side. The way they held each other's hands while they waited for Skylar to return with their credit card.

Moments later, Skylar slipped the black check holder back to them and waved goodbye as they left. Then, she proceeded to bring the ceramic mug filled with steaming coffee to me. Taking a chance, I asked, "Do you know them?" I gestured to where the couple had been sitting.

"The Addingtons? Of course. Their daughter was one of my best friends." Her bright features suddenly faded into repressed pain.

"*Was?*" I asked, brow furrowed.

"You don't know about Grace?" she asked, her voice tinged with sadness. She lowered her head. "You're not from around here, are you?"

I shook my head, playing dumb. My dark eyes locked in on her green ones, and I wielded my control over her mind. "Tell me about her."

Since she had no choice but to comply, the waitress slipped into the seat across from me. "Grace and I were best friends in high school... until she went missing."

"How long ago was that?"

"I don't know. Seven years ago, maybe?"

"I see. So, what happened to her?"

Skylar shrugged. "No one knows. Most people think she's dead. When she vanished, the whole community searched for her. People were looking for months. It was devastating."

"Do you? Think she's dead, I mean?"

She thought about it for a moment. "No. The Addingtons haven't given up on finding her. They believe she's still out there somewhere. And since they still believe she may be alive, so do I. She might have run away. Or she might have been kidnapped. Who knows? I just hope she's okay, wherever she is."

"The Addingtons are still looking for her?"

"Yes. Of course. They love her." Skylar cocked her head to the side. "Why are you so curious about Grace?"

Getting annoyed, I leaned in. "Don't ask questions."

"Okay," she said, her green eyes glazing over in submission.

"What do you remember about her?" I asked, realizing I didn't know much about what Grace's life was like before she was brought to Crescent Cape.

"She was fun. A little devious. Whenever we had sleepovers, she'd always insist we sneak out of the house. We didn't do anything too crazy. We usually just toilet papered the houses of guys in our class. Ryan, mostly."

"Who's Ryan?"

"He's her boyfriend. Or, he *was* her boyfriend."

Interesting. Grace had never mentioned Ryan before. I wondered why...

"What happened to Ryan?"

"I haven't kept up with him. He's not on social media. Last I heard, he had become a private investigator. I think Grace's disappearance really messed with his head."

"Is there anything else you can tell me about Grace?"

"She was a good friend. The best friend anyone could ever hope for. She put on a tough exterior. I think knowing her birth parents had given her up made her feel like she had to prove herself to people. To prove that she was worthy of being loved. And when *she* loved someone, she loved them with her whole heart."

My throat bobbed as I swallowed. "Forget this conversation, Skylar." And I released my hold over her.

Confusion contorted her features. Warily, she glanced around. "What—what am I doing?" Cheeks flushing, she swept her dark hair off her shoulder and stood. "Sorry about that." She glanced back at the seat, having no idea why she'd been sitting with me.

I slipped her some cash to cover the coffee, along with a generous tip, before downing the drink and heading outside. Maybe I wouldn't find Grace in Portland. Her parents would have mentioned it to Skylar if she had returned. But I wondered if I should stick around a bit longer... I knew how much Grace missed her parents. How she only stayed away from them in order to make sure they stayed safe from the supernatural world. But since I was here, it wouldn't hurt to pay them a little visit. Maybe being able to update Grace on how they were doing would help me earn her forgiveness. It was worth a shot, wasn't it?

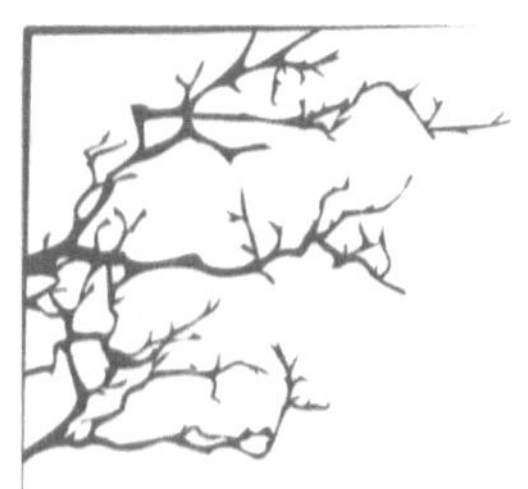

Xander

From what I'd gathered, Grace's dad had recently retired from his job as an orthodontist. Which I hoped meant that he would be at home in the middle of the day.

I strolled up to the Addingtons's front door. I hoped I was doing the right thing here. That getting her information about what her family had been up to since she left would bring her some peace about the situation. I'd compel them to forget everything when I was done and leave them with a sense of peace, too. Grace wasn't a fan of me using compulsion, but surely she'd agree that making sure her adoptive parents didn't spend the rest of their lives fretting over her was the most merciful thing I could do.

Straightening my posture so that I was standing tall, I knocked on their front door. Mr. Addington opened it, oblivious to the fact that there was a vampire at his doorstep. He tilted his head and smiled. "How can I help you?"

"I'm a reporter with the Portland Herald," I lied. "I was hoping to talk to you about your daughter."

Mr. Addington's face lit with hope. He sucked in a sharp breath. "Do you have any information about Grace? Have you found something?"

"Do you mind if we talk inside?"

"Of course," he said, gesturing for me to enter. "Come on in." He led me to the living room where his wife was enjoying a plate of assorted macaroons and lavender tea. It was hard to believe Grace had grown up here. The place seemed so *normal* for such an extraordinary girl.

I pulled out my phone and hit record, keeping up the guise that I was a reporter, but also thinking Grace might appreciate hearing her parents' voices again. I shifted my weight in the plush floral loveseat and began questioning them. "Let's start at the beginning. What do you remember about Grace's disappearance?"

Mr. Addington frowned.

His wife's features turned stern. She looked at her husband. "George, honey. Who is this man?"

"A reporter with the Herald," Mr. Addington explained. "He has questions about our daughter."

Mrs. Addington's eyes glistened with tears, and she nodded, signaling that it was okay to proceed with the interview, although it was clear she wanted no part in it.

Answering my question, Mr. Addington recalled that fated evening. "Grace was staying at a friend's house. The girls decided to sneak out and head to a local park to meet up with friends. And they did." He wiped his brow as if recounting what he knew was bringing up emotions he'd much rather bury. "The last thing anyone remembers, they were hanging out by the swing set when Grace thought she heard something. She went to investigate, and she never came back." Mr. Addington covered his mouth in a failed attempt to hide the fact that he was crying. "I'm so sorry," he said, wiping away his tears with the back of his hand. "It's still so hard to talk about."

I nodded, giving a respectful pause before proceeding with my next question. "So, what do you think happened to her?"

"I don't know. But Grace was a good kid. She wouldn't have just run away."

He wasn't wrong. Grace was fiercely loyal to the people she cared about. Even to me, until recently. And she hated hurting people.

Grace never talked about how she was taken. Though, to be fair, I never asked her. I'd spent more time than I cared to admit trying to remember if I had been the one who had taken her. But hearing Mr. Addington's version of the story brought me great relief. Because I knew without a doubt that I'd never been to a playground in a park in Portland, Maine.

Releasing a breath, I continued with my questioning. "What do you think happened to her?"

Mrs. Addington placed down her tea and left the room, not wanting anything to do with this conversation. I wasn't trying to upset her. I'd make it right soon enough.

Mr. Addington shrugged. "All I know is that my daughter is still out there. And I have to find out what happened to her. One of her worst fears growing up was that she was unlovable. I think her birth parents giving her up did a number on her." His lower lip began to quiver, and he took a deep breath to calm himself. "That's the hardest part about all of this. I'm terrified that she's out there somewhere thinking that we gave up on her. Or, worse, that we didn't care enough to keep looking. That's why we've never given up on her search for her. And we never will."

I swallowed down a lump in my throat.

I heard a knock at the front door, and Mrs. Addington called out that she would get it. So, I continued with my final question. "Mr. Addington, if there was anything that you could tell Grace right now, what would it be?"

He hung his head, pondering the millions of things he no doubt wanted to say to her. Finally, his chin lifted. "I'd tell her that her mom and dad love her. I'd tell her that we believe in her. And if someone took her from us, which I suspect they did, then I'd tell her to fight. Because she deserves so much better out of life than this."

"Anything else?"

He glanced up, his eyes meeting mine. "Finally, I'd tell her to come home."

With that, I turned off the recording. "Thank you for your time, Sir," I said as I stood to my feet. "Do you mind if I take a picture before I go?" I thought Grace might appreciate getting to see them again.

Obliging, Mr. Addington called for his wife to join him in the living room. She quickly entered, and a young man in his early 20s followed in behind her. He had dark skin and a wide smile, and yet there was a hardness in his eyes. Pain or grief, perhaps. I wondered if he knew Grace, too.

Mr. and Mrs. Addington situated themselves in front of the fireplace, posing in front of the mantle where pictures of their daughter were arranged in a beautiful display. I snapped a picture and thanked them profusely. Glancing over my shoulder at the stranger, I said, "Do you mind giving us a moment?"

"It's okay, dear," Mrs. Addington said to him.

Hesitantly, the stranger nodded, reluctantly humoring me. He slid back into the hallway out of sight.

I placed my hands on the Addingtons's shoulders, locking my gaze in on theirs, the powers of my mind overwhelming theirs. "Grace is alive, and she's perfectly safe," I told them. "She started a life of her own. But she can't come back here. You don't need to know why. It's time to stop looking for her. Just know that your daughter is okay. And that she loves you more than anything. She wants you to be happy. *It's okay to be happy. And it's okay to be at peace.*"

I let go of their shoulders, and, dazed, the Addingtons stared blankly at me. They blinked, looking at each other. Soon, the harsh lines in Mr. Addington's face relaxed, and I knew with certainty that my compulsion had worked.

Satisfied with myself, I said my goodbyes and started out the door.

As I headed back down the sidewalk, I sensed somebody following me. Expecting it to be Mr. Addington, I turned around only to find the same stranger from before rearing his arm back.

By the time I realized that he was holding a knife, the silver and wooden blade was already lodged into my stomach. Blood poured from my belly, and I let out a threatening snarl, staring my attacker down.

"You missed," I hissed at him. In a flash, I ripped the knife out of my torso and tackled the man, pinning him on his back. He let out a whelp as his head hit the cement, but it wasn't hard enough of a fall to knock him out. "Who are you?" I said through gritted teeth.

The stranger spat in my face. "The name's Ryan Tanner. And you may have no idea who I am. But I know *exactly* what you are."

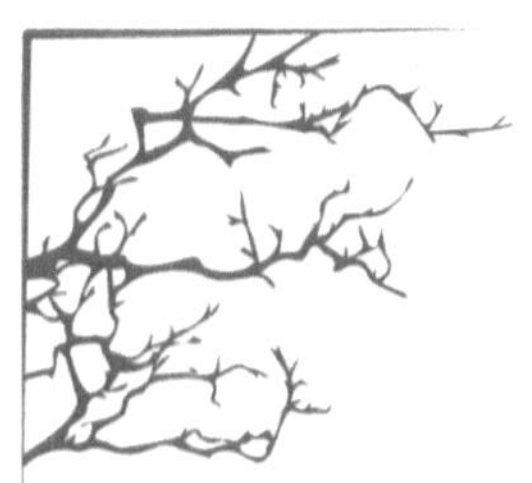

Grace

I tugged at the collar of my uniform, watching the clock. A couple more hours and my shift would be over, and I could go spend time with Bellamy. He had checked himself out of the hospital and was recovering at his apartment now. I still didn't understand why he'd suddenly become so insistent on getting out of there, but there wasn't anything I could do about it.

I arched my back and stretched out my arms. The muscles in my shoulders were screaming in pain after the bizarre contortions I'd found myself in trying to get comfortable yesterday in that sad excuse for a chair the hospital provided. But I was happy to have been able to be there for Bellamy. Thankfully, my boss had been understanding about Madison and me both missing work yesterday. One of our co-workers had been asking to pick up extra shifts anyway and another didn't mind helping out, so it all worked out.

I covered my mouth with the back of my hand while I let out a yawn. These next two hours couldn't go by fast enough. I brushed past Madison, who was carrying a tray full of drinks to one of her tables, and poured myself a cup of coffee. One of the few perks of working at the Sunny Side Grille was that we were allowed to help ourselves to as much coffee as we wanted.

I had just finished downing the liquid energy boost when a customer came in. He quickly took a seat and buried his head in the menu. Seeing as that I wasn't doing anything of importance, I marched over to his booth and pulled out my pad and pencil to take his order. "Welcome to the Sunny Side Grille," I said with a smile, trying to look more alert than I felt.

The man slowly pulled the menu down and gaped at me, jaw hanging wide open.

"I'm sorry," I said. "I didn't mean to startle you."

"Grace?" he asked.

I nodded cheerfully, pointing to the snazzy new name tag I'd been given last week. "How'd you guess?" I said with a wink.

The stranger furrowed his brow. "Grace, what are you talking about? It's me." I frowned, staring at the middle-aged man sitting before me. I had no idea who this guy was, but he sure seemed certain he knew me. "*Ben*," he added in a tone that suggested that should mean something to me.

I glanced around the room, not knowing what to say. "I'm sorry," I said, shaking my head. "I don't know who you are."

I started to walk away, but he grabbed my wrist. "Very funny," he said sternly. "Grace, we've been looking everywhere for you. If you're mad at Xander, I can—"

I snatched my wrist out of his hold. I had to admit, there was some part of me that was curious to hear more. After all, I was missing out on *years* of my memories. But how could I trust that he wasn't just some lunatic? "Look, buddy. I don't know who you think you are, but you can't just stroll in here and try messing with my head."

"What happened to you?" he asked, his hushed voice filled with sadness. "Did the Albrights do something to you? What's going on, Grace?"

"Who are the Albrights?"

"The Albrights," he said, growing frustrated even though, to his credit, he was trying not to show it. "As in Sofia Albright. As in the woman who attacked you and Xander in New York."

I frowned. "I've never been to New York," I confessed. "And I don't know what you're talking about. You've got the wrong girl."

Part of me wanted to walk away, but the other part of me was screaming for me to press him with questions. He sounded crazy. And yet, something deep in my gut, some primal part of me, told me I could trust him.

It didn't make any sense.

What connection could I possibly have to this guy?

And why would he show up here out of the blue *now*?

And yet... what if he did know something about my past? Shouldn't I hear him out?

"You really don't remember, do you?" he asked under his breath. Something about the sincerity in his voice made me profoundly uncomfortable. "Your memories," he said as if a lightbulb had gone off in his head. "I didn't think it was possible, but... Sofia said she'd make sure you wouldn't come back for Xander, but that you were fine." He was standing now, piecing together this bizarre puzzle in his mind. "That's because she altered your memories, didn't she?" My breath caught at that. Yes, I had those memory gaps. But someone couldn't *alter* my memories. Could they? "I *knew* it. I knew you wouldn't have just left us."

I scratched the back of my head. "How do you know about—?"

He cut me off before I had a chance to finish my sentence. Taking a step closer to me, he took me by the shoulders, and in the most serious tone possible said words that sent a surge of frost down my spine: "Everything you think you know is wrong."

I shook my head, not wanting to believe him, yet somehow knowing every word he said was true.

"Come with me," he said, motioning for me to follow him outside.

And, like a fool, I did.

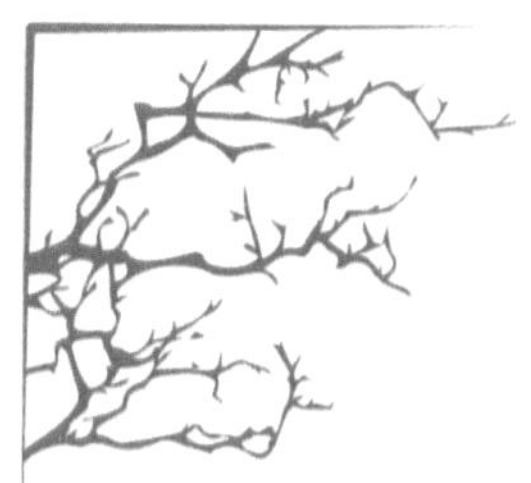

Grace

I startled awake. I'd had a strange dream, but it was better than the nightmares I was used to. I stretched out my arms until they hit against something. My eyes popped open, and a surge of adrenaline coursed through my veins. Breathing rapidly now, I looked to my side and found the man from the dream sitting behind the steering wheel.

Then it dawned on me. That hadn't been a dream.

A chilling scream tore from my lungs, ripping through the air.

He startled at that, but then flashed me an assuring smile. "Grace, everything's going to be fine. I'm bringing you home."

Acting on instinct, I scooted as far away from him as my seat would allow. I took a quick inventory of my surroundings. We were on the outskirts of Amber Falls on a narrow street in the middle of nowhere. There was no one else around.

Heart pounding, I reached for my phone, but it was gone.

Horrified, my gaze met my captor's.

"Grace, I promise I'm not going to hurt you. I don't know what the Albrights did to mess with your head, but Xander, Aiden and I are going to find a way to help you. Okay?"

"You... you kidnapped me," I hissed. How did he even pull that off? I didn't remember getting in the car with him. And I was getting really sick and tired of not remembering things.

He held up a finger in protest. "No, technically, I rescued you. I swear, it will make sense soon. For now, you're going to have to trust me."

I shook my head in defiance. "No. No. No way." Ben started to say something, but I cut him off. "My coworkers will realize I'm missing. And my boyfriend will come looking for me."

Ben offered me a pitying look. "Boyfriend, huh? Well, rest assured, I've already called Aiden, and he's on it. Your coworkers will be none the wiser."

I scrunched my eyebrows, not following at all.

That was it. I wasn't going to just sit back and do nothing.

I was going to get away from this guy—or die trying.

I checked the dashboard. He was only going forty miles per hour. I could survive a jump at that speed, right?

I guessed I was about to find out...

Praying I wasn't about to make the dumbest decision of my life, I unbuckled my seatbelt and threw the passenger door open. Not giving myself enough time to run through the mental checklist of all the ways this could go terribly wrong, I jumped from the moving vehicle and slammed into the hard earth before rolling across the grass and gravel.

The wheels of Ben's car screeched as he skidded to the side and made an abrupt stop. My whole body was throbbing, and I thanked my lucky stars I hadn't suffered serious damage. Just scrapes and bruises, if I had to guess. Terrified of what he'd do next, I scrambled to my feet. When I stood, I realized that I had a huge gash on my thigh. Warm blood was oozing down my leg. It wasn't a deep cut, but man, it hurt. I wasn't going to give up that easily, though.

I started hobbling, limping as I hurried to get away from the nutjob. I cupped my hands around my mouth and screamed for someone, anyone, to help me. But there was literally no one around. Other than Ben.

I picked up my pace, dragging my leg behind me as I let the adrenaline take over.

Every inch of me was throbbing, and I wanted to do nothing more than to collapse into a ball and sob uncontrollably, but there wasn't time for that. I could let the tears fall later.

First, I had to *survive.*

"Grace," Ben shouted, panting as he chased after me. I risked a glance over my shoulder and saw that he was pulling something out of his pocket. My heart skipped. *Please don't be a weapon. Please don't be a weapon.* "Just look at this," he said, holding out his phone.

I knew I shouldn't have looked back.

But I did.

He was only a couple of feet behind me now—thanks to my stupid leg—so I got a good look at the screen. It was *me.* And him. And some unthinkably attractive guy. We all had our arms wrapped around each other as we posed for the shot. We were smiling.

Against better judgment, I slowed to a stop. Ben brushed his graying ginger-brown hair away from his face, catching his breath, too. "I know this doesn't make any sense to you right now. But you're practically family, Grace." He held out the phone for me to get a better look. "You can look through the pictures if you want. There are plenty of you in there."

Warily, I took the phone from him. Sure enough, as I swiped through the album, I found picture after picture of me—usually posing next to the James Dean-esque dude. You'd think I'd remember a face like that...

Brow furrowed, I kept swiping, my eyes widening as I realized the photos went back for *years*.

I began to wonder if what he'd said about that Sofia woman wiping my memory was true... It sounded crazy, but just because I hadn't met any before didn't mean supernaturals didn't exist. Whoever that Sofia was, what if she had the power of mind control or something? It wasn't out of the realm of possibility.

Though I had absolutely no idea why she would have come after me. I was nobody.

"I imagine you have a few questions," Ben said, his eyes turning into half-moons as he spoke in a fatherly tone. "I'll tell you whatever you want to know. After that, if you still want to return to Amber Falls, I'll drive you back myself if you want. Just hear me out first, Grace. Okay?"

I swallowed down the lump in my throat. I couldn't understand why I was believing the man who had just kidnapped me, and yet... I could see as clear as day that we had known each other at some point. It was feasible that the pictures could have been edited somehow. But there were videos, too. And that was *definitely* me in them.

Ben had promised he wouldn't harm me. And if he intended to kill me, wouldn't he have done so already? He'd had every opportunity.

I chewed the inside of my cheek, thinking. I *desperately* wanted to get to the bottom of my missing memories. And if there was a chance this guy had answers, then I owed it to myself to hear him out, didn't I?

It wasn't like I had much of another choice anyway. There was no way I was going to be able to hobble all the way back to Amber Falls. And there wasn't another person, car or house in sight. No one was coming to swoop in and rescue me.

Eventually, I nodded, handing him his phone back as I started limping in the direction of his car. "Fine," I said briskly. "Start talking."

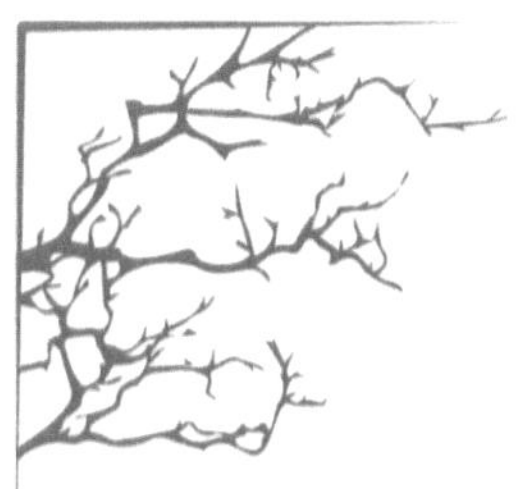

Xander

It turned out that Uncle Ben, Aiden and I weren't the only ones looking for Grace.

It didn't take much to overpower Ryan Tanner after he attacked me. He'd missed my heart. And I was a Blood Heir, an original vampire—made, not turned. Plus, I'd just fed. Which meant I was *strong*.

And as for Ryan, he was only human.

I saluted his effort. Pretty gutsy to assault a vampire in broad daylight in the middle of a well-to-do neighborhood. But also incredibly stupid.

Once I had him pinned, I grabbed him by his whiskered jaw and forced him to look into my eyes. Seething, I overpowered his mind, forcing him to succumb to me. To tell me *everything*.

"My name is Ryan Tanner," he said again, features slackened now. "Grace was my high school girlfriend."

"And you still care about her?" I asked, because I was curious—not threatened. "Seems kind of pathetic to me."

"I was in love with her." I snorted at that. I couldn't help it. "I've never given up looking for her," he continued, his beetle black eyes blazing. "I became a private detective. I've dedicated my life to uncovering the truth about what happened to her."

I frowned at that. "Why did you attack me?"

"Because you're a *vampire*."

"Do you always go around attacking vampires?" I pressed.

"I heard you using compulsion on the Addingtons. I think you know what happened to Grace. I think *you're* the one who kidnapped her."

I pursed my lips. "Afraid not, buddy. And unfortunately, I have no idea where she is, either. You're lucky that I care about Grace. Because if I didn't, I'd have my fangs buried in your carotid artery right now." I helped the lovesick detective up to his feet and wiped the dirt off of his shoulders for him. Patting him on the cheek, I added, "There. Much better. Now, be a good boy and forget this conversation ever happened. Go back about your business. And don't you even think about following me. Got it?"

Ryan nodded.

"Oh, and lay off the cologne. You're trying way too hard," I pointed out. Hey—I was just helping the guy out.

"Okay."

I flicked my hand, ushering him to return to the Addingtons.

After readjusting my T-shirt, I brushed my hands through my hair and started heading in the direction of my car. I hadn't gotten any closer to figuring out where Grace had run off to, but I was certain she wasn't here.

I reached into the glove box and grabbed myself a stick of wintergreen gum. I blew a massive bubble as I backed out of the Addington's driveway, wondering if I should have gone farther with my compulsion of Grace's ex. Maybe I should have made him give up the search for her, too.

I shook my head. One problem at a time.

Hours later, I was nearing Quarter Square when my cellphone buzzed. I answered it without bothering to check to see who it was. "Hello?"

"Xander," Uncle Ben said, sounding like he was catching his breath.

"Hey. I was just about to call you. Portland was a bust. I'm heading back to Quarter Square now."

"Good," Uncle Ben said, his voice getting softer now. "Because I found Grace."

My heart leaped. "Seriously? How?"

"Luck," he answered honestly. "I stopped in a diner in Amber Falls, and she was my waitress."

A deep wrinkled split my brow. "She's waiting tables? Why?"

"Grace is... different than you remember her."

Growing frustrated, I huffed as I took a left turn. "Can you stop talking around whatever is going on and just spit it out already? I just got staked, and my patience is wearing thin."

"Staked? Are you okay?"

"Uncle Ben!"

"Right, right. Grace. I'm almost positive the Albrights wiped her memory."

I glanced around at nothing in particular, processing that. "They can do that?"

"Apparently. Grace has no idea who she is. She has no idea who I am, who Aiden is... or who you are."

My throat bobbed as his words sank in. "Does she know *what* I am?"

"As far as I can tell," he said between hushing his dog in the background, "she doesn't even know what *she* is."

The car rolled to a stop as I came upon a red light. "Well, this should be fun."

"I wanted to warn you, too," Uncle Ben continued, "that she's scared. She thinks I kidnapped her. I mean, technically, I did use some sleeping powder on her—I had a stash in my collection. When she woke up, she thought I was going to hurt her and jumped out of the car."

"Please tell me she didn't—"

"She's fine. A little banged up, but fine."

I released a pent-up breath. Great. This was just great. "How'd you get her back in the car? More sleeping powder? Is she asleep now?"

"No, she's downstairs. She decided to come with me after I showed her pictures of her on my phone. She could tell it was her in the photos, but she has no memories of taking them. I need to get back to her, but I wanted to give you a heads up. She's... different, somehow. You'll need to tread lightly with her for now. At least until we get her memories back."

"And how do you propose we do that?"

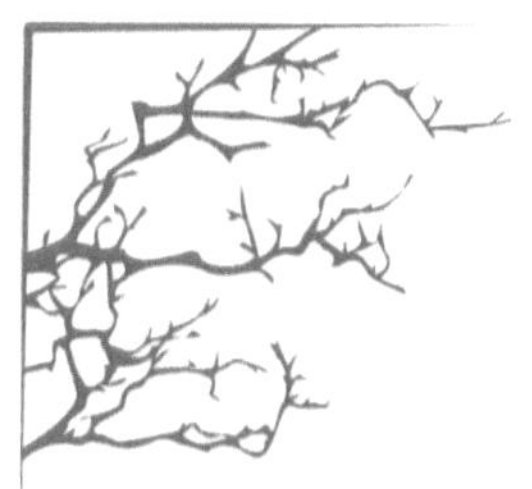

Grace

While Ben was upstairs making a phone call, I snooped around his living room. And I didn't feel bad about it. I wanted to know what kind of guy this *Ben* was.

First things first—I needed to think ahead in case things went south. Unfortunately, he didn't have a landline, so making phone calls was out of the question unless I could get my hands on his cell. But I didn't know Bellamy's number by heart. Or anyone else's for that matter...

I could always call the police. I hoped it wouldn't come to that.

I also took note of where the doors and windows were so that I could make a quick escape if needed.

Weirdly, though, I didn't think I'd have to.

Other than having a ridiculous number of family albums lining the shelves that bookended his fireplace, the guy's place seemed pretty normal. Hearing his heavy footsteps skipping down the stairs, I plopped myself on his couch, tossing my blonde hair over my shoulder, trying to act casual. He had promised to tell me everything once we got to his place, and I was ready to hear what he had to say.

"Find anything interesting?" he joked.

My eyes widened. I thought I'd been quiet while snooping, but maybe I hadn't been as sneaky as I'd thought. "How'd you—?"

"Because I know you, Grace. You're smart. And you've been brought to the house of someone you don't remember who says he knows all about your past. Of course you were going to go through my stuff." He gave an innocent wink. "I'd expect nothing less."

I cleared my throat, unsure of how to respond to that.

He shrugged. "The good stuff's all upstairs anyway." He headed toward the kitchen to pour himself a glass of water. "Want anything?"

"No, thanks." I wanted to keep a clear head. I needed my wits about me in case anything went wrong.

"No problem," he said. "Something tells me you'll change your mind, though."

Carrying his glass back into the living room, he eased into his La-Z-Boy recliner. He was about to start talking when a bark came from one of the back rooms. He set the glass down. "Oh, I almost forgot..." He got back up and disappeared into the hall, returning moments later with a fluffy cream-colored dog. The Goldendoodle jumped onto the couch the second she saw me, squealing uncontrollably like she had missed me. I glanced at Ben warily, but all he did was nod. The dog kept pawing for me to pet her.

"She recognizes you," Ben explained.

I couldn't argue with him. The dog sure did seem to know who I was... "What's her name?" I asked, petting the massive pup as she licked my arm up and down.

"Fangs."

I giggled at that. "She doesn't seem very aggressive," I pointed out.

"She's not. Her bark sounds impressive, but she's just a big old lovebug. The worst she would do is lick you to death."

I smiled at that, still petting the dog. "Good to know."

Ben downed his water and then rubbed his forehead, deep in thought. He let out a sigh like something was weighing heavily on him. "Where to start?" he said, mostly to himself.

I lifted my chin so that I could look him dead-on. "Start with the beginning. The last thing I remember is being with my family in Portland."

He nodded. "Grace, how much do you know about the supernatural world?"

Caught off-guard, I straightened at that. "I know there was a war."

He frowned. "That's all?"

"Pretty much. Why? Is there something else I should know?"

He hesitated. "There's no other way to break this to you other than just saying it outright." He looked me in the eye, unblinking. "Seven years ago, you were taken from your family and brought to Crescent Cape."

My throat suddenly felt dry. "Okay..." I wasn't sure what I'd expected him to say, but it certainly hadn't been that. Already, I had a thousand questions. But I kept my mouth shut. I could drill him for information after he told me what he knew. I wanted to hear *his* version—the way he told it.

"I didn't meet you until three years later, so I don't know what all happened to you while you were a blood slave. Same as what happened to the others, I presume. Blood slaves lived in the village and once a week would offer themselves up to the vampires on Donation Day. The vampires would take their fill of blood for the week, and they would return to their business while you returned to yours."

Okay, I know I said I wasn't going to ask questions. But how could I not? The dude had just said I was a *blood slave.* "That doesn't make any sense. Why would I let them do that?"

"You were compelled," he explained. "You didn't have a choice in the matter. And before you ask, no, running away wasn't an option. You would have been killed."

I swallowed. "Oh." I was in shock. Days ago, I had gone to Crescent Cape with Bellamy—on a date, no less. The very place where this guy was telling me I served as a blood bag for vampires. I felt sick to my stomach.

He continued his story. "So, a few years later, Julian concocted this hair-brained scheme to usurp power from Prince Aiden."

"Wait—who's Julian? And who's Prince Aiden?"

Ben dragged his fingers along his unshaven face. "I'm sorry. I forget that there is so much to fill you in on... Bear with me, okay? Centuries ago, Queen Rosa and King Leopold, two humans who ruled over Crescent Cape, were struggling to produce an heir. They adopted a boy named Julian, but Queen Rosa desperately wanted a true blood heir to the Crown. So, she made a deal with a witch. She became pregnant with quadruplets: Aiden, Xander, Charlotte and Natalie. But unbeknownst to her, the witch had cursed the children. Twenty years later, the curse took hold. The four siblings were turned into vampires—true Blood Heirs to the throne. And their older brother Julian was transformed into a werewolf—a failsafe to the curse."

My head was spinning. I'd heard one of those names before. "Wait... wait a second. Who were you speaking to upstairs?"

"Xander," he answered truthfully.

I shook my head, trying to process this. I knew the name sounded familiar. Instinctively, I scooted back. "You're not a... a... *vampire*, are you?"

"No. I assure you. I am very much a human."

My throat bobbed as I swallowed. Part of me wanted to run, but some other demented part of me desperately wanted to hear what else he had to say.

Picking up on my cue, Ben continued. "Anyway, about four years ago, Julian came up with the Choosing Ceremony—a scheme to distract Aiden and keep him busy selecting a bride. That's where you came in."

I clasped my hand around the armrest to keep the room from spinning.

"You were summoned to compete for Aiden's heart. While there, you befriended another blood slave—Danielle Parker. Aiden fell for her, but through a bizarre series of events that would take way too long to explain here, Danielle was turned into a hybrid and ended up falling for Julian instead."

"Please tell me I'm not married to a vampire prince," I said, hardly believing the ridiculousness of the words coming out of my mouth.

"No. But... there is something you should know about yourself."

I swore, if this dude was about to tell me that *I* was a vampire, I was going to lose my mind.

"Around the same time, you came into your powers, Grace."

"Powers?" I had no idea what he was talking about. I didn't have any powers. Believe me, if I did, I would have used some woo-woo magic to spell me up a heck of a nicer life than the one I was living.

He nodded somberly. "You're descended from a long line of powerful witches, Grace."

I stood, knowing this was crazy talk. "I assure you that isn't true. My parents are perfectly normal."

His eyes caught mine, and the seriousness in them made my spine tingle. "I'm not talking about the Addingtons, Grace."

He knew I was adopted then. Maybe he really was telling the truth. I sat back down.

"Your father was Reed Carlisle, the leader of the Carlisle coven. He was a terribly evil man. He was the one who dropped the boundary to Crescent Cape, setting off the series of events that led to the war."

My mouth fell open. I didn't know how to respond to that. I had made up a million versions of my birth parents, trying to rationalize why they had given me up and what they must have been like. Never in my wildest imagination had I expected *that*. "Did I ever get the chance to meet him?"

He gave me a look that suggested I did and that it didn't go well. "You have a twin brother," he added, trying to soften the blow.

I sat upright. "I have a brother?"

"His name's Nick. A decent guy, from what you've told me. Surprising, considering Reed raised him."

"And my mother?"

He shook his head. "I'm sorry. I'm afraid you never told me about what happened to her. Perhaps you never knew."

My head was spinning. I had a twin brother? And my father was... the leader of a coven of witches? How was that even possible? I hugged my arms around myself, even though I wasn't particularly cold. "I think I'll take that drink now."

Happy to oblige, Ben headed back into the kitchen and pulled out a bottle of champagne from the refrigerator. "I bought this for your birthday," he said, holding the bottle high in the air. "Happy twenty-first, by the way."

I forced a smile. This was so weird. This guy knew my whole life story—or at least claimed he did. But I had no memory of him. Of any of this. You'd think I'd remember being food for vampires or having magical powers.

I glanced down at my hands, wiggling my fingers. I didn't know what I expected to happen.

Ben brought a flute of champagne over to me. He had a flute for himself in his other one. "I know this probably seems like a weird thing to celebrate, Grace, but you have no idea how good it is to see you again. I'm just glad you're okay." He raised his glass to me.

I took a long sip, savoring the bubbles as they tingled down my throat. "I still don't understand how we met, though. Where do you come in?"

"I forgot that part, didn't I?" he said to himself. "The Blood Heirs and Julian are my ancestors. They refer to me as their uncle now to keep up appearances. When chaos ensued after Julian's Choosing Ceremony backfired, he brought you and Danielle here so that I could keep you safe. Because of your friendship with Danielle, you found yourself entangled in my family's drama."

I set my flute down on the coffee table. "Where are all of these people now, anyway?"

He sighed. "Natalie is dead. Aiden is happily married. And then, when the boundary fell, you used your powers to burn the castle down to the ground. But Julian's photograph was discovered in the ashes. You helped him, Danielle and Charlotte escape through a portal to a faerie realm, which was sealed behind them. And as soon as the war was over, you dedicated every second of your life to figuring out a way to *unseal* the portal."

I blinked. What was I supposed to say to that?

"You and Xander became good friends over the years. Weeks ago, you'd gotten a lead on a woman who might have access to faerie dust—an ingredient you need to open that portal. The two of you went to investigate, and that's when Sofia Albright attacked the two of you. We can only assume that she found some way to wipe your memory clean. She knocked Xander out cold and brought him back to her coven, where he spent weeks strapped to a hospital bed while they did who-knew-what to him. And until recently, Aiden had been enjoying his new human life with his wife Victoria. I called him when I realized you and Xander weren't coming back. Together, we rescued Xander. And then, the three of us split up to look for you."

There was so much to take in. I didn't even know where to begin. "I don't understand. Why would this Sofia woman erase my memories?"

"Maybe because she's from your father's rival coven. Maybe because she is afraid you'll become like him. Who knows?"

The doorbell gave an ominous ring, and Ben's eyes flicked toward the door. "That's either Xander or Aiden."

Great. Wonder who it will be? My vampire BFF or the monster who ruled over me?

"Well, Grace," Ben said as he went to open the door, "I hope you're ready to face your past..."

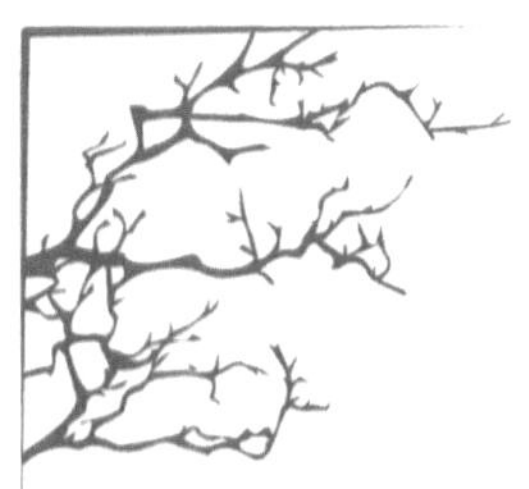

Grace

I followed Ben to the door, and when he opened it, the handsome man from the photographs locked his eyes with mine. I let out a gasp and then immediately felt a rush of heat pooling in my cheeks. I swallowed hard, unnerved by the look he was giving me. He marched in, brushing past Ben, and wrapped me in his arms. His hold was protective and strong, and I found my heart racing.

And then I remembered that he was a vampire and that a racing heart was probably a really bad thing to have around him.

His fingers tangled in my hair as he pulled me in close. I tried to steady my nerves, but a dizzying explosion of sensations took over. "I, uh," I stumbled, unsure of what to say—scared to say the wrong thing. I didn't care what Ben told me about me and my past. It didn't make the idea of being hugged by a *vampire* any less terrifying.

"I'm so sorry, Grace," he whispered, his breath tickling my ear.

Cautiously, carefully, I pulled away and looked up at the man, or being, or whatever he was, standing before me. He looked like a perfectly ordinary person. I mean, devastatingly good-looking with a chiseled physique and a one-sided smile that had probably made countless girls swoon. But he didn't have freakishly pale skin like the vampires in movies. And he certainly wasn't sparkling.

And he was hugging me. Apologizing to me.

Weird.

"Xander, I presume?" I asked, lashes fluttering like I was some ditzy schoolgirl. I did *not* like the effect this guy had on me.

His deep brown eyes clouded with sadness, and he looked over his shoulder at Ben. Like he'd expected me to be thrilled to see him.

But he was a stranger to me.

He removed his hands from me and slid them into the pockets of his leather jacket. "I... I'm sorry," he said, clearly regretting ever touching me.

"It's okay," I said, because what else was there to say?

Ben cleared his throat, the tension in the room palpable. "Aiden should be here soon, too. Xander, why don't you show Grace upstairs?" I looked at him quizzically, so he added, "I told you, all the best stuff is up there."

With a nod, Xander strode toward the staircase, motioning for me to follow. When we were halfway up the stairs, he asked over his shoulder, "How much did Ben fill you in on?"

"Oh, just that I'm a witch, I have a twin brother and psychopathic father. And that my best friend and your family are trapped inside some sealed portal. You know. Totally normal stuff."

He smirked. "I see you still have your sense of humor."

I pressed my lips together and tried to smile. I wasn't sure what to say. This whole situation was so confusing. And overwhelming. And bizarre. "Does that about cover it?" I asked.

"Yep. Pretty much sums it up."

Once upstairs, I followed him into one of the bedrooms. Well, perhaps bedroom wasn't the right word. Sure, there was a bed in there. But there were also weird trinkets—shrunken heads, clunky jewelry, glass orbs. And books. Tons and tons of musty, old books. It was like Ben had raided some Halloween-themed gift shop.

For such a normal-looking guy, he had some pretty strange stuff.

"Did Uncle Ben happen to mention he's a Collector?"

I blinked, having no clue what that meant.

"I take that as a no," Xander said, picking up various items and examining them before putting them back. "He and his line of the family have spent centuries collecting magical objects. Mostly to keep them out of the hands of people like me." He winked.

I instinctively hugged my arms across my chest.

"I'm joking," he added. "Well, kind of. But you don't have to worry about me, Grace. I would never hurt you."

"Ben said I used to be a blood slave," I pointed out.

He cocked his head to the side. "A lot has happened since then. And anyway, you're a witch. Once a witch comes into her powers, any vampire stupid enough to feed from her will be rendered violently ill."

"Oh," I said, tucking my hair behind my ear. "That's, uh, good to know."

Xander stood there for a moment, making heat blossom in my chest as he gave me a once over. His nostril twitched, and his eyes fell on my leg. "You're bleeding," he pointed out.

I brushed my hair away from my face. "Well, it's a good thing you can't drink from me then, huh?" I joked, my voice rising higher than I meant for it to.

"Oh, I could. But I won't. Do you want something for that?"

"Ben already gave me some antibiotic cream for it."

"I meant my blood."

Was that some sort of sick joke? By the way that he was holding out his wrist, exposing his veins, I didn't think so. I thought I was going to puke. "Excuse me?"

"I take it you aren't aware that vampire blood can heal wounds?" he asked. I shook my head. If that was true, how did more people not know about this? "We look out for each other," he continued. "You've saved my life more than once, and I've saved yours, too. It's kind of our thing."

Great. The handsome vampire and I have a *thing*.

He pulled a book from the shelf and handed it to me. "Look familiar?"

I shook my head. "Should it?"

Xander chuckled. "You've only read it cover-to-cover a thousand times."

Curious, I took the heavy, leather-bound book from his hand and opened it. The pages were old and worn and filled with frantic scribbles and intricate drawings. "What is this?"

"A grimoire." Realizing that word meant nothing to me, he added, "It's like a reference book for spells."

I pursed my lips and flipped through it. Tracking spells, levitation spells, reanimation spells, body-jumping spells. None of it looked familiar to me. And honestly, looking through a book filled with spells gave me the heebie-jeebies.

This was all getting to be too much.

Needing to get some air, I shoved the book back at Xander, eyes pleading for him to take it, and whirled around, heading for the door. I hurried down the staircase, clomping with each step, but came to an abrupt stop when I saw another man downstairs deep in conversation with Ben.

The recognition in his ocean-blue eyes gave him away. He was the other vampire from the photos Ben showed me. The one who had reigned over Crescent Cape. The one who I could have been forced to marry if what Ben told me about the Choosing Ceremony was true.

"Grace," he said, his tone a mix of relief and sadness.

I lifted my chin. "Aiden."

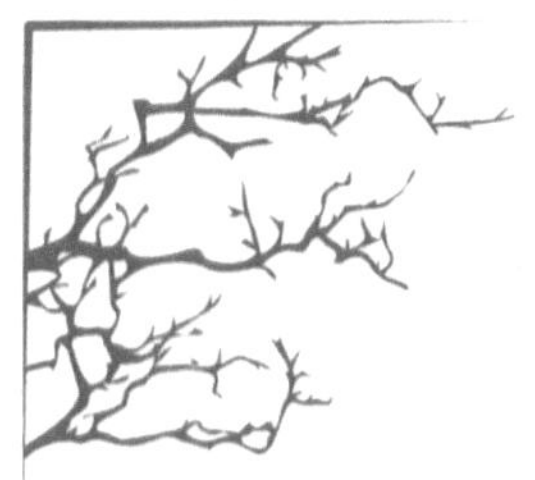

Grace

Before I had the opportunity to get some fresh air, Aiden cut me off, stepping in front of me. He reached into his pocket and pulled out a golden trinket. He handed it to me.

"What is it?" I asked, cradling the object in my hands.

He frowned, having expected me to recognize it. "Uncle Ben told you about the portal, right?"

I nodded warily, unsure of where he was going with this.

"Before the portal was sealed, you used magic to enchant two matching compact mirrors. You gave one to your friend Danielle, and you kept the other. Thanks to your magic, we can use these compacts to communicate with Danielle, Julian and Charlotte."

I examined the compact while Aiden spoke, trailing my fingers along the swirly design on top. Curiosity got the best of me, and I opened it. When I did, I felt a surge of power thrumming from the case. As I studied my reflection, the mirror rippled, replacing my image with that of a young woman about my age. She had deep brown hair that flowed past her shoulders and a wide grin. She seemed happy—genuinely happy to see me. "Grace! Where have you been? Is everything okay? I've been trying to reach you for weeks. I was worried something happened to you."

"I... uh... Danielle, right?"

"Of course it's me. Who else would it be?"

Ben reached for the compact. "May I?" he asked.

I handed it over, feeling completely weirded out at this point.

"Hey, Danielle," he said. His voice trailed off as he headed for a room down the hall to speak with her in private.

"Okay," I said, clasping my hands together. "I guess magic mirrors are a thing, too. Cool, cool."

"I found it when I was looking for you in New York," Aiden explained. "The witches must not have noticed you dropped it. You have no idea how important that compact is to you."

"No kidding." Feeling like I was going to be sick, I walked past the vampire, trusting that he wasn't going to attack me when I turned my back on him, and headed out the door.

"Grace?" he and Xander called out simultaneously.

"I'm not leaving," I said over my shoulder. "I just need a minute to think."

I stepped outside, shutting the door behind me before leaning the back of my head against it. Wanting to crumple into a ball, I did basically just that, sliding my back down the door until I was in a sitting position. I bent my knees and kicked my legs out to the side since I was still wearing my waitress uniform, which was covered in dust, dirt and a little blood, too. I cradled my head in my hands—not crying. Processing. Or, trying to anyway.

Everything I heard today sounded crazy. Like this was some sort of new nightmare or like I was hallucinating somehow. But I knew it was real. I didn't know how. But I knew. And I believed what they were saying was true.

Or... I thought I did, at least.

I was sitting here, trusting in magic and vampires and all of these wild stories I was being told. But I hadn't actually seen any of it. For all I knew, the mirror thing could be a trick. Maybe Ben was some tech wizard and had managed to pull up a video chat on a device that was designed to look like a mirror—and Danielle was just in some house on the other side of town.

I needed proof.

I needed a reason to believe what I was being told was true.

Pictures weren't cutting it. Even videos *could* be edited. I needed hard evidence.

Letting out a deep breath as I worked up my nerve, I got back to my feet and went back inside the house. Xander, Aiden and Ben were waiting for me, crowded around the kitchen which was right beside the foyer.

"How do I know any of this is true?" I asked, placing my hands on my hips. "How do I know this isn't some elaborate prank or that you aren't just psychopaths toying with me? How do I know these two are really vampires?"

The three men exchanged knowing looks amongst themselves. Ben, shaking his head at what he was about to do, held out his arm. Aiden's face contorted, and his lips curled back as fangs ripped through his gums. I took a reflexive step back. I knew I'd asked to see it. I just hadn't thought through how I'd handle it if I confirmed that I was standing in a room with two vampires. Aiden took Ben's wrist and held it in front of him, eyeing it with pure bloodlust.

"Better not," Xander said, placing his hand on his brother's shoulder. "Uncle Ben's got the synthetic stuff in the fridge if you need to top yourself off." He looked at me before explaining, "He has no self-control when it comes to feeding off of humans." He flashed a wicked smile, teeth bared, before sinking his fangs into Ben's flesh. Ben gave an instinctive grunt, his face contorting into a grimace. Xander quickly pulled away, and Ben cupped his hand around his wrist, looking at me as if to say *do you believe me now?*

I did. I believed every word.

But this didn't make me feel any better.

I blinked, trying to think, as I watched Xander wipe the blood from the corners of his lips.

If they were really vampires, was I really a witch? I glanced down at my own hands, rotating them back and forth.

"Any word from your friend?" Ben asked Aiden. "About how to get Grace's memories back?"

"Starla refuses to talk to me. She was adamant that she wants nothing to with interfering with the Albrights's business."

Xander propped his elbows on Ben's counter while he fiddled with the salt shaker. "I can have the Book Slayers look into it."

"The Book Slayers?" I asked.

"Some librarians I turned into vampires a while back. They love researching this kind of stuff. They'll be happy to help." His eyes caught mine, and he added, "Plus, they're your friends, too."

Oh. More supernatural friends... Who knew I was so popular?

Aiden's phone rang. "It's Victoria," he announced. He stepped aside to speak with her privately.

"Another friend of mine?" I asked, taking a few steps closer to Ben and Aiden.

"She's Aiden's wife," Ben explained. "A human, if you were wondering."

"Another blood slave?"

"No, no. The whole Choosing Ceremony thing went out the window when word of the competition spread to other vampire kingdoms. Victoria was the love of Aiden's life."

"Was?"

"It's a long story," he said, suggesting he'd explain it another time.

"And she doesn't mind that he's a vampire?"

Xander turned around and leaned against the counter, folding his arms across his chest. "Well, he was a vampire when they first met. Then he became a human again when our werewolf brother bit him."

"Right. Julian?" I guessed.

He nodded.

"But if he's a human, how did he—?"

"He gave it up to save us. He had one of the Book Slayers give him his blood, and then Uncle Ben let Aiden feed from him." *So that's how people turned into vampires.* Grinning, Xander patted Ben on the back. But based on the look on Ben's face, it was a memory he'd rather forget.

I couldn't believe that Aiden had given up a life as a human to help save me. I mean, Xander was probably the real reason behind it. He was his brother, after all. But still...

All this time, I thought that I had no one in this world who cared about me.

And all this time, they'd been looking for me.

Moments later, Aiden returned. He explained that he was going to head back home to be with his wife. There was something she needed to discuss with him.

"Is she upset about you turning?" Xander asked.

"No. Something unrelated. She said it wasn't an over-the-phone conversation, though."

Xander eyed his brother questioningly. "How do you feel about it? Being a vampire again, I mean."

Aiden shrugged. "I've been a vampire most of my life. I have to admit, it beats my muscles aching all the time. It is what it is for now. When we get Julian back, I'll have him bite me again. And then Victoria and I can get back to being perfectly ordinary humans." He winked.

My chest caved. From what they told me, all of this hinged on *me* finding a way to unseal that portal. And I had no memory of ever using magic before.

"You really think that'll work?" Xander asked his brother.

Aiden smiled. "Why wouldn't it?" He jerked his head toward me. "And anyway, I've seen what this one's capable of. I have no doubt she'll get that portal open again."

I forced a smile. It was nice that he had so much faith in me.

But I feared I was giving them false hope...

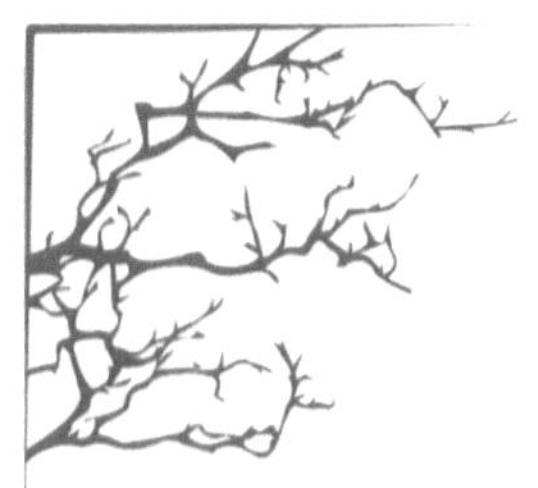

Grace

I missed Bellamy so much it hurt. I didn't have my phone, which meant that I didn't have his number. The thought of him thinking I had flaked out on him while he was recovering from an injury killed me.

Now that Ben had told me everything, he'd offered to take me back to Amber Falls. He even told me he could have Xander compel away my memories of the past day.

But my memories had already been tampered with once. And how could I walk away now that I knew I had people who cared about me? And that I had a family?

I had to know more.

Truth be told, I probably could have asked Ben if I could borrow his cell and looked up the number for Bellamy's bar. But even if I did, what was I supposed to tell him? *Hey, Bellamy. You're the perfect boyfriend, and I know you're recovering from a terrifying attack, but I'm going to hang out with some vampires and witches in Quarter Square for a bit.*

No. He'd think I'd lost my mind.

Instead, I decided to write him a letter. It would be easier that way. I could tell him everything I needed him to know—without leaving a return address. I didn't want him to come looking for me. He didn't need to get tangled up in this supernatural mess I had apparently been in the middle of. I could send it to his work, figuring it would get to him.

Letting out a sigh, I sat down to write.

Dear Bellamy,

Do you remember when I told you I felt like I was living someone else's life? Well, as it turns out, in a way... I was. Someone from my past got ahold of me. I can't explain why, but I had to leave town on short notice. It's a long story, and I promise I'll share it with you one day. But this letter isn't about that.

I'm writing to tell you that I'm sorry. I'm sorry that I left you. I'm sorry that I can't tell you why.

I promise I never had any intention of hurting you.

I promise it was nothing you did or didn't do.

I promise that I'm okay.

You don't need to come looking for me. You don't need to wait for me. There is something important that I have to do, and it may take some time.

In the meantime, just know that I care about you deeply.

I'm sorry for the mess I made. I hope that one day I can explain everything to you and that you'll understand. And maybe even forgive me.

-Grace

I read the letter over a thousand times. Part of me wanted to crumple it up into a ball and chuck it in the trash. But even though it wasn't perfect, I knew there was no right way to tell your boyfriend that you were ditching town and couldn't tell him why.

He would hate me after this.

But I had to figure out a way to get all of my memories back. I had to track down my birth family. And I had to find a way to unseal a portal to a faerie realm.

But I couldn't do that if I knew doing so would potentially put Bellamy in harm's way. He was human. And he deserved a normal life.

And anyway, I had a feeling he wouldn't like the idea of dating a witch.

Things were better this way. Maybe if I kept telling myself that I'd start believing it.

I waved my hands in front of my eyes, trying to fan them to keep from crying. Lower lip quivering, I folded the letter and slid it inside the envelope. I scribbled the address on it, added a stamp and then handed it over to Ben. He dipped his head, acknowledging the inner torment I felt, and headed outside to stick it in the mailbox.

Meanwhile, Xander was reclining in Ben's La-Z-Boy with his hands folded behind his head. "Finish your letter to your boyfriend?" he asked, his voice tinged with emotions I couldn't quite decipher.

"Yeah," I said, hugging my arms around myself. I felt sick to my stomach. Bellamy was the last person in the world I ever wanted to hurt. I couldn't bear the thought of imagining what he'd think of me when he read it. I glanced at the clock that hung over the front door. He was probably worried sick by now. He'd probably tried my cell a hundred times. And had no doubt called the Sunny Side Grille, too. I wondered what Madison would think...

Xander looked like he had something else on his mind, but he held his tongue. "I was thinking we could head to my bookstore."

I snorted. "You own a bookstore?" Here I was on the verge of tears, but the thought of this ancient vampire owning a bookstore of all things made me laugh. He didn't strike me as a bookworm.

"Is that funny?"

I shrugged. "No, just unexpected."

Ignoring my comment entirely, he continued, "The Book Slayers work on the second floor. I thought it might be good for you to meet them. There are a bunch of grimoires there, too. I'm hoping maybe they can help you remember how to use magic."

"Are they witches, too?"

"No, but they've read the books a hundred times. If anyone can help you, it's them."

I scrunched my nose, remembering an earlier conversation we'd had. "Why don't you just call my brother? Nick, was it?"

Ben walked back inside, soaking wet. "It's raining," he announced, wiping his hands on the blue kitchen towel that had been sitting on the counter. "In case you were wondering."

"Anyway," Xander went on, "the problem is that we still don't have your old phone. So, we don't have a way to call Nick."

That was a bummer. I had been looking forward to learning more about him. "What about my dad? You said he was in charge of a coven, right?"

Xander and Ben shot quick looks at one another, and I could tell there was something that they weren't telling me. "What?" I asked. "What is it?"

Xander shook his head.

Realizing what that strange look in his eyes was implying, I blurted out, "He's dead, isn't he?" My world felt like it had imploded. One second, I *finally* had a family. Even if he was a complete jerk, he was my father. And I had hoped to meet him. I had so many questions for him. And now, I'd never get any answers. Lowering my head, I asked, "How'd he die?"

"Uh, that's a story for another day, I'm afraid," Xander said, clasping his hands as he stood up from the seat.

"Xander," Ben interjected. "Don't you think she—?"

Xander silenced him with a look. "Say another word, and I swear I'll kill you." His eyes narrowed. "No. Better yet, I'll *turn* you."

Ben rolled his eyes at that.

"You think I'm kidding?"

I stood there, gaping. Why didn't Xander want me to know what happened to my father? I wanted to press him further, but if he was willing to kill his own family, what was he willing to do to me?

I decided I didn't want to find out.

Reading the emotions on my face, Xander took a step closer to me. "I'll tell you when you're ready. I swear. Just trust me on this, okay?"

For people who were complete strangers to me, they sure did ask me to trust them a lot. But then, I remembered that we did, in fact, have a history together. So, even though current-me was wary of the whole family, old-me not only trusted them but cared about them. I didn't have to have faith in them. I had to have faith in *her*. In myself.

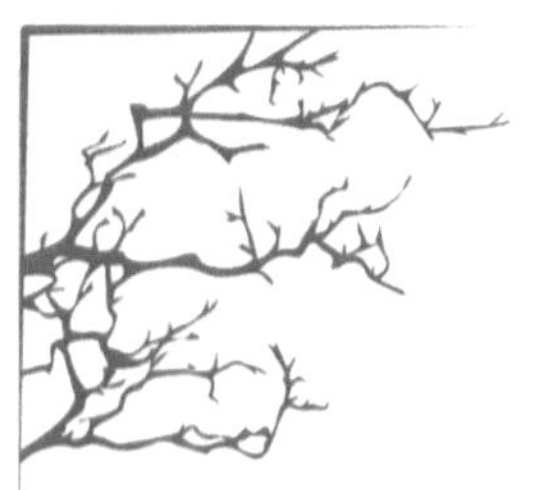

Xander

Thunder thrashed in the cool night air as sheets of rain pummeled from the sky. With an umbrella in my other hand, I pulled open the door to Books & Brews. Grace and Uncle Ben went inside, and I followed after them. Jasper, one of the Book Slayers who helped look after the shop, was busy restocking the thrillers shelf when he looked up to greet us. Startled, he hurried over. Trying not to draw too much attention from the customers, he greeted us. Flipping his wavy brown hair away from his eyes, he stuffed his hands in his pockets. "Xander?" he said under his breath, hardly believing his eyes. "How are you?"

"I'm still here, aren't I?" I said with a wink as I squeezed his shoulder. "Thank you for coming to my rescue, by the way."

He nodded, and then his eyes drifted toward Grace. He immediately wrapped her in a hug. Jasper and Grace had hit it off pretty well. Aside from me and Danielle, he had become one of her closest friends. "Grace!" he said, squeezing her hard. "I missed you so much." He had a lot of questions for her, but he bit his tongue, not wanting the human customers to overhear. Realizing that she hadn't spoken a word, he pulled away. "Grace?"

She blinked at him, and it hit me then that she didn't remember him at all. I took a step forward and gestured between them. "Grace, this is Jasper."

Bewilderment flashed across Jasper's deep brown eyes, and he looked at me, waiting for an explanation. "She knows who I am... doesn't she?" He looked like a wounded puppy. Well, more so than usual. He was shy by nature, but becoming a vampire helped him settle into himself. After all, he'd had *plenty* of time to grow into his own skin. He had an innocent look about him, which was one of the reasons I'd picked him to man the front of the shop. He was approachable. And, given the way he chose to live his life, he was mostly harmless. Still, Grace was one of the few people he opened up to outside of the Book Slayers—and, of course, me.

Growing impatient with my lack of an immediate explanation, he looked back at Grace. His mouth stretched into a wide smile, wrinkling his whole face. "You're messing with me, aren't you?" he said, wagging his finger at her.

She frowned. "I'm sorry," she said, without much emotion behind it given that she had no idea who he was. "I seem to have forgotten a lot lately."

I dipped my head in appreciation for her remembering not to openly discuss any of our supernatural business in front of the customers.

Jerking my head toward the bar, I told Jasper I could use a drink. On cue, Jasper asked Grace and Uncle Ben if they wanted anything and then promptly headed toward the bar to grab our drinks of choice.

I scanned the room, happy to see my bookshop-slash-bar booming with business. Uncle Ben thought it was strange for me to combine books and booze, but hey—who didn't like to relax with a drink and a good book?

There was no point in us awkwardly waiting here, so I suggested we head upstairs. I motioned for Uncle Ben to lead the way, and I followed behind Grace. I shook my head as we walked, baffled by how much Grace's memory loss had changed her. The Grace I knew was headstrong and confident. But this version of her was... muted. I supposed it made sense. All of those negative experiences—being a blood slave, being dragged to the castle to partake in the Choosing Ceremony, learning her father was the infamous Reed Carlisle and then subsequently killing him in an epic battle changed her. They toughened her up. Hardened her. She was intense and fiery.

But without any memory of those events, there was this lightness to her that I'd never seen before. It was like this version of Grace was what she would have been like had her life been... good.

I wondered if it was wrong of me to take that from her by reintroducing her to her past.

And yet, the Grace I knew hated being compelled because she hated the idea of changing someone's memories. It was like stealing from them. The Grace I knew would want her memories back, even if that meant bringing the pain back, too.

I still didn't know how I was going to break it to her that she was the one who killed her father. I was hoping to avoid the topic and let her remember it on her own if and when the Book Slayers helped us figure out how to restore her memories.

When we finally reached the top of the staircase, we slipped inside the common room where the Book Slayers spent much of their time. Melissa was the first to sense our presence, and in a flash, she was standing before us, squeezing her book in excitement. Before she got ahead of herself, though, I explained the situation to her. The other Book Slayers gathered around to hear. They were furious that the Albrights had taken so much from us. But they vowed then and there to help get to the bottom of how to restore Grace's memories.

By the time I'd finished my spiel, Jasper had caught up with us. He brought a martini for me, a margarita for Grace and a cabernet for Uncle Ben. We chatted with the Book Slayers for a while as we sipped from our drinks.

But then, it was time to begin.

Being the daughter of Reed Carlisle *and* being a twin born of his coven meant that she was powerful. *Crazy* powerful.

Perhaps having her perform some spell would remind her of who she really was.

And maybe that would be the key to bringing back her memories.

Hey—it was worth a shot.

So, it made sense to start at the beginning.

One of the spells Grace had performed countless times over involved her controlling fire. She'd even been the one to set the castle in Crescent Cape ablaze after my siblings and I fled to keep us from being discovered. What's more, when she'd killed her father in order to protect me, she'd set his *veins* on fire. *Yeah... she did some dark stuff.* But her intentions were always pure. And she had never *wanted* to hurt anyone. Even Reed. We had confronted him intending for her to use a spell that would soften his heart and force him to change his ways. But it all went terribly wrong.

Anyway, being as that controlling fire came so naturally to her, it seemed like a good place to start.

While we had been drinking, Melissa had been busy thumbing through an old grimoire. Finally, she found one with the spell she had in mind. "Hang on a second," she said, handing the grimoire over to Grace, who stared at the pages in bewilderment while Melissa rummaged through some cabinets. Sighing with satisfaction, she retrieved two white pillar candles and placed them on the table in the center of the common room. "Here you go." She looked at Grace expectantly.

Grace's eyes widened, realizing that everyone was now focused on her. "What am I supposed to do?"

"Reading the page would be a good start," Melissa teased.

"Right." Grace cleared her throat. Kneeling before the coffee table, Grace held her hands in the air while reciting the spell laid out for her. I watched with great interest as a hard line formed in the center of her brow. All at once, flames shot up from the candles—way higher than should be possible. What's more, flames roared from the fireplace to her left. She jumped back, realizing what she'd done. The rest of us stepped back, too, in response to the intense heat emanating from the table.

"Okay," Grace said breathlessly, laughing to herself as the brilliant light flickered across her face. "I have to admit... that was really cool."

I took a step closer to her, hoping that performing a spell would trigger a rush of memories. She looked back at me, reading my thoughts, and shook her head.

"You always were a fast learner," Uncle Ben pointed out.

"Yeah?" she asked.

He nodded. "It's not normal, you know, for witches to pick up on spells so quickly. For many, it takes years of practice to hone their abilities."

"To be fair, it sounds like I've done this one a time or two already," she pointed out.

Uncle Ben chuckled. "True."

While Melissa and the other Book Slayers were busy blowing out the candles, Grace clasped her hands together, her blue eyes sparkling with excitement. "So, what's next?"

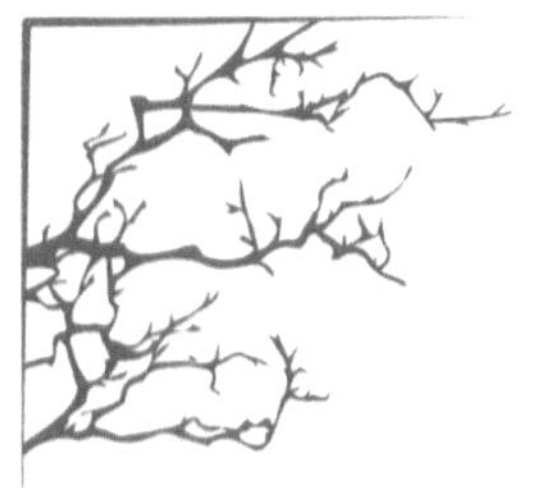

Grace

I'd spent the past days splitting my time between the upper level of Books & Brews and Ben's place. Now, I could easily control fire, make objects move across a room and make things float, to name a few tricks. And for some reason, it didn't freak me out like I thought it might. I felt powerful. More like myself than I had since... well, since I could remember.

I'd spent every waking second practicing spells and reading through the ancient grimoires, absorbing as much information as I could. I'd been told I was a fast learner. It turned out that was true. Naomi had spent countless hours helping me memorize spells, and Jasper ran drills with me, encouraging me to practice what I was learning.

While I couldn't say that any of this had helped jog my memory, it did solidify my confidence that everything Xander and Ben had told me was true. Not only was I a witch, but with each passing day, it became clearer just how well these people knew me.

The Book Slayers hadn't had much luck with figuring out a solution to my memory problem. Spells often had loopholes, they explained. But without asking the person who cast it, there was no way to know for sure what it might be. And it was possible Sofia Albright herself wouldn't even know.

So... *that* was encouraging...

Meanwhile, Xander was on edge. He couldn't figure out why Sofia and the others hadn't tracked him down since his escape. From what I understood, Aiden, Ben, Jasper and Naomi had left behind a pretty gruesome scene at the Albright compound when they broke Xander out of there. Honestly, the details wreaked havoc on my psyche. I couldn't sleep at all the first night I heard about it. I knew they were trying to rescue Xander (and me, even though I wasn't there), but still... It was hard to wrap my head around the fact that I was now a part of the dark and twisted world of supernaturals.

Anyway, Xander had expected revenge. But he hadn't noticed any sign of trouble, which somehow made him *more* worried. And an ancient vampire being worried made me worried, too.

Xander was driving Ben crazy with his various theories on what Sofia could be up to. So, Ben suggested the three of us take a trip out of town. He had Collector business to attend to in Virginia, and he thought it could be a good learning opportunity for me. A chance to practice magic in a *real* setting. So, we went along.

It turned out that Virginia was much more progressive than Maine when it came to supernaturals. Back home, even after supernaturals had been outed, they still lay low. You didn't see rival wolf packs brawling in parking lots or witches casting spells in the streets. You rarely even saw vampires drinking the "red drink" out in public. We sold some at the Sunny Side Grille, but no one had ever ordered it. But it made sense. The Book Slayers, for instance, didn't want anyone to know what they were. And neither did Xander. Anonymity was a form of protection.

But here, things were different. When we first got into town, we stopped at a diner. The place was crawling with vampires—one of whom was feeding on a waitress. The staff must have been compelled because no one even batted an eye. Werewolves were there, too, sitting at tables piled high with rare hamburgers.

Ben's intel had been right. I just hadn't expected the fact that there were supernaturals here to be so obvious.

Xander and I slid into a booth together, situated across from Ben. After taking a long sip from my milkshake, I said, "Go over it with me one more time, will you?" This was just a typical day for Ben, but I had no memory of trying to steal magical objects out from under the noses of supernatural beings. Granted, I was just tagging along as backup. And I didn't know how helpful I'd be if we did run into trouble. Practicing with Jasper was one thing... but this was on a whole different level. Ben had given us a vague gloss-over of the plan before, but if I was going to tag along for this, I wanted to know exactly what I was walking into.

Obliging, he slid his milkshake away. "We're looking for a woman named Ruby Drake. She's a werewolf. It turns out that she and a local witch had some beef."

My brow wrinkled with intrigue.

"You know how most werewolves can shift at will?"

"Yeah." It had been mentioned in one of the books Melissa had encouraged me to read.

"Well, ever since supernaturals were outed, Ruby and her pack have taken over this town. So, a witch named Isadora Wenbrook cast a spell to bind Ruby to the moon once again." He glanced around before leaning in to continue the story.

"Understandably, Ruby wasn't too pleased about that. So, she ransacked the witch's place, getting her hands on anything she could find in order to hold the items as ransom until Isadora undid the spell."

"And Isadora refused?" Xander guessed.

"She didn't have to. A vampire got to her first."

I gulped. It made sense that the vampires would want Ruby to be a slave to the moon. Vampires and werewolves weren't known for getting along. They tolerated each other at best. "So, she was murdered?"

Ben nodded somberly.

"How did you find out about this, anyway?" Xander asked.

"Believe it or not, I'm not the only person in the world amassing magical objects. There are others like me. There's a whole network of Collectors."

"How many magical objects are out there?" I asked. His attic was filled with them. All kinds of crazy things...

"Plenty," he assured me. "They've been around as long as supernaturals have."

"And these Collectors? Are they all descendants of supernaturals?"

"Official Collectors, yes. Of course, now and again a human will get wind of what we're doing and try to get in on the action. But you'll notice that we're called *Collectors*, not users. We have the option to use the objects when necessary for protection. But for the most part, we try to stay out of the supernaturals' business. We look after our loved ones when we can, but we don't insert ourselves unnecessarily."

"That must be hard having immortal relatives."

"Sometimes, they forget that no one is truly immortal," he said, now making eye contact with Xander.

Xander merely gave a coy smile and sipped from his milkshake.

I swallowed hard, not having ever considered that before. "So, the whole vampire and werewolf rivalry is real?"

Ben nodded. "You have to remember, Xander's family situation is a unique one. He and his siblings weren't turned, they were made."

I nodded, remembering the story. I thought, too, about how his brother Julian's bite had turned Aiden into a human again. Curious, I turned to Xander and asked, "Would you ever want to become human again?"

Ben leaned in, intrigued by the question. "I think he's forgotten what it's like to be human," he offered.

Xander leaned back against the cushioned seat, casually draping his arm across the top. I scooted forward a bit, not liking being so close to the vampire. "Oh, I remember," he said. "I remember what it was like to be weak. Helpless. Useless. I can't fathom a reason I would ever subject myself to that willingly."

I gaped at him. "Wow," I said sarcastically. "I didn't realize I was such a waste of a life. How kind of you to enlighten me."

The corner of his mouth tugged into a grin. "First of all, you're a witch through and through. And second of all…" He started to say something, but he stopped himself.

"What?" I asked, growing annoyed by his smugness.

He wagged his finger at me. "That. That right there."

I blinked, having no idea what he was alluding to.

"It's good to know you're still in there."

I wasn't sure what to say to that. So, I decided to ignore the comment entirely. Turning to Ben, I asked, "Anyway, where do we find this *Ruby Drake*?"

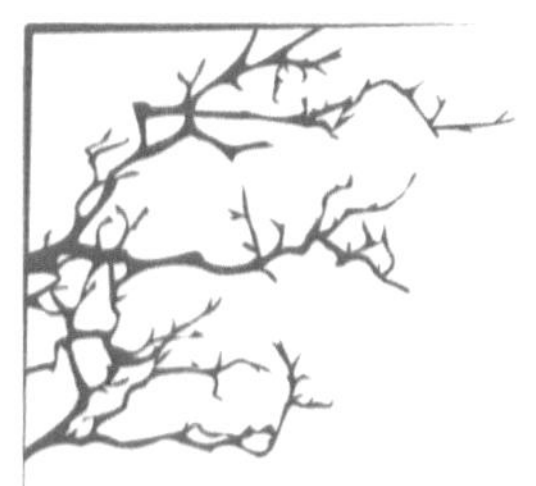

Grace

It turned out that Ben had no intention of finding Ruby. Last he'd heard, she'd taken a trip out of town. Something about recruiting wolves that didn't belong to a pack and bringing them back to her hometown. From what I gathered, werewolves looked after their own.

Being a werewolf was usually an inherited trait. But not always. And "packs" could mean many things. Sometimes people turned without having anyone around to guide them.

That's where Ruby came in.

Which was why we were here now. Because with her gone, we could make our move.

While we were in town, Ben had discreetly asked around about Ruby—making sure he was questioning humans and especially *not* werewolves. He learned that she worked the night shift at a local bar. We decided to go and check the place out for ourselves. What we *really* needed to know was where Ruby lived, but, unfortunately, we hadn't been able to dig up anything about her current residence online. So, we were going to have to do this the old-fashioned way.

Rather than just barging in the place and demanding information about Ruby, which would only draw unwanted attention, we sat at the bar and ordered a round of drinks. Plus, with Xander here, he could compel the information out of people if needed. He'd offered to do it straight away, but Ben insisted it would be good for me to watch and learn how *he* did things.

The bartender brought our drinks to us but had forgotten to return our IDs. He assured us he'd grab them and bring them right back.

Ben was nearly done chugging a bottle of an IPA when a striking woman with catlike features appeared behind him, resting her hand comfortably on his shoulder. "Ben Sullivan, is that you?"

Ben's eyes widened in recognition. "Jessica? What are you doing here?"

She shrugged coyly, tucking her short black hair behind her ear. "Following up on a lead." Her eyes squinted. "I'm guessing that's why you're here, too."

"The ring?"

Her bright red lips curved into a smile. Jerking her head to the side, she asked, "Who's the kid?"

Ignoring the dig at my age, I offered her my hand. "Grace."

"A friend," he added. "She's tagging along for the trip."

"And Mr. Handsome over there?" she said, lifting her chin to gesture toward Xander.

"My nephew. Sort of."

Her eyes sparkled with understanding. "I see," she said, keeping her obsidian eyes locked in on Xander.

"So," Ben chimed in. "How's this going to go down? Two Collectors? One ring? Whoever gets to it first gets to keep it?"

She chuckled at that. "May the best woman win," she said with a wink. She turned on her heel and started walking away, her curvy hips swishing with each confident stride.

Rolling his eyes, Ben took another swig. I was just about to say something to him when the bartender approached us. "You're Grace Addington," he said, eyes bugged out as he handed me my ID.

"Yes... And you are?"

"The name's Jason." He propped his elbow on the bar, and, eyeing Ben and Xander with suspicion, said to me, "I knew you looked familiar... We went to the same high school."

As if on cue, the door to the bar burst open, the harsh light from the streetlamps in the parking lot pouring inside. Police officers swarmed the building. Xander stood, getting ready to intervene. But Ben cautioned him against it. "Your anonymity is everything," he reminded him.

Scanning the room, I realized just how many people had their phones out, obviously recording what was about to go down.

Xander didn't like holding back, but he decided to play along. At least for now.

And before I knew it, Ben, Xander and I were being taken in for questioning. The officers led us outside toward their vehicles. But, with no more witnesses around, Xander broke free from their hold. He tried compelling them, but another officer fired a wooden shot into his stomach. I instinctively lurched toward him, and Ben cried out in horror.

Xander drew his hand to his stomach and groaned in agony as he plucked out the wooden bullet. The officer standing over him placed a hand on his hip, staring Xander down as he said, "We live in a town crawling with supernaturals. You really think we don't have ways of making you comply?" With that, he fired another shot for good measure. Then the three of us were separated and shoved into the backs of their vehicles.

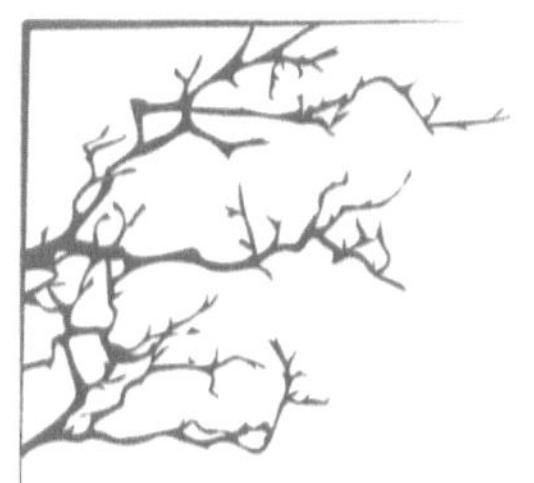

Grace

There was no way our stories were going to match up. We never prepared for this scenario. What were the chances that someone from my *hometown* would recognize me?

Maybe it was stupid of me not to change my name. But it was too late to worry about that now.

I considered my options. I could always tell them the truth. Now that vampires had been outed, I wouldn't sound like a certifiable crazy person if I told them that I'd been kidnapped and taken to Crescent Cape.

But I didn't want to connect Xander to my disappearance should *his* identity ever be discovered. What's more, I didn't want the truth of what happened to me getting back to my parents. I had succumbed to a worse fate than even their worst imaginations could conjure. I had no clue how they would take learning that their adopted daughter had been serving as vampire convenience food for years.

The other option was to lie. To say that I'd run away.

I hated pretending like I would be so heartless to the people who raised me. We didn't have the best relationship, but I would never up and leave without saying goodbye.

But I didn't see another feasible option. I didn't want the police thinking *Ben* had taken me.

It'd been so long, though. Maybe he could just tell them that he didn't know anything about me and my disappearance. After all, why would he? For all the police knew, we could have just met a few days ago...

The questioning dragged on, and I was becoming emotionally drained. Coming up with lie after lie was exhausting. I tried to think about what Ben would tell me to do if he were here beside me. I figured he'd remind me that I was a witch and to use that to my advantage. So, because I could, I started messing with my interrogators. The spill of their coffee here, the flickering of the lights there. Little things like that. I didn't want to hurt them. I was trying to throw them off their game to give myself more time to think.

I worried about what they must be doing to Xander. If they knew how to incapacitate a vampire, his supernatural abilities were useless.

Finally, when they felt like they had all the information they needed, one of the burly officers told me they were going to go give my parents a call. They asked if I wanted to speak to them.

Warily, I nodded.

This was *not* how I was expecting my day to go.

I got up and followed the men out the door and rounded the corner. I was busy scrambling to come up with a way to explain this to my adoptive parents when, of all people, *Jessica* cut us off. Her red lips twisted into a satisfied smirk. And as quick as a flash of lightning, two men appeared at her side. "Eddie, Jackson," she said, speaking to the vampires. "Do your thing."

Before the men had the chance to draw their weapons, the vampires split up and compelled them to let me go. They told them not to question who any of us were or why we had been at the station.

Hurrying to get away why still could, I scrambled down the hall. Panting, I found Ben, who had been released, too. I glanced over my shoulder while Jessica held an object in her hand that looked like a glass ball. Securing her hands around it, she started to give it a twist, but then she stopped. Realizing we were still standing there, she shouted, "What are you waiting for? Get out of here! We'll handle the rest."

"But," Ben argued, "Xander's still in there."

Visibly annoyed, Jessica ordered her vampire lackies to search the place until they found him.

Luckily, vampires moved quickly.

We heard clashing and screaming, and moments later, Eddie emerged from one of the rooms with Xander's arm flung over his shoulder. Xander's face was twisted and he was holding his stomach, which now had multiple wounds.

"Where is everyone?" Ben asked, realizing how profoundly odd it was that we were able to walk through the place without anyone noticing.

"We're not the only ones here," Eddie answered in a gruff voice.

I didn't know who this Jessica person was or how she'd managed to get so many vampires to team up with her, but I was grateful for her help. I didn't understand why she was helping us considering she and Ben were after the same object. But hey—I wasn't about to complain about being rescued. I was just glad she'd found us before they'd called my parents.

Eddie nudged Xander toward us, and we helped him out of the station. As we walked toward the exit, I noticed a couple of officers lying on the floor while the others meticulously focused on their work as if we weren't there at all.

I would never get used to this.

Once outside, we realized that we didn't have any transportation now. We hurriedly removed the bullets from Xander's belly, which was way more gruesome of a task than I even imagined it to be. With help from Ben's blood, he healed. At first, Xander started heading back in the direction of the station. But Ben pleaded with him to use reason. "It's over. Let Jessica and her guys handle it. We need to get out of here. Now."

Xander was about to argue with him, but then he looked at me and shook his head. "Fine. Let's get out of here."

So, we made a run for it, vaguely remembering where the bar was. I didn't know why Xander was running at the same pace as us—maybe so as not to leave us in the dust. But anyway, it turned out that it was a much longer trek than we remembered, so we decided to catch a cab to make it the rest of the way.

Once back in the parking lot, we climbed in Ben's car and sped off. "Want to tell me what the heck that was about?" I asked. "Why did that woman help us?"

"Jessica said that she wanted to beat me to the ring fair and square," he answered as if that explained everything. "She got her vampire friends to compel the bartender as well as the police officers and everyone else in the station to forget we were ever there. She and her friends are going to go through the records and destroy any evidence they may have about you."

"Seriously? Just like that?"

"Just like that."

"But that doesn't make any sense. She wants the ring, too, so why would she help us? Why isn't she just using this time to get it for herself?"

"Jessica and I are old friends. We've been running in the same circles for years. I would have done the same for her—assuming I had the resources. And anyway, it's not like she wants the ring for herself. All that matters is that we get it out of Ruby Drake's hands. Werewolves are fearsome enough. The last thing we need is them collecting magical objects and amassing an arsenal of weapons on top of their supernatural powers."

His explanation made sense, and honestly, I didn't care why Jessica was helping us. I wasn't ready to face the Addingtons yet, and I would gladly take any excuse I could to avoid a confrontation altogether. I missed them terribly. But now that I was learning more about the dangerous world I'd found myself tangled up in, I knew they were better off without me in their lives. "But," I pointed out, "we still don't know where Ruby lives. How are we going to find her?"

Ben flashed an uncharacteristically devious grin. "I've already got that covered. While Jessica and her vampire friends were making the rounds compelling our way to freedom, I broke into the computer system. Turns out the werewolf has had some traffic violations."

"Wait. You have her address?" Xander asked, thoroughly impressed.

He nodded in satisfaction. "Now, let's go get that ring."

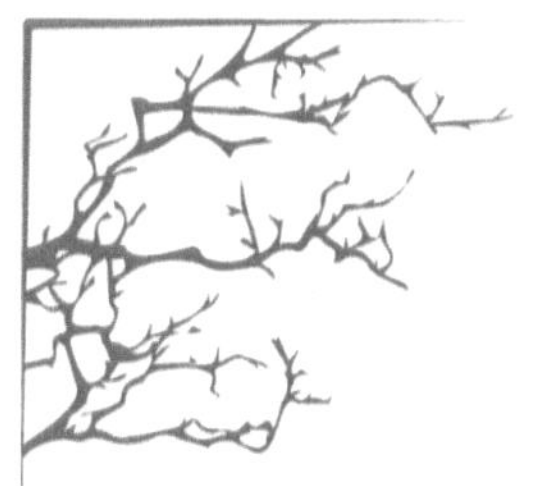

Grace

I stood watch while Ben and Xander broke into the house. It was a dinky little place far on the outskirts of town, a mishmash of reddish-brown colored bricks and crooked shutters situated in the woods. I shivered, but I wasn't sure if it was from the cool night air or my nerves. I was quickly learning that being caught up in the world of supernaturals forced me to bend my morals—sometimes multiple times in a day. The normal, human me would have been horrified at the thought of breaking into someone's place—let alone *stealing* something from them.

But if what Ben told me about Ruby was true, which I was sure it was, then we were doing the right thing.

We scanned the home, looking for places where we thought she might have stored the ring. We didn't have much time. While Jessica wasn't a threat to us—after all, she and her vampire companions had come to our rescue—Ben still wanted to beat her to getting that ring. Apparently, he was way more competitive than I'd realized.

I had no idea why this ring was so important, and Ben wasn't sure what it did, either. But that didn't matter. His network of Collectors said someone needed to get it out of Ruby's hands, so that's what we were going to do. After that, we'd take it back to Ben's where he would keep it safe.

We wandered through the shotgun-style house, passing through the tiled kitchen. I lifted my brows in surprise at the '50s-style refrigerator. Interesting. This place wasn't anything like I expected. I guessed werewolves didn't have the luxury of spending lifetimes amassing riches like the vampires did. But still, I'd expected more from the leader of a wolf pack. You'd think the job would come with some perks...

"Where should we look first?" I asked Ben.

He marched ahead, knowing exactly what he was doing. "Her bedroom. It's always the bedroom."

Xander and I followed him down the long hallway and hooked a left. The bedroom door was wide open. A bed was situated flush against the far wall. Ben headed for it, reaching toward the nightstand beside it.

"I'll take the closet," I offered. I pulled the door open and tugged at the chain hanging from the lightbulb overhead, illuminating my view. "I'm guessing her favorite color is red," I mused to myself sarcastically.

"What makes you say that?" Xander asked while he shuffled through some bags on the floor, half-listening.

"Oh, I don't know. Maybe because her closet is overflowing with red shirts." I wasn't exaggerating. T-shirts, tank tops, hoodies, jackets. You name it, she had it in red. Was it a werewolf thing to wear different colors to signify which pack they belonged in? Or was she taking the name *Ruby* a bit too seriously? I hadn't a clue.

I stood on my tiptoes and reached for a box on the top shelf. Being fairly tall myself, I was able to grab it comfortably. I carried the cardboard box over to the bed and sifted through its contents. I refrained from judging her when I realized it was a collection of love letters, all signed with the letter K, or maybe R.

Meanwhile, Ben was busy disassembling her dresser. He stuck his hand in one of the empty slots and felt around. Pleased with himself, he announced, "I got it." He held the ring in his palm, and I stepped closer to get a better look.

I frowned. "It's..." I started, searching for the right word.

"Garish? Hideous?" Xander offered. "Either one will do."

I scrunched my eyebrows. "Is that a *bird* on top?"

"I think so," Ben replied.

"What do you think it does?"

He shook his head. "No idea. We'll research it when we get back to my place." He stuffed it in his pocket. "Let's get out of here."

We started to leave, but then we heard a noise coming from the front of the house.

Teasingly, Ben called out, "Sorry, Jessica. You're a little late."

"Oh," a dry, feminine voice called out—one that definitely did *not* belong to Jessica. "I'm right on time."

THE MYSTERY WOMAN STEPPED into view. It was Ruby Drake, all right. Red shirt and all. Processing out from the shadows, the werewolf pack leader stared us down. "Who are you? And what are you doing in my house?"

My pulse raced. Her very presence was intimidating. She was stunning in a terrifying way. Bronze skin. Penetrating eyes. Thick, perfectly manicured eyebrows. Brown hair tied up into a high ponytail. She looked like she'd slit your throat and be selfie-ready two seconds later.

Before we could answer her, her eyes ping-ponged between Xander and me. They widened with recognition. "The witch and the Blood Heir together again," she said to herself, mindlessly thumbing an onyx pendant that hung from her neck. "Oh, he's going to *love* this…"

"He?" I asked, clenching my fist to hide the fact that I was shaking. She knew who I was. And if she knew who I was, then maybe she knew why my memories had been stolen from me…

"How do you know who I am?" Xander said, stalking toward her. He towered over her, fangs bared.

"Back up, *vampire*," she said, emphasizing the word with pure revulsion. Her eyes flicked toward me for the briefest of moments before falling back on Xander. "Shouldn't you be in a lab somewhere anyway?"

Warily, I glanced over at Ben. The ring was tucked in his pocket, out of view. He reached for his other pocket, and I knew he was about to make a move.

But if Ruby had information about what had happened to us, maybe she knew how to help me. It was a long-shot, but it didn't hurt to ask. "My memories—do you know how I can get them back?"

She smirked at first and then shook her head, laughing to herself. "Sorry, you're going to have to take that up with the boss."

Xander flew toward her, pinning her against the door.

"Bite me," she snarled, daring him.

"My pleasure." Xander opened his mouth, but then she slid out of his hold. She may not currently have access to her full range of supernatural powers, but she had clearly been trained as a warrior. She had Xander's arms pinned behind his back, and she thrust him forward, slamming his head against her door until it drew blood.

I didn't have time to scream before she grabbed him by his neck and gave it a snap.

My fingertips twitched at my sides as I ran through a filing cabinet of spells in my mind that could get us out of this situation. That was why I was here, wasn't it? To serve as backup.

But Ruby was already two steps ahead. Watching me as if she could sense my magic, she curled her lip. "I may not have orders to kill you," she said, snarling, "but that doesn't mean I can't make you suffer." She pounced on me, pinning me to the floor. She was still in human form—thanks to the witch Isadora, she couldn't turn at will. But I had a funny feeling that wasn't going to stop her from having fun with me. "Why are you in my house?"

I squirmed, crying out as she reared her arm back and punched me in the jaw. Pain seared through my entire head. Ben was shouting something in the background, but I couldn't make out the words. My mind was too fuzzy to think, but on instinct, fire erupted from my fingertips. Forcing my arms out from under her strong frame, I placed my fingers against her forehead.

Startled, she jumped back. "Stupid witch," she hissed.

At that exact moment, Ben emerged from the kitchen, and I winced in anticipation as he reared a cast-iron skillet back and swung.

But to my horror, he missed.

She slugged him in the gut right before kneeing him. Ben curled over, writhing in pain.

Just then, Jessica and her vampire friends stormed inside. "How many times do I have to save your life today?" she said to Ben before she signaled for her friend to handle the werewolf. The strange man tore Ruby off of Ben and flung her against the wall. Her head slammed into a picture frame, knocking it to the ground. Glass shattered around us, and then Jessica closed in on Ben.

Panting, Ben managed to utter, "Thank you."

But then Jessica slinked even closer to him and offered him her hand. She helped him to his feet. Her thin fingers trailed along his chest as she straightened his shirt. Then she dipped her finger into his shirt pocket and plucked the ring out. She flashed her teeth before winking. "I see you found the ring."

He snatched it out from her fingers. "Fair and square, right?"

"Fair and square." She nodded.

"Want me to finish her off?" a vampire hissed from across the room, referring to Ruby who was out cold.

"No!" I blurted out. The others looked at me, surprised. "We were the ones stealing from her. She was just protecting her house."

"She has a point," Ben offered, sliding the ring back in his pocket where it belonged.

Annoyed, the vampire stormed outside.

"Do you always drag vampires along for your exploits?" Ben quipped.

"Do you always drag along teenagers?"

"Hey," I interrupted. "I'm twenty-one."

Jessica laughed at that. "Still not any less creepy."

Ben started toward the door, motioning for me to follow. "Grace is like a daughter to me," he said sternly, daring Jessica to question our relationship again.

Jessica held her hands up in mock surrender. Following her vampire friends, she stepped over Xander's body.

Now that the adrenaline was fading and I could think, I knelt beside him. "He's going to be okay, right?" I asked Ben. I thought I'd read something about it being hard to actually kill a vampire, but hearing his neck crack like that certainly sounded deadly to me.

"He'll be fine," Ben said, crouching down beside him. "Just give him a few minutes."

Sure enough, minutes later, Xander's eyes opened. I was startled at the sight of him moving again. This was so... unnatural. He stood and brushed himself off like nothing happened and half-listened while Ben explained what he'd missed.

Xander started toward Ruby, who was unconscious in a pool of her own blood. But Ben put his hand on Xander's shoulder to stop him. "Are you joking?" Xander scowled. "She just snapped my neck."

"After we broke into her house," Ben reminded him.

Xander crossed his arms as a deep line formed on his brow. "Fine. I won't kill her. But I do have some questions for her." I watched with bated breath as he lurched toward her. He bit into his wrist and gave her a drop—just one drop—of his blood. Moments later, she blinked. "Who are you working for?" he hissed. He grabbed her by the collar and lifted her to her feet. "I gave you enough blood for you to regain consciousness. I can give you more to heal your wounds. But you're going to have to start talking."

She let out a deep, throaty cough. Her penetrating eyes locked in on his. "Over my dead body," she muttered.

So, he let her go.

As Ruby collapsed into a heap on the hard floor, Xander brushed past Ben and me and headed for the car.

We followed after him. I glanced back over my shoulder at Ruby before closing the door behind me. A storm of emotions brewed within me. It turned out that reading about the supernatural world and witnessing it were two very different things.

Maybe the old me had been okay with all of this.

But maybe the new me didn't want to be a part of this world after all...

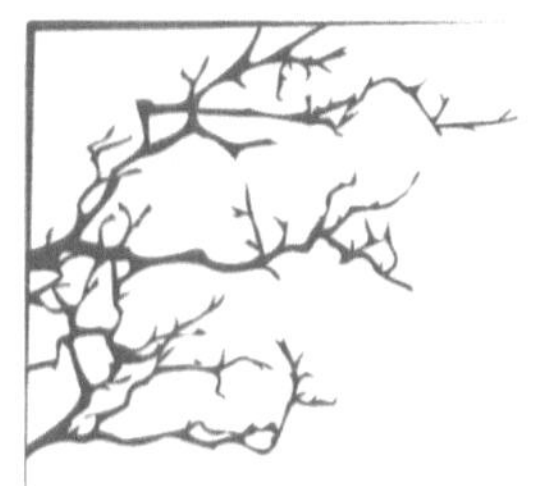

Grace

I didn't know how to break it to them that this was all too much for me. In one day alone, I'd been taken into police custody, freed by a Collector and her vampires, helped steal a magical object and was attacked by a werewolf.

I didn't even know who I was anymore.

I thought that tagging along with Ben and Xander would give me clarity. That using my powers in a real setting might trigger a flood of memories to return. But all it did was leave me with more questions.

Ruby was clearly working for someone who wanted Xander and me out of the picture. They'd gone to great lengths to wipe my memories and drain him. Who knew what they were up to? Did I even want to find out?

I had a feeling I didn't.

Things were so much easier just a couple of weeks ago. Life was easy. I was happy. My biggest worry was how to get that awful smell out of my apartment. I wanted to go back to that. To go back to *Bellamy*.

Thinking of him made my stomach turn to lead. I had no doubt he hated me. As far as he knew, I'd abandoned him at his weakest moment. He probably never wanted to see me again... And yet, I had to try to make things right.

Now, it was a quarter after midnight. Xander was off tending to things at Books & Brews, and even from upstairs, I could hear Ben snoring in his La-Z-Boy. He had planned to stay up late researching, but the events of the day must have finally caught up to him.

I debated whether I should leave a note explaining why I was leaving. Heck, I didn't have to run away. Ben had promised he'd drive me back to Amber Falls himself if I still wanted to return after learning the truth. I'd tried bringing the idea up at dinner, but when push came to shove, I couldn't get the words out. He and Xander were counting on me getting that portal open so that they could get their family back. And that Danielle girl, too. Me walking away meant that I was also saying no to helping them. Even though I felt like going back to Amber Falls was the right choice, I couldn't bring myself to watch their faces when they realized I had let them down. I was a coward, through and through.

And so, I did the cowardly thing. I carefully unlatched the window, climbed down the trellis and headed toward downtown Quarter Square where I caught a cab and returned home.

"THAT'S NOT WHAT THE prophecy said," Xander pointed out when we were on our flight to Lisbon. "Remember? It said one of you would kill the other one. And both you and Nick are still here."

"He'll never forgive me," I said, staring out the window.

"Grace, he let you go, didn't he? He could have ratted you out to the others, but he didn't. And anyway, he saw what his dad was doing to you."

"And he made his choice," I snapped. "He chose Reed. Not me. He only helped me because you made him."

Xander was quiet for some time. Part of me wished he would say something to give me an excuse to snap at him. To get some of this anger out.

I replayed the evening's events over and over again in my mind, torturing myself. I leaned my head against the window, staring out into the starry abyss. Saying goodbye to Danielle was going to be hard enough. Now I had guilt layered on top of it. And the memories of what I'd done.

I woke up in a cold sweat, panting, shivering. My heart felt like it was going to explode. Panicked, I looked around. It was dark, though a yellow haze from the streetlights slanted through the windows.

I relaxed when I realized I was in my apartment.

It was just a nightmare.

Or was it a memory?

I pressed my fingertips to my temple, taking shallow breaths.

I tried putting the bits and pieces of the dream together, but they were already slipping from my mind. All I could remember was the feeling of utter devastation over something I had done. But what could I have done that was so bad?

I remembered, too, the care and concern in Xander's eyes. Like we had been close once. I mean, like, *close*. There was a gentleness about him. A warmth...

I didn't remember him looking at me like that in the last couple of weeks. Mostly, I seemed to be getting on his nerves. He'd been nice enough—or nice for him, from what I gathered. Yet...

Who was I to him? And who was he to me?

I shook my head. It didn't matter. It was just a dream. And after time away playing witch, I was finally back in Amber Falls. I knew I had a lot of explaining to do to my boss. I hoped I could get my job back. But that could wait a day or two.

First, I had to find Bellamy.

IT WAS CHILLIER THAN I'd expected. I regretted not thinking to grab a sweater before I left. I hugged my arms around myself, shivering. The morning sun was peeking over the horizon, casting the sky in brilliant orange and yellow tones. It was breathtaking, and yet my chest caved with sadness as I stood outside Bellamy's apartment. I thought back to my first date with him. I thought back to our first kiss. I longed to see him look at me the way he'd looked at me that night. I was terrified to face him. Terrified to see the disappointment, the anger, in his eyes.

But I had to apologize after what I'd put him through.

"Grace?" his familiar, raspy voice called out from behind.

I whirled around, bracing myself for whatever harsh words he may be ready to unleash on me—I deserved them all.

But instead, he ran toward me and wrapped me in a bear hug. "Where have you been? I've been looking everywhere for you."

He pulled away just far enough to look down at me, and my eyes swelled with tears. "Did you get my letter?"

"Yes, but there was no return address. And you weren't answering your phone. I've been worried sick about you."

I chewed my lip, overwhelmed with emotion. "Aren't you mad at me?"

"No," he said emphatically, shaking his head in disbelief. He drew me back in for another hug. "No, I'm just glad you're okay." He rested his chin on top of my head.

Feeling safe in his embrace, I said the words that had been weighing on me. "I'm so sorry for leaving you."

"You said in the letter that someone from your past came back into the picture..."

"Yes."

"An ex?" he asked, and I wondered how long that question had been spinning in his mind.

"No, not at all."

He paused for a moment. "Did you take care of whatever needed to be taken care of?"

I let out a sigh. No, I hadn't. Because I had been referring to opening that portal. But instead, I'd abandoned my once-friends without so much as saying goodbye. Because I was scared. Scared of becoming like the monsters from the storybooks. Scared of becoming like the Albright witches or the werewolves or the vampires. Scared of how powerful I might become if I stayed in Quarter Square. And scared of who

I might have to hurt along the way in order to get the others out of that faerie realm.

"Grace?" he asked again, pulling me back into reality.

"Not exactly," I said, burying my face into his chest. "It was all too much." I knew I was being vague and that wasn't a real answer. But what was I supposed to say to him?

Suddenly, I felt stupid for running back into his arms.

Sure, Bellamy cared for me. Here he was, having every right to be furious with me, and he was *hugging* me. But would he still feel the same way if he knew the truth about me?

I wasn't ready to find out.

And I didn't want to be that girl anyway.

I wanted to be normal and forget everything that had happened.

"Hey—I'm going to let the others know you're okay." He pulled out his phone.

I nodded and found a spot under a maple tree to wait while he called Madison and Nathaniel. I ran my fingers through my hair, hoping I was doing the right thing. The realization that Ben had probably woken up by now and noticed I was gone occurred to me, but I had to push those thoughts away. I had to look out for myself and what was best for me.

And being here with Bellamy was what was best for me.

Before long, Bellamy was strolling down the sidewalk wearing a full-face smile. "I'm taking the day off," he announced.

"Just like that?"

He snapped. "Just like that. Nathaniel suggested it."

I smiled. "Thank you."

"Now, how about we catch up over some coffee? I want to hear *everything*."

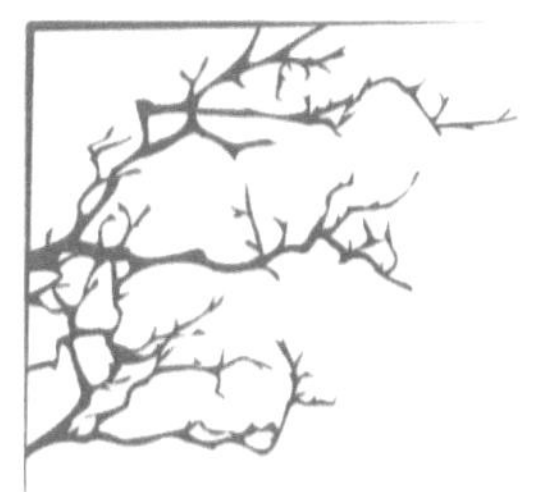

Grace

"Just promise you won't disappear on me like that again," Bellamy said, his hazel eyes turning into half-moons. He sank into the metal chair, his spoon clanking as he mindlessly stirred his coffee. "I'm not the jealous type, and I'm so glad to know you're safe. But I have to know... Where *were* you?"

He waited for an explanation. One I wasn't ready to give. Not fully.

I bit into the warm chocolate-covered donut, buying myself a couple of seconds to think. I hated keeping secrets from Bellamy. I was going to be honest with him. Today. I just had to work up the courage first. He didn't need to know everything—at least not yet. But perhaps I should give him a glimpse into the world I was an unwilling participant in. How could I even think of a future with this guy if I couldn't be honest with him about who I really was?

"Grace?" he pressed.

"I was on a trip with a friend," I said. Which was technically true.

His left eyebrow arched. "Oh?" I nodded, hoping that would satisfy him. But, of course, it didn't. He shifted in his seat. "Which friend?"

"His name's Ben. He lives in Quarter Square. He's a travel blogger." I cleared my throat, growing more uncomfortable with this conversation by the second. "I tagged along with him on a trip to Virginia."

Again—technically true. Ben was a travel blogger, and I had been with him. But that had nothing to do with why we had gone there.

Bellamy's brow relaxed. "Wait—wait, did you say he was a travel blogger? Are you talking about Ben Sullivan?"

"Yeah. You know him, too?"

"Not exactly, but Nathaniel's mom is a huge fan of his," he said, shaking his head at the coincidence. "She knew him back in high school and has been following his blog for years."

I scratched the back of my neck. "Small world."

"So, why are you and Ben going on trips together? He's old enough to be your dad. You two aren't—"

I suppressed a gag at the suggestion. "No. Not at all," I shivered, trying to get that image out of my head.

"So, he's the *someone important* from your past? I don't get it. What did he need you to do that was so urgent?"

I looked at the ceiling, hoping for a reasonable explanation to pop out of the air. I didn't have one. So, here went the truth. "I've had this problem going on for a while. I should have told you sooner. But... There are entire *years* of my life that I can't remember."

He reached his hand across the table and placed it on top of mine. "Why didn't you tell me sooner? Did you have a concussion or something?"

I shook my head. "I don't know what happened. But Ben showed up, and he knew exactly who I was. Like, really knew me. I had no memory of him, but he had photos, videos, texts, all sorts of evidence that he and I had been like family once.

I thought he might have answers about my past and that he might be able to fill in the gaps."

Bellamy's brow furrowed deeply as he tried to follow along. "Where did he take you?"

I shook my head, realizing the conclusions he was drawing. "You don't have to worry about me, Bellamy. I can take care of myself."

"How can I not worry?" He spoke softer now, leaning in as he spoke. "When you disappeared like that without so much as calling or texting, I was afraid—"

My gaze slid to the glass door as it burst open behind Bellamy. I immediately stiffened. It was Xander. He was storming into the café, jaw clenched.

He marched toward me, and I shifted in my seat. What was he doing here?

He spotted Bellamy and gave him the once-over. By the time he reached our table, he was stifling a mocking laugh. "This must be the boyfriend I've heard so little about."

"I take it you two know each other?" Bellamy was now standing, his thumbs hooked through his belt loops. I nodded, so he offered Xander his hand. "Bellamy Mortimer."

Xander left him hanging, eyeing him with suspicion. "Xander Dumont." Xander slid his attention back toward me. "I need you to come with me."

"I'm sorry I left without saying goodbye, but I can't go back there," I said, being purposefully vague since I hadn't told Bellamy about the whole *witch* thing yet. "I'm not the same person you remember."

"Grace," Xander said through his teeth. "It's Uncle Ben."

"Whoa, whoa, whoa," Bellamy said, holding his hands up. "Ben? Ben Sullivan is your *uncle*? I didn't know he had any relatives in town."

"My family's full of secrets." He winked at Bellamy, and then he took my arm. Lowering his voice, he said, "I'll explain everything on the way. But I need you to trust me."

Bellamy stepped forward, his hand now protectively resting on my lower back. "What you *need* is to get your hand off my girlfriend."

"Listen. You need to back off."

"And if I don't?"

Xander's dark eyes flashed, and the corner of his mouth pulled up into a wicked half-smile. "Then I'll make you."

Xander wasn't stupid enough to bite him in a café. But he could compel him.

"It's fine," I interjected, shaking out of Xander's hold. I turned my attention to Bellamy. "Xander's a friend. Kind of."

Xander placed his hand on his chest, feigning wounded pride.

Bellamy folded his arms across his broad chest in protest.

"We don't have time for this," Xander growled. "Grace—Uncle Ben's in the hospital. And you *need* to come with me."

My face slackened. "What?" I asked, taking a step back. "How did that happen? I was just with him last night."

When he stole a glance at Bellamy, his jaw twitched. He didn't offer up any explanation, but concern clouded his eyes. This couldn't be a typical illness. Supernaturals were at play. That's why he wasn't giving any details in front of Bellamy. Bellamy would ask questions. And him asking questions about what happened would only lead to more questions. About Ben, Xander and me.

Now understanding his sense of urgency, I grabbed my jacket and slid it on, pulling my blonde hair out from under the collar. "Okay, let's get going."

Bellamy pushed his chair in. "I'll go with you."

"No, thanks," Xander said, raising his palm to stop him. Xander cocked his head to the side. He took a step closer and peered down at Bellamy. "You're not coming." He didn't have to raise his voice to sound threatening.

I shifted my weight, chewing the inside of my cheek. He was compelling him. And... I was letting him. What was I thinking? "Stop," I asserted.

Xander looked at me over his shoulder, scowling. "He's not coming."

Growing frustrated, I pulled Bellamy aside.

"What's going on here, Grace?" he asked.

"Look, I planned to tell you everything, but it's going to have to wait. If Ben's in trouble, I need to be there for him."

He looked past me, staring Xander down. "I don't trust that guy."

"Then trust me," I said. I felt like a jerk for playing that card. I'd vanished without a trace, leaving him to worry about me when he should have been focused on healing. And here I was now, leaving again. He had absolutely no reason to have any faith in me. "If something happened to Ben, I need to be there for him."

"I do trust you, Grace." He slid his hand around the small of my back and kissed my cheek. "Just don't disappear on me again this time, okay?"

"I won't," I promised. I patted my pocket, frowning as I realized I still didn't have a phone. "I lost my phone. I don't know how long I'll be gone, but you'll be the first to know when I'm back. I'm sorry. I have to go." I bit my lip as I walked past him and caught up with Xander.

Xander was shooting Bellamy daggers with his eyes. Hardly looking back at me, with a wave of his hand, he said, "After you."

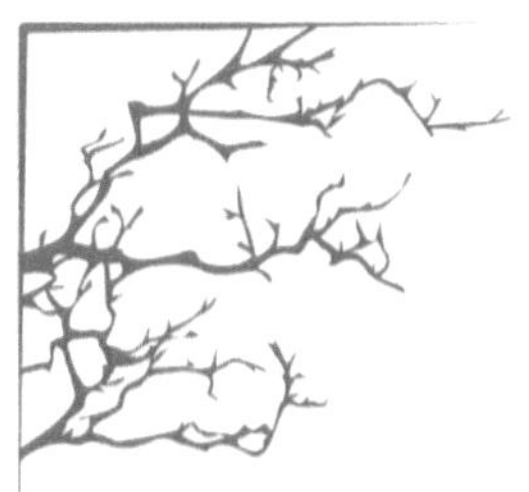

Xander

"**G**et in," I said, opening the car door for her. I tried concealing the frustration in my voice, but I knew I was doing a crappy job.

I climbed into the driver's seat and revved the engine.

"Look," Grace said. "I know you're worried about Ben, but I can do without the attitude. What's your problem anyway? Why were you being such a jerk to Bellamy? He didn't do anything wrong."

My jaw clenched, and I gripped the steering wheel hard as I sped in the direction of Quarter Square. "I don't like the way he looks at you."

"Excuse me?"

"He looks at you like you're some fragile doll. Some damsel in distress waiting for a knight in shining armor to come and rescue you." I looked over at her, eyes blazing. "But you're not some damsel, Grace. You're a witch. And a powerful one, I might add. You're a force to be reckoned with. If he can't see that, he doesn't deserve you."

"Well," she said contemplatively, "as someone who was locked in *your* castle at one time, I think it would have been rather nice for someone to have come to my rescue."

I didn't like what she was implying. "That was before... and anyway, I had no part in that."

"And yet, you did nothing to stop it."

I growled, growing more agitated by the second. I wasn't going to have this conversation with her.

It was pointless.

The Grace I knew was gone.

Yes, every once in a while, bits of that fiery spirit would blaze through. But our entire history had been erased from her mind. Maybe the facts were there. But the emotions? Without those, our friendship meant nothing to her.

When I'd first heard Uncle Ben was in the hospital, my first thought, first fear, had been about Grace. The person who'd made the call didn't have any information about her. I was afraid she was dead—or worse. It'd all been too convenient—me escaping the Albright compound and us tracking Grace down all without so much as a peep from Sofia Albright. I worried my worst fears had come true.

I'd rushed to the hospital in the middle of the night—though, technically, early morning was more like it. Uncle Ben had told me Grace was gone. He'd realized she'd left just before someone broke into his place and attacked him. They beat him up, dragged him out of his home and left him for dead on the side of the road. He hadn't told the investigators much—he didn't want them snooping around his home with all of the grimoires and magical objects up there. And anyway, he didn't know who had done this to him. But it didn't take a genius to put two and two together.

It was Sofia Albright.

Or maybe Ruby Drake...

Either way, I'd offered to give him my blood to heal him and get him out of that awful hospital room, but he'd refused. He didn't want to raise any suspicion.

I'd asked him if he had any idea what happened to Grace. He told me he suspected she'd freaked out after our encounter with the werewolf and had run back to Amber Falls.

He was right.

I just hadn't expected to find her running into the arms of that Bellamy guy.

I didn't know who Grace was anymore. But I knew that I needed her help.

Now, Grace Addington was nothing more than a means to an end.

Because I was going to get my siblings back. They were all I had left.

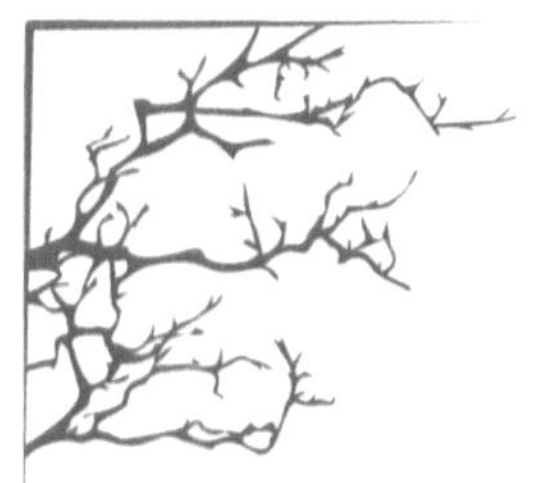

Grace

I didn't understand what Xander's problem was. Was this about me running away without saying goodbye? Was he worried about Ben and taking his emotions out on me? I hadn't encountered this side of him before. And I wasn't sure that I liked it.

The drive to Quarter Square seemed to drag on forever. After our little spat, neither of us spoke a word for at least twenty minutes. Xander kept his eyes on the road, deep in thought. I watched him, recalling the bits and pieces of my dreams. Those *had* to be dreams. He'd spoken to me with such compassion, such gentleness. I wasn't sure the guy sitting beside me was capable of such emotions. Part of me regretted ever getting in the car with him in the first place. But I knew that I had to see Ben. I owed him that. And seeing that I was on an apology tour today, I owed him one, too.

"Why are you staring at me like that?" Xander quipped.

"I'm not staring," I insisted.

"Oh, you're definitely staring." He glanced over at me and batted his eyelashes in a playfully obnoxious manner.

He was seriously getting under my skin. But... I couldn't help but wonder... "Have we ever been on an airplane together?"

His eyes lit with intrigue. "Why do you ask?"

I shook my head, knowing how stupid my explanation was about to sound. "I had a weird dream last night. It felt so real, but it doesn't make any sense. We were on an airplane and you were trying to comfort me. There was something about my brother and dad…" I couldn't recall the exact details.

Xander's jaw twitched, and I knew at once that it wasn't just a dream. "That was a long time ago."

"What was that about? I remember feeling guilty, but I don't know why. What was I so upset about?"

"It's not important," Xander said, keeping his eyes on the road.

"Not important? That's the first thread of a memory I have, and you don't think that's important? You were there. You claim to be my friend. What are you hiding from me?"

At that, Xander swerved to the side of the road. I instinctively pressed my heel against an imaginary pedal as I braced myself for a crash. The car screeched to a halt, and Xander turned to face me, eyes blazing. "Let's get something clear. I'm not hiding anything from you. I'm protecting you from the truth."

"So, you admit you're keeping secrets from me?" I shook my head in disgust. "Then we aren't as close as you claim we are. That, or I was an idiot to ever trust you in the first place."

He exhaled deeply, and it looked like it was taking every ounce of willpower he had to keep from screaming at me. In an eerily calm voice, he said, "You'll know everything when you're ready to handle it."

"What could I have possibly done that was so horrible?" I spat. "What could I have done that was so horrific that I can't even know about it?" It didn't make any sense. And he wasn't offering any explanation. I closed my eyes. I was so frustrated I thought I might cry—but I would never give Xander the satisfaction of seeing me so vulnerable.

Growing angrier by the second, a rush of fire flooded my veins...

And then I remembered.

I remembered the recurring nightmare I'd had.

The one with the man burning to death.

The one where he smiled right before I killed him.

What if that was a memory, too?

And then I remembered how Xander had reacted when I asked what had happened to my father. It was a similar reaction to the one he was having now. This... protective rage.

I drew my hand to my mouth, understanding the answer to the secret Xander had tried so desperately to keep.

"I killed him, didn't I?" I said, turning to face him. I could feel the color draining from my face, and my voice was faint, like I was a mere shadow of myself. "*I killed my father.*"

"IT'S MORE COMPLICATED than it sounds," Xander said. And there it was. That look. That look that revealed there was more to him than being the charming and smug and sometimes downright obnoxious Blood Heir. That look that suggested that he really did care.

I wanted to try to understand. But it felt like my entire world had crumbled. I'd waited my whole life to find out who my father was. To meet him.

And now, I was learning that I was the reason he was dead...

"Your father was a bad man, Grace," he said. "And that's coming from a vampire."

I curled my lip in disgust. "Is that supposed to be a joke? Because your timing sucks."

"He gave you a choice: you were either with him or against him. He threatened everyone you cared about. He threatened *you*. And when he dropped the boundary, he unleashed a supernatural war. I know you don't remember it, but it was bad. And it was only the beginning of what he had in store. You knew that."

"And so, I killed him?" I asked, trying to understand.

"No. You wanted to stop him." He lifted his wrist, revealing the weird bracelet he always wore. "Do you know what this is?"

I shrugged. I decided against offering my theories.

"This is the Bracelet of Wynstar. Years ago, Reed put a curse on me. Like you, your dad was freaky powerful, even for a witch, and he'd found a way to overpower my mind. He was bent on getting revenge against my family. And he took it out on your friend Danielle. He wanted me to kill her. And I would have if it weren't for you." He held the bracelet out so that I could get a better look. "Thanks to your spell, Danielle was safe. And I got my life back."

"That's nice and all. But what does this have to do with anything?"

"You were planning to use a similar spell on him. You wanted to overpower his mind—but instead of making him do evil things, you wanted to make him be *good*." He paused for a moment. "You were trying to save him, too, in a way."

I hugged my arms around myself, taking it all in. "So, what happened?"

"We infiltrated a party he'd thrown and conspired with your brother, Nick. You and I waited for Reed in his hotel room, thinking we had the upper hand. But Reed saw right through it. He tried to kill me, and you saved me. But then, he turned on you. You took your brother's hand—and because you were Carlisle twins, doing so amplified your power. You killed Reed, yes. But it was self-defense."

"Is that supposed to make me feel better?"

"It's the truth. That's what you wanted, wasn't it?"

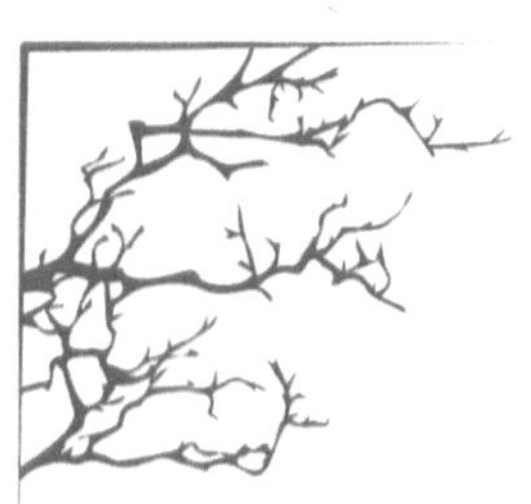

Grace

Xander and I barged into the hospital room, eager to speak with Ben. The muscles in Ben's face relaxed when he saw me, and in a faint voice, he managed to say, "*Grace*. You're safe."

The sincerity in his tone made my chest cave. I felt awful for running away like that. "I'm so sorry," I said, crossing the room until I reached his bedside. "I should have told you I was leaving."

He reached for my hand, and I took it. "You don't owe me an apology, Grace. All that matters is that you're safe."

"From whom?"

Not knowing the answer, Ben shook his head.

"It has to be Sofia or Ruby," Xander offered, stepping closer so that he was now standing over my shoulder. "Either Sofia was taking revenge against Ben for rescuing me and finding you or Ruby discovered he stole her ring."

The reality of the situation hit me dead-on. I was stupid for thinking I could run back to Bellamy and pretend like all of this never happened. Sofia and Ruby knew who I was. Which meant that as long as Bellamy and I were together, he'd be in danger. I cared about him too much to do that to him. He might be capable of taking care of himself when dealing with humans. But witches? Werewolves? It was selfish of me to think we could be together.

And as much as I didn't fully understand my past, I knew that Ben was a good person. A person who would do anything to protect me. And if I had the power to help him, I owed him that much, didn't I? I couldn't run away again knowing that someone was after him. I wasn't a monster.

Lifting my gaze, I locked eyes with Ben. "What do we do now?"

"We?" Xander asked. Even though he was standing behind me, I could sense his smirk.

I spun around, raising my chin to look him in the eye. "That's why you brought me here, isn't it? You need my help. I'm the all-powerful witch, aren't I?" I asked, raising my hands in question. "So, what's the plan? Go after Ruby? Face off against the Albrights?"

"The plan," Ben said in a strained voice, "is for me to heal. Once I am well enough, we can regroup and come up with a plan of attack." He erupted into a coughing fit and then slid his hand to his side, groaning. "Have you had a chance to check my place out?" he asked Xander.

"Not yet."

"Would you two mind going there and assessing the damage? If any of those objects got into the wrong hands..." He didn't have to explain further. "I keep a log of all the objects in the attic. I need you to go through it and see if anything's missing."

I had been so fired up about avenging Ben that it hadn't even stopped to consider the fact that he had an entire arsenal of magical objects at his disposal that might have been tampered with. "Of course," I said, trying my best to sound reassuring. "Whatever you need."

A RUSH OF CHILLS ROLLED up my arms as we neared Ben's door. Xander gave the front door a couple of knocks before pushing it open. Ben's dog Fangs started barking—you'd never guess such a cute, cuddly pup could sound so intimidating. She pounced on me when we stepped inside.

I was relieved to see Fangs appeared unharmed, and I bent down to pet her. She licked my hands and cheek and practically climbed into my lap. "It's okay, girl," I said, trying to comfort her. "Your dad's okay. He'll be home soon."

While I was busy tending to Fangs, Xander was surveying the damage on the first floor. The family albums were strewn across the room, and Ben's La-Z-Boy had been thrown to its side. There were splatters of blood on the floor—Ben's, Xander determined.

I should have been here. I could have stopped this.

I blinked away the tears that were threatening to come. "Is anything missing down here?" I asked, still tending to Fangs as Xander went through the many books.

"No," he said, shutting one of the albums and placing it back on the shelf, "but if whoever did this had any doubt that he was related to vampires before, they definitely know now." He held up another album that was opened to an old sketch of him and his siblings. It was hundreds of years old, if I had to guess, based on their attire and the deep yellowing of the paper.

I finally got to my feet and helped him clean up the downstairs. I'd been shown an album or two already, but seeing them all laid out in front of me was hard to wrap my head around. Xander had lived through so much. I couldn't decide whether it was a blessing or a curse.

I stumbled upon one of the more recent albums. One picture in particular caught my eye. It was of me and Jasper laughing together in one of the booths at Books & Brews. And Xander was there off to the side in the background, his lips curving into a smile. The way he was looking at me almost made me think... "Is there anything else you haven't told me?" I asked him.

"What?" he asked, busy focusing on the task of getting Ben's place back in order.

"Were we ever, you know, *together*?"

He stopped what he was doing and turned to look at me. "Why would you ask me that?"

I shrugged. "I don't know. You just seem to care about me, that's all. And in some of these pictures..." My voice trailed off. "I'm just trying to make sense of it all."

He blinked.

"So, were we?"

His throat bobbed as he swallowed. "No," he sighed. "We were never together." And then he got back to work.

And so did I. I suddenly felt embarrassed about bringing it up. I must have read into things too much. And why would we have been together anyway? He was a vampire—and a ridiculously handsome one at that. With those cheekbones, he could have any girl he wanted. Why would I have thought he would have wanted me?

It didn't matter anyway. I had Bellamy.

For now, at least.

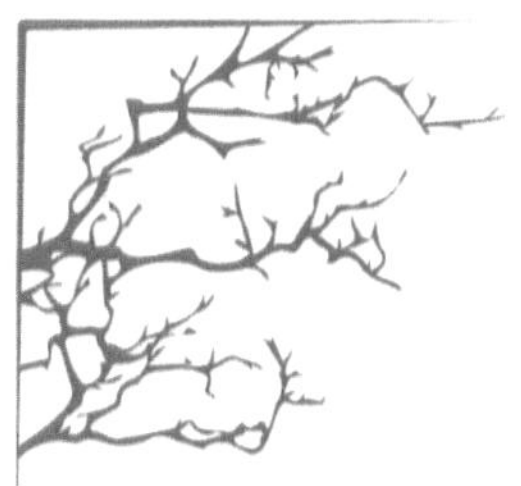

Grace

Once the living room was in order, we made our way upstairs, Fangs practically attaching herself to my legs all the while. I couldn't blame the poor thing. She must have been terrified.

The upstairs was just as much of a wreck as the downstairs. Maybe worse.

We went to the attic first since that's where Ben kept his log and stored most of his artifacts. Xander rummaged through the many boxes until he found the log Ben had said would be there. His eyes widened as he flipped through it, realizing just how much work we had in store for us.

"This is going to take days," I said after he'd flipped through five pages or so.

"Maybe not," Xander said. He handed the log over to me. "It's all categorized. And there are pictures, too. That'll make it easier."

"I guess," I said, feeling overwhelmed. It wouldn't have been such a daunting task if these objects didn't look so foreign to me. It felt like I was in a real-life version of an *I Spy* book. And I was terrible at *I Spy* books. Thankfully, though, Ben had at least categorized the items by their location. So, we started in one corner and made our way around the entire attic. We began by sorting through an assortment of jewelry—amulets, rings, you name it.

I realized Xander was eyeing the tattoo on my shoulder. I swiftly readjusted my jacket to cover it better. "You wouldn't happen to know where I got that tattoo, do you?"

"It's not a tattoo," he said, flipping to the next page of the log. "It's a Mark."

"What does that mean?"

He let out a heavy sigh. "When witches kill, they're Marked."

I grimaced, mindlessly drawing my hand to my shoulder. "Why?"

Xander shrugged. "Who knows? Something about balance, blah, blah, blah. You know how witches are."

I scowled at him. "No, I don't. Please elaborate."

"There's a price for everything, or so they claim. I always figured the Marks were the price for taking a life. Like a constant reminder that you carry with you forever."

"Great." I frowned, thinking of my father. "Did I ever kill anyone else?"

"No. Just Reed."

We moved on to the rest of the attic. Multiple objects were missing. My heart began to race as questions arose in my mind.

Once we had finished checking out the attic, Xander pointed out that we needed to check the bedrooms, too. While Ben took care to hide most of the magical objects, there were a select few that he kept on display. Luckily, he'd made note of those on his log, too.

We eventually made our way to the guest bedroom where I'd been staying and quickly rummaged through the dresser drawers. The bottom drawer was filled with more jewelry. The middle drawer was mostly stones, vials and powders. And the top drawer was filled with random boxes etched with runes, loose papers with notes written in code and ancient grimoires. Everything was right where it was supposed to be. Finally, we checked the top of the dresser. Ben kept a few random magical objects up there, too: a dagger, a wooden stake (which Xander had a few choice words to say about), silver bullets and—"Where's the siphoning tool?" Xander asked.

"The what?"

"It's a golden ball used to siphon magic," he explained as he pointed to the log, his voice rising in panic. "Where is it?"

I slowly turned around, surveying the room. "It has to be here somewhere."

"Does it?" he snapped.

Good point.

"What would Ruby or Sofia want with a siphoning tool?" he wondered to himself, referring to our two prime suspects.

I thought on it for a moment, trying to recall the contents of the various grimoires I'd read in recent weeks. The siphoning tool had a specific purpose: to siphon dark magic. But in the wrong hands, the magic wouldn't necessarily stay stored. It could be *used*. Worry creased my brow. "I'd say someone's planning something big."

"Care to explain?"

"If they're siphoning magic from something, one would think they'd have a use in mind for that magic..."

He grunted. "Let's keep looking. Once we go through everything and see what else is missing, we can decide where to go from there."

He was right. We needed to go through everything and see what else had been taken. Then, we'd know what we were up against.

"Why didn't Ben have some sort of security system installed in his house?" I wondered aloud. "Seems like it would have saved him a lot of trouble."

"The problem with security systems," Xander explained, moving on to the closet, "is that when they go off, the police come." He gestured vaguely to the room. "This wouldn't be easy to explain now, would it?"

"Fair enough. But you'd think he would have had a witch put up a boundary spell around his place or something."

He glanced at me over his shoulder. "He did."

"Oh," I said, realizing he was referring to me. "Then how did whoever did this get in here?"

"They must have have been working with a witch who's even more powerful than you."

I decided not to press the issue. It didn't do any good to think about what he should have done. It didn't matter. He'd been attacked in his own home and was now in the hospital. And multiple magical objects had been stolen from him... I wished I knew of a spell to pick up magical fingerprints or something. What's more, I'd have to look into setting up an even stronger protection spell for Ben's home.

Xander shook his head. "You're right," he said. "This stuff should be kept somewhere safer than this."

"Such as...?"

"I'll come up with something."

And with that, we got back to work.

WE HAD WORKED THE ENTIRE day, and we still hadn't finished going through everything. Xander ordered a pizza, and we made awkward small talk while we waited for it to arrive.

"So," he said, searching for something to talk about that didn't involve witches, "how did you and Belly meet?"

"His name's Bellamy," I scowled. "And we met on my birthday."

"Let me guess," he grinned. "You met at a bar."

"He was saving me from some jerk who was hitting on me."

Xander pressed his finger to his lip and tapped it. "So, he saved you from someone who was hitting on you... by hitting on you?"

I rolled my eyes. "It wasn't like that."

"And your first date?"

I swallowed, knowing telling him would only lead to jokes. "It's none of your business."

"Come on, it couldn't have been that bad."

"It wasn't bad. It was wonderful."

"So, where'd he take you?" he asked. "Come on, don't make me compel it out of you."

"You wouldn't do that..."

He raised a brow. "Wouldn't I? I guess I could always get it out of him..."

"He took me to Crescent Cape," I blurted out.

"What?!" He clutched his stomach and burst into a fit of hysterical laughter. "You can't be serious."

I should have just kept my mouth shut.

Xander was in tears. "You're telling me he took you to the place where you were a *blood slave*? How romantic."

I wanted to argue with him. Maybe I had a dark sense of humor, but in spite of myself, I smiled, too. "Shut up. It wasn't like that."

He was laughing too hard to hear me.

"Seriously, Xander. He's a good guy. Better than I deserve." I propped my elbows on the counter and rested my head in my palms. Now that I thought about it, nothing about this was funny.

"He can't be that great."

"He is," I asserted, staring down at the counter. Bellamy was the epitome of everything that was right in the world. A world I now questioned whether I belonged in... "He's a perfect gentleman. He's protective. He's compassionate. He's understanding. He's forgiving. He's as dependable as they come."

"Dependable, huh?"

"Yes. Oh, and speaking of being dependable," I started, "can I borrow your phone? I want to call him."

He scoffed. "Absolutely not. What if he traces my number? If you really care about this guy as much as you say you do, then you'd better get used to letting him down. Because the only way you can guarantee his safety is if you keep him as far away from the supernatural part of yourself as possible."

As much as I wanted to debate him, I had a terrible feeling he was right...

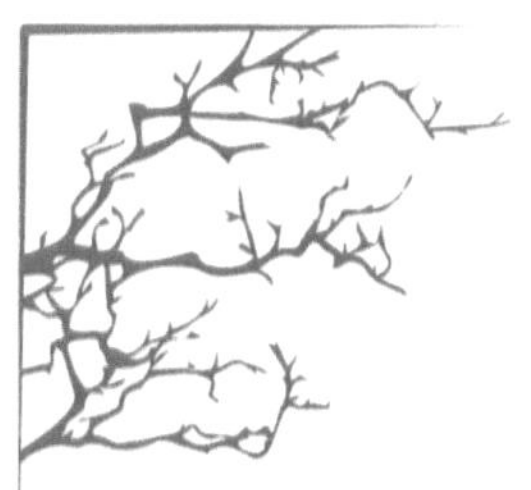

Xander

We'd spent all day and much of the night cataloging Uncle Ben's collection of magical objects. A variety of objects were missing. The most concerning item that was missing, in my opinion, remained the siphoning tool.

I don't know why I hadn't ever suggested Ben find a better place to store these items. Honestly, I hadn't paid much attention to how he conducted his business. Though, to be fair, it had never been an issue before.

I couldn't do anything about the past, but I had an idea about how to rectify the situation in the future.

Whoever broke into his home had seen our family albums. Whatever anonymity Uncle Ben had before was long gone now. He was now officially connected to the Blood Heirs. And word traveled fast in the supernatural community. Which meant that he'd never be truly safe.

Crescent Cape had been vacant for years. Ever since the fire and the raids, the government had taken over the property. But it wasn't like it benefitted the government in any way. Other than weirdos like Bellamy apparently, most people didn't want to visit the land once reigned over by vampires.

A year or so ago, I saw that the land was up for auction. Not surprisingly, there hadn't been any bidders. First of all, the land itself was worth a fortune. After all, it stretched for acres along the Cape. Second of all, well, *you know.*

Now, I hadn't made a move to buy back the land because of my name. After Julian's photograph ended up plastered all over the news, it seemed like it'd be a bit obvious if I purchased it. I could only imagine how the public would react. And, believe it or not, I liked keeping my identity under the radar. It made feeding much easier when people didn't scream in terror at the sight of you.

What's more, with Grace and I on the never-ending search for faerie dust, I hadn't had time to look into it too closely.

But now, I had another idea.

Perhaps I could give Uncle Ben the money. Have *him* buy the property. Have *him* rebuild our family home. He had a different last name, after all. No humans would know he was connected to us. And now that supernaturals had been outed anyway, even if people did put two and two together, it wouldn't matter.

Granted, building another castle in its place might be pushing it.

But a mansion? I could settle for that.

What's more—we could create an armory for him. In addition to locks and alarm systems, Grace could spell up stronger protection wards. And I'd offer my services of protection, too, of course.

Uncle Ben could live there with me. Aiden and Victoria, too, and the rest of my siblings if we made it big enough. We had the financial means. So, why not? We may not be able to bring Crescent Cape back to its former glory. Now that the world knew of what had transpired there, there was no going back. Not in this day and age. But still... Crescent Cape had been our home for *centuries*. Someone would claim the land eventually. We might as well get to it first.

I wondered if Grace would consider moving in, too. It would be the safest place for her, undoubtedly. The one place where I could keep an eye out for her. To protect her.

The only problem was Bellamy.

I was banking on him running for the hills as soon as she told him she was a witch... but what if I was wrong?

She kept emphasizing the word *dependable* earlier. Was that supposed to be a dig at me? No, it couldn't be. She didn't remember our history.

And yet... our fight that night in New York was forever etched into my mind.

I know you run away when things get tough. So, is that what this is about? Is that what's happening now?

I dragged my hands down my face, knowing that none of it mattered anymore. But I vowed then and there that if I ever *did* get the old Grace back, I'd make certain she never had to doubt my loyalty again.

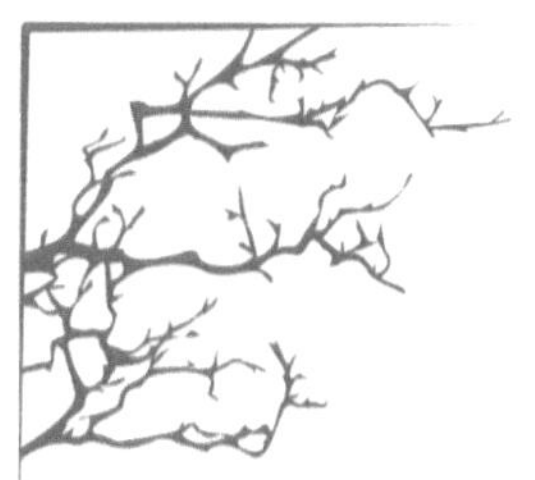

Grace

Today was the big day—Ben was returning home from the hospital. Xander had left a while ago to pick him up, but I offered to stay behind. I wanted to do my part to make things right with Ben. He said there was nothing to apologize for, but still... I felt awful that he had been attacked *right after* I'd left. If I'd been there, maybe I could have stopped whoever did this to him.

So, here I was in the kitchen doing my best not to accidentally burn the place down.

Back at the diner, I didn't touch anything other than the coffee maker. But I did remember my mom's famous casserole. Everyone that had ever tried a bite had fallen in love with it. Hopefully Ben would accept this as my peace offering.

I had just finished topping the casserole off with crushed crackers when the last of the crumbs slipped out of my hands. Fangs was there in a flash, lapping up the remnant. I chuckled at her and, after drizzling melted butter over the top, popped the meal in the oven.

Needing something remotely healthy to serve alongside the heart attack-inducing dish, I wandered over to the refrigerator and rummaged around looking for lettuce and some veggies to toss into a salad. But then the doorbell rang, taking me by surprise.

Fangs unleashed a ferocious bark, and I jumped and slammed my head against the refrigerator door. Shutting it and pressing my palm to my forehead, I looked through the peephole.

My heart jumped. *It couldn't be.*

Even through the distorted glass, I could make out the features of the young man standing before me: deep blue eyes, hair as bright as the sun and a thin nose.

My memories of him might have been gone, but even without them, I knew who the person on the other side of the door was: my brother. My twin.

Hurriedly, I unlocked the door and pulled it open. "Nick?" I said breathlessly.

Fangs was barking at him, so I did my best to settle her.

Nick smiled and said, "Grace, it's so good to see you again." He gave me an awkward hug—I guessed that was how we typically greeted each other in the past. But I couldn't help myself. I flung my arms around his neck and pulled him in close, hardly believing I was touching my own flesh and blood. He chuckled. "Whoa, what's that for?"

My lashes grew wet, and I blinked, trying to compose myself. "It's just really good to see you."

I released him from my hold and he stared down at me quizzically. With a whiff of his nose, he asked, "What are you cooking?"

"Casserole," I said. "It's an old recipe from my mom. My, uh, adopted mom." I sounded like a bumbling idiot. "I'm sorry, this is super weird."

"What is?" he asked, making himself comfortable at the kitchen table.

"This is going to sound crazy." I sat down across from him and let out a heavy breath. "I know that we've met before," I started, "but I don't remember any of it."

"Oh?"

"Memory powder, we're guessing." And then I realized I hadn't even asked why he was here—or how he knew where to find me. I swept my hair away from my eyes and tucked it behind my ear. "Anyway, what are you doing here?"

"I was looking for you," he said flatly. There was something disconcerting about his tone. A coolness in his voice that I hadn't expected. "I tried calling..." he started.

"I lost my phone," I explained, not bothering to bore him with the details. As I was sitting there with him, I realized he was the first witch that I'd come across since learning about what had happened to me. Maybe he could help. "Hey—you wouldn't happen to know anything about memory powder, would you? Do you know how I can get my memories back?"

He was about to speak when his phone buzzed. I happened to see the name that flashed on the screen before he swiftly silenced the call and tucked the phone in his pocket: Phoebe Mather. The name was strangely familiar, but I couldn't place where I had heard it.

"So, you were saying something about your memories being wiped. Do you know who did it?"

I shook my head.

"And you really don't remember *anything*?"

"Nothing of the past seven years. I wouldn't even know about you had it not been for Ben and Xander."

The lock on the front door jostled. Ben walked inside, followed by Xander. "Ben," I said, jumping to my feet and hurrying over to greet him. Fangs brushed in front of me and jumped up, pawing lovingly at her owner while she licked him to death. She looked back at my brother and snarled before giving a whine and nuzzling against Ben's leg. Once she calmed down enough for me to get a word out, I asked, "How are you feeling?"

"Never better," he said, and he glanced back at Xander.

"I gave him some of my blood in the hospital parking lot," Xander explained.

"Oh," I said. "I see. Well, that's good... right?"

"Yeah, as long as no one tries to kill me in the next twenty-four hours," he joked. He spotted my brother sitting at the table. He walked over to greet him. "Hey, Nick," he said, giving my brother's shoulder a squeeze. "Long time no see. What are you doing here?"

"I heard my sister was back in town," he said, glancing over at me and smiled. There was something oddly familiar about his smile. Maybe, deep down, I really did remember him. "I hadn't been able to get in touch with her for some time. Thought it would be best to come by and make sure she was okay."

"I'm fine," I said, though I didn't know why. Nothing about what had happened to me in the past weeks was *fine*.

"Back in town?" Xander asked, stepping forward. "How'd you know she was out of town?"

Nick flicked his hand. "Oh, I'd tried to call her a while back. Went to her place and saw that no one was there. Figured she'd skipped town."

"And you didn't think to ask us?" Xander asked, gesturing to himself and his uncle. "And who told you she was back in town anyway?"

Nick shrugged. "I did a tracking spell. And what difference does it make? It's not a crime to visit my sister."

"Don't worry about Xander," Ben said to Nick. "You know how he is." Then he sniffed the air and asked, "Is something in the oven?"

"It's a casserole," I explained. I crossed the room and flicked the oven light on so that he could see. "It's my way of saying sorry and that I'm glad you're okay."

"Grace, how many times do I have to tell you that you don't have anything to apologize for? This wasn't your fault."

"I shouldn't have just left like that," I asserted. "And anyway, call it an *I'm sorry casserole* or a *get well casserole*. Whatever you want. I just felt like I needed to do something. You know?" I hugged my arms around myself, staring at the floor.

"I know," he said, and though I wasn't looking directly at him, I could feel the smile in his voice.

Xander pulled out a chair and plopped himself across from my brother. The way they stared at each other made it seem like they were arch enemies. There was clearly some bad blood there. I wondered what that was all about. Maybe Nick blamed Xander, too, for what happened to our dad. "So," Xander said, his gaze unflinching, "you wouldn't happen to know anything about what the Albrights are up to, would you?"

Nick blinked. "I don't know what you mean."

He jerked his head toward me. "Memory powder for her. Blood draws for me. If you ask me, the witches are up to something." He folded his hands and rested them on the table before leaning forward. "And then someone breaks into Uncle Ben's place. Attacks him and steals his magical objects. Pretty weird coincidence, huh?"

"Super weird," he admitted.

"So, I'm asking you one more time: do you have any guesses as to what they're up to?"

"I couldn't say. Rival coven and all."

Xander locked his gaze in on my brother's. "Tell me the truth. What are the witches up to?"

"I already told you. I don't know."

"Xander," I said with a scoff, realizing what he was doing. He was *compelling* my brother. "Stop it. If he says he doesn't know, he doesn't know."

Xander stammered back, holding his hands up in mock surrender. "Fine," he said, his gaze dark and murderous.

Nick scooted his chair back, getting ready to stand.

"Seriously, Nick," Ben started, "don't mind him. Stay for dinner."

"Please, Nick," I said, eyes pleading. "Please stay. I'd love to get to talk with you. I have so many questions for you."

Nick sighed. "Actually, I should be going. I just came to make sure Grace was alright," he said, straightening out the hem of his shirt as he stood. He offered his hand to Ben. "Glad to see you're on the mend."

"Wait," I said, chasing after Nick as he headed for the door. I grabbed a pad of yellow sticky notes and a black pen from the edge of the counter and handed it to my brother. "Can I get your number again?"

His mouth tugged into a smile. "Sure." And he scribbled the digits on the paper before handing it back to me. "Take care of yourself, Grace."

I nodded. "I will." And I stood in the doorway as I watched my brother slide into his car and drive away. Frustrated, I spun on my heel and marched straight toward Xander. "Why you do have to be such a jerk? Do you have any idea what him being here meant to me?"

"Grace—"

"Stop it! I don't want to hear it. I only came back because of him," I said, pointing to Ben. "I can't begin to fathom how we ever ended up being friends before. Because, quite frankly, you are selfish and rude and completely insufferable." My fists were clenched so hard that I drew blood. I noticed his nostrils flare. Part of me wanted to shove my hand into his stupid mouth to force him to drink witch's blood and make him sick. But I refrained.

"Grace," Xander started in an unsettlingly stoic voice. "Did you find anything strange about that whole interaction?"

"What?" I said, scrunching my face in exasperation. "What are you talking about?"

"Seriously," Ben chimed in. "What *are* you talking about?"

"What did he say to you before we got here? Did he say anything strange to you?"

I crossed my arms defensively. "No. I asked him about getting my memories back, but someone called before he could answer."

"Did you hear his conversation? Who was he talking to?"

"Someone named Phoebe called, but he didn't answer it. And then you walked in and ruined everything."

"Did you just say *Phoebe*?"

"Yes..." He and Ben exchanged a tense glance. "Why? Who's Phoebe?"

Ben cleared his throat. "She's a witch from the Kingdom of the Silver Seas. She's the one who secured the Silverleaf sapling for Reed—the ingredient he used in the spell to drop the boundary to Crescent Cape."

"Why would Phoebe be calling Nick?" Xander pondered.

I shrugged. "I don't know. Maybe she was a family friend?"

Xander was pacing now, mind spinning. "You told your brother that your memories were wiped clean, and he didn't help you." It was more of an observation than a question.

"That's only because you barged in here and picked a fight with him."

"And he got a call from Phoebe... And he said he knew you were here because he did a tracking spell on you. But why didn't he do that in the first place when he hadn't been able to reach you?"

"I don't know." I really didn't. I had no idea what my relationship with Nick was like. He seemed a bit on edge, but maybe that was normal for him.

Xander brushed his dark hair away from his face, letting his fingers dig into his scalp. "Grace, who were you texting right before we were attacked in New York?"

I shrugged. "How would I know?"

"Oh, right." He flicked his hand dismissively. "Doesn't matter. It was a rhetorical question. The answer is Nick. You didn't see each other often, but you always checked in with him. And you always told Nick where you were going. And you texted him to let him know you'd made it alright. I thought it was a weird twin thing you'd picked up, but now, I'm not so sure..."

"What are you getting at?" I planted my hands on my hips.

"What if Nick was thwarting our attempts to find faerie dust the whole time? Every single lead we had came up short. What if he was beating us to the punch? How did the Albrights of all people know we were in upstate New York anyway?"

"What would Nick have to do with that? I thought that the Albrights and Carlisles were rival covens..."

"I haven't figured that part out yet," Xander said, pacing faster now. "Nick knew where we were going before we got there. He knew you had been out of town. He knew you had returned to Quarter Square. Not to mention, someone with magic would have had to break down those protection spells you had put around Uncle Ben's magical objects."

"Someone like Nick?" I asked, eyes narrowing.

"What if... what if he's behind all of it?"

"Xander—" Ben started, trying to talk some sense into him.

Xander whirled around. "I couldn't compel him," he said, chest rising and falling hard.

"How do you know?" Ben asked.

"You live long enough, you get pretty good at reading people. Trust me. Something's not right. I don't know what it is... but I'm going to get to the bottom of it."

"And how do you plan to do that?" I asked.

A devious grin crossed his face. "I'm going to follow him. But first, you're going to do a tracking spell."

"Absolutely not. He's my brother. That may not mean much to you, but it means something to me."

"He's also Reed's son," Xander pointed out.

"And I'm Reed's daughter. What's your point?"

Xander huffed. "Why are you being so difficult? If I'm right," he said, pointing to the door in desperation, "he's been deceiving you for years. Which means he can't be trusted. And if he's anything like your dad, no one is safe. Not even you."

My arms were crossed. I couldn't even look at him.

"Don't you want to know the truth?"

"Grace," Ben started, "he has a point. If you do the tracking spell, Xander can follow him and keep an eye on him. See if he's up to something. I can go with him if that would make you feel better. I'll make sure he doesn't get into too much trouble." He smirked at Xander.

"Fine," I said—only for the sake of proving Xander wrong. "I'll do the spell. But I'm coming, too."

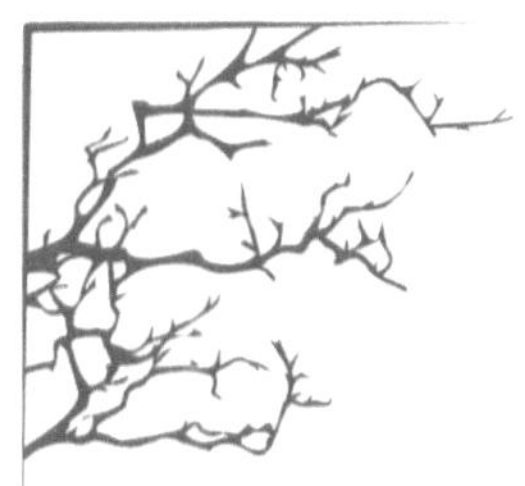

Grace

We waited an hour or two for Nick to get wherever he was going. We spent that time eating dinner and listening to Xander's absurd conspiracy theories. And then I performed the spell. "He's in Crescent Cape," I told Xander. Ben was upstairs now, rummaging through his magical objects. I wasn't sure of Nick's exact location, but Xander had his suspicions.

"He went to the Carlisle coven's compound."

"I thought you said he left the coven."

"I thought he did. I thought a lot of things..."

I shook my head. "You're jumping to conclusions. Maybe he's visiting an old friend or something."

"Or maybe he's been conspiring with them all along."

Just then, Ben came hurrying down the stairs with Fangs trailing close behind. He didn't explicitly show them to me, but I could tell he had weapons on him, hidden under his sleeves. As if reading my mind, he explained, "I promise I won't use them unless I have to. But Xander's right—if there's a chance that Nick was the one who broke into my house and stole those objects... if he was the one conspiring with the Albrights... we need to be prepared. *You* need to be prepared."

I may not have remembered my brother, but none of what they were saying jived with what I'd been told about him. Why would he be plotting against us? And to what end? He hadn't caused any problems in the last four years. So, what was different now? If he'd been against us all along, I had to hand it to him for his dedication to playing the long game.

"Grace," Ben said. "I'm serious. I hope we go there and prove Xander wrong. But if he's right, you need to be ready."

"To learn that my brother is secretly an evil mastermind?"

"To defend yourself if things go wrong."

I nodded, though I couldn't accept that possibility. I was only going to make sure Xander didn't do anything stupid. And I looked forward to seeing the look on his face when he realized just how wrong he was about Nick.

WE STOOD UNDER THE velvet sky, ironically lit by a crescent moon. Ben, Xander and I had parked the car a good way back and were currently trekking through the woods on foot. The trees were tall and thin—they'd hardly provide much cover in daylight. We weaved between them, steering clear of the long gravel road that led to the coven's compound.

Ben had a strange look on his face. "What's wrong?" I asked.

He swallowed down the lump in his throat. "It's been a long time since I was here."

My eyebrows lifted. "You've been here before?"

He nodded somberly like he was reliving a memory he'd much rather forget. "I came here to confront your father—before I knew you were his daughter. He had used dark magic to murder Freya, the Albright witch who had volunteered to keep up the boundary in Crescent Cape. And spell up artificial blood for Aiden. Anyway, Evanna—the Albright witch who had volunteered to take Freya's place—and I went to confront Reed about what he had done. Let's just say it didn't end well."

"Oh."

Xander, who was walking a few feet ahead, lifted a hand to silence us. He tilted his head, tuning into his supernatural hearing. "Someone's here."

My nerves prickled, and a swarm of conflicting emotions consumed me. I didn't know why I was so confident that my brother hadn't turned against me. But I couldn't let go of hope. Hope that I had one piece of my biological family to hold onto. Hope that being his own flesh and blood meant something to him. And yet... Xander and Ben had been right about everything else thus far.

We trekked further on, and I noticed the tension in Xander's shoulders release.

"Hey!" a twenty-something guy called out from up ahead. He had his arms tangled around a girl. I had a feeling we were interrupting something. "What do you think you're doing out here?"

In the blink of an eye, Xander stood before them, locking his gaze on them. "Go back to whatever it was you were doing, and forget you ever saw us. You'll tell no one of this."

The couple had a dazed look about them for a moment or two, but then they went back to kissing as if we weren't there at all.

We walked around them, since they were now oblivious to us, and headed on toward the compound.

I didn't know what it was that I was expecting. A hut? Spiderwebs? Cauldrons? This definitely wasn't *that*. The compound was, in fact, a massive house that was big enough to house multiple families. And a rather nice house at that. It even had a porch swing which seemed... random. I couldn't picture witches who were known for dabbling in dark magic relaxing on a porch swing and sipping lemonade.

Then my eyes slid toward the gravel driveway, and I spotted the same car Nick had been driving. It shouldn't have surprised me. I had tracked him. But still... I had been so sure I was right about him. Now that I was here, though, I couldn't shake the sinking feeling in the pit of my stomach.

I shuddered as we drew nearer and wondered if I had ever been here. After all, I'd met Reed before. I closed my eyes, grasping at faded memories. But none came.

The lights inside the mansion were on, and we could see silhouettes passing by the windows. The witches were still bustling about inside, so we found a spot behind some bushes and decided to wait them out. Once they were in bed, we'd sneak in.

The plan wasn't to confront Nick directly. If he was working against us, he wouldn't outright tell us. And Xander was convinced that, for whatever reason, my brother couldn't be compelled. So, we were going to sneak in through the back and find Reed's old office. Whoever was running the place, be it Nick or someone else, would have taken up Reed's old room. And if they had, by chance, stolen the magical objects, chances were we'd find them in there.

Hours had passed, and even though we'd eaten a huge dinner, my stomach started to rumble. Xander looked away, undoubtedly pretending he hadn't heard it. But Ben reached into his pocket and handed over a snack bar. "This isn't my first stakeout," he whispered with a wink.

I unwrapped the chocolate chip oatmeal bar and gobbled it up. I could have gone for a glass of water, too, but that would have to wait.

My knees were aching from sitting for so long. I readjusted, trying to give my joints a break. I groaned as I shifted my weight, keeping an eye on the compound all the while. Then I took in a sharp inhale. "The lights are out," I pointed out.

I blinked, waiting for my eyes to adjust to the total and complete darkness. I was startled by the feeling of a large hand on my shoulder, but relaxed when I realized it was just Ben. "Slow down. Lights out doesn't mean they're actually asleep."

Good point.

I sat with my arms hugging my knees, and eventually fell asleep. The nightmares came, as they always did. This time I was hugging a girl—Danielle. I was saying goodbye. Nothing terrifying happened in the dream, per se. It was more of the way it made me feel that was the problem... completely and totally alone in the world.

"Grace," I heard, and the familiar voice pulled me out of my dream. It was Xander. His face was close to mine, his hand on my shoulder, rattling me awake. "Grace, it's time."

Nodding, I got to my feet and followed him and Ben toward the back of the compound.

I pressed ahead of them, seeing as that we were betting that I'd have to use a spell to unlock the door anyway. Letting out a heavy exhale in a failed attempt to calm my nerves, I reached out my hand and tried the knob.

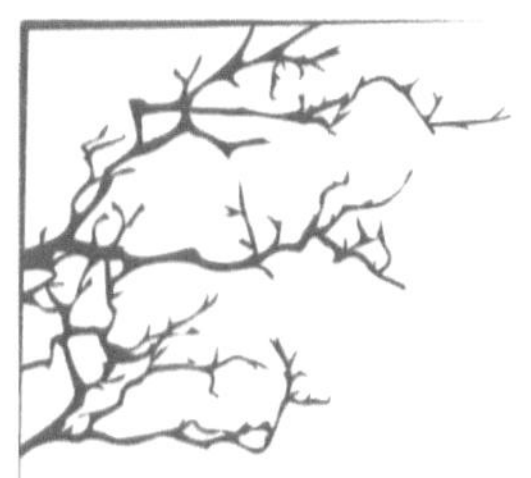

Grace

As expected, the door was locked. It was a good thing I'd insisted on coming. I didn't know how Xander and Ben would have managed to break in. Maybe Xander figured I'd come all along since he "knew me so well" and all.

I closed my eyes and recalled one of the spells I'd studied with the Book Slayers. A surge of energy rushed through me, and then the lock clicked open. It was strange how easily the spell had come to me. And how *right* it felt to recite it. I wondered how much I was really capable of. I reached for the door, but then realized it made more sense for Ben to go in first since he'd been here before. He'd told us where Reed's office was, but he could find it faster than I could.

Ben twisted the handle and pulled the door open. And then, an invisible force slammed into us, throwing us through the air. I landed on my back, writhing in pain. The wind had been knocked out of me, and it was all I could do to gasp. I felt a strange sensation on the side of my head and reached for it. When I drew my hand away it was covered in blood.

Xander was to my right, hand pressed to his ear. I had a feeling he was hearing the same ringing sensation I was. As he turned to push himself up off the ground, our eyes caught. They narrowed for the briefest of moments as if to say *See? I told you something was wrong here.*

But we were the ones trespassing. Of course the witches would defend their home.

A guy that couldn't have been older than seventeen stalked toward us, and the sliver of moonlight glinting off his bright eyes revealed a murderous look about them.

He was holding something in his hand, and as he tossed it to the other, I realized what it was: a wooden stake.

He shook his head. "You really thought you could break in here?" He smiled a dangerous smile. "How stupid are you?"

Ben was scrambling to his feet, reaching for his dagger. As he charged toward the witch, he said something to me: "We'll keep him busy." He said it so quickly that I almost didn't realize what he was telling me to do.

Ben charged at the witch, dagger raised, but the witch blasted him with that same invisible force. Everything in me screamed at me to stay and help—but if I didn't go in there and prove Nick's innocence, all of this would be for nothing.

So, while the witch was distracted with Ben and Xander, I made my move.

Running as fast as my legs could carry me, I slipped inside the house and skidded to make a sharp left turn. I fumbled in the dark until I found the knob and twisted it. Warily, I stepped inside, flicking the light on as I did so.

I scanned the room, taking it all in.

It was hard to imagine *this* was Reed Carlisle's office. Or had been.

I wondered if these were his old things... But that was a silly thought. Surely this stuff belonged to whoever was running the coven now.

I heard a grunt from outside, and I realized I needed to hurry. I rushed toward the desk and started sifting through drawers, looking for anything that resembled the objects that had been stolen. Or anything else that might help prove Nick's innocence.

There was nothing. Just papers and spell books. A few magical objects, but not from Ben's place.

Growing exasperated, I spun around. I wasn't sure how much time I had left—and I needed to get out of here before someone ended up dead outside.

Behind the desk was a filing cabinet. So, I opened it. The first drawer contained a mishmash of random things—one of which made my mouth fall open. I reached inside and retrieved the photograph. It was of two men, one much older than the other. They were smiling, their sunshine-yellow hair glowing in the morning light. The older one had a hardness about him, and yet an undeniable charisma. And I knew at once that that was my father. The other one was my brother.

The rustling was still going on outside, and since I hadn't found anything of note, it was time to get out of here before anyone realized I was in here.

I was sliding the drawer closed when files fell forward, revealing a small safe tucked behind them. I bit my lip, and I reached for it. It was locked, of course. But if I could open a locked door, it stood to reason that I could open a locked safe, too. I closed my eyes and recited the same spell.

And then I jumped when a voice behind me said coolly, "I'm afraid even your magic won't work on that, Grace."

My heart was pounding so hard it felt like it was going to explode. I set the safe down and turned on my heel, mortified that my brother had caught me snooping.

"Look at you," he said. He padded toward me, smiling an off-kilter smile. "I have to admit this isn't nearly as fun as I thought it was going to be."

He veered off-course and reached for a drawer on the wall. He pulled it open and retrieved a rope, which he tightened around his fist. "Sit."

I swallowed. "Nick, please. It's not what you think. I was trying to prove that—"

"I said SIT!" he roared in such a tone that I dared not defy him.

He pinned my hands behind my back and fastened the rope around them. "You're hurting me," I said, which only made him squeeze tighter. The rough texture of the rope scraped against my skin, and I lifted my gaze to look at my brother as he stepped out in front of me. "Why are you doing this?"

"Why am I doing this?" he laughed. "I almost killed you once, you know. But then I thought it might be better to let you live. After all, death is swift. Too easy a fate for you. I wanted you to suffer. And anyway, you being alive made things easier. You were so intent on opening that portal. And all along, I was one step ahead of you. And you never knew, did you?"

A harsh breath escaped my lips. Xander was right. "No," I said, shaking my head in disbelief. "No."

Nick rolled his eyes, as if bored by my bewilderment. He walked around behind me and clasped his hands bony hands around the back of my neck, sending a chill of terror racing down my spine. His fingers trailed along my collar, and he tugged at it, revealing my Mark.

"What are you doing?" I asked.

"Messing with you has been fun and all, but this version of you is rather... boring. I want to see the look in your eyes when I tell you what you've done. And I want you to *understand*."

He pressed his palm against my Mark, what I had until recently presumed to be a tattoo, and uttered a spell under his breath. Everything went woozy, and a rush of memories flashed across my mind's eye all at once. I remembered serving as a blood slave. I remembered the night I met Danielle at the Choosing Ceremony and the unlikely alliance we'd made. I remembered my time with the family that had once ruled over us. I remembered my long history with Xander. I remembered Nick and Reed. I remembered just how evil and demented my father was, and how he'd threatened me and my friends. And I remembered the night I killed him. I remembered that strange smile that had flicked across his face before he mumbled something to himself. I remembered *everything*.

All at once, the flood of memories stopped. And I realized I was shaking.

Nick placed his finger under my chin and lifted it, forcing me to match his gaze. And there it was again. That smile.

"*You*," I said, voice quivering. "It's been you all along, hasn't it?"

A sense of pride washed over him, and he straightened. "Welcome back, my daughter."

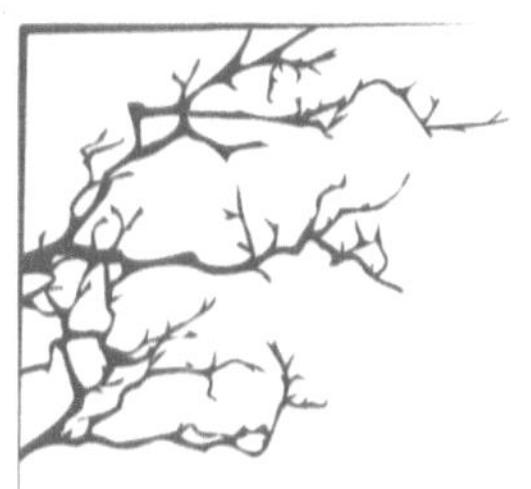

Bellamy

Nathaniel banged on my door. He hadn't told me he was coming over, but I knew it was him by his distinctive knock. Two quick taps followed by a pause and two slower taps. With a sigh, I set my comic book on the nightstand and got up to let him in.

Nathaniel was sporting one of his signature preppy looks with perfectly coiffed hair to match. He looked me up and down, his brown eyes filled with judgment, and shook his head. "Come on, Bells. Why are you still moping?"

"I'm not moping."

"You're in your *Star Wars* PJs—and you only wear those when you're moping. Did you and Grace break up?"

"What? No."

He walked past me, inviting himself in. "Everyone at work keeps saying you look like a zombie. You're spacing out constantly. It's like your head is somewhere else. And you already told me you're not on the pain meds anymore, so what's going on? If you and Grace didn't break up, what's the problem? I thought she came back and things were okay."

I plopped myself on the leather couch and rested my face in my hands. "She was back. But then she left."

Nathaniel scrunched his eyebrows, looking as confused as I felt. "What do you mean she left? She's flaked out on you twice now?"

I shook my head. "She didn't flake out. Her friend was in the hospital."

He narrowed his brown eyes, not buying any of it. "Weren't you in the hospital when she first ditched you?"

"Actually, I was here."

Nathaniel placed his hand on my shoulder. "How are you healing, by the way?"

I lifted my shirt, revealing my abdomen. Nathaniel leaned back, cocking his head to the side. "That looks gnarly." He shivered. "So, anyway... we were talking about Grace. You said that she came back to tell you that she was leaving again?"

"No, she planned to stay. But then some guy named Xander showed up and told her that his uncle was in the hospital. Then she got all weird and left."

"An uncle, huh?"

"No, really. His uncle is that travel blogger in Quarter Square. Apparently, he's an old friend of Grace's."

"Wait. You don't mean that blogger my mom is all googly-eyes over?" Shaking his head, Nathaniel got up and helped himself to a beer in my fridge. He brought one over to me, too. He took a long swig before setting it down on the coffee table and resting his hand on his knees. "Have you texted her?"

"She lost her phone."

He looked at me for a moment as if he were debating what to say. I knew the whole thing must sound stupid from his perspective. I trusted Grace, though.

"How much do you really know about this Grace girl anyway?"

"What are you getting at?" I asked, a defensive tone rising in my throat.

"Madison said she just showed up at the Sunny Side Grille out of the blue one day."

"So?"

He shrugged. "Maybe it's nothing." He started tapping his finger on his kneecap. "Have you stalked her on social media?"

"That would require me using social media, remember?"

"Oh, right. I forget you're still living in the Dark Ages." He pulled out his phone. "What's her last name again?"

"Addington."

He typed in the name and frowned. "She's not on Facebook." He began pulling up other apps, too. "Or Twitter. Or any other social media site."

"Maybe she's not into that stuff either."

He shot me a look, then got back to typing.

"What are you doing now?" I asked, growing bored with sitting and waiting for him to find whatever it was that he was looking for.

"Googling her."

"Seriously, Nathaniel?"

"You can't just date someone without looking up everything about them. What if she's some sort of psycho?"

I was starting to get angry. "She is *not* some psycho. She left to go visit someone in the hospital. She'll come back." I snatched the phone out of his hands. I was sick of this. I cared about Grace, and I didn't need to Google her past to prove that she was trustworthy. But the first search result caught my eye when I jerked the phone from Nathaniel, and I couldn't help but read it.

"What?" he asked, leaning in closer so that he could see, too. "What did you find?"

"Oh," I gulped, "just about a hundred articles about a missing person who perfectly fits the name and description of my girlfriend."

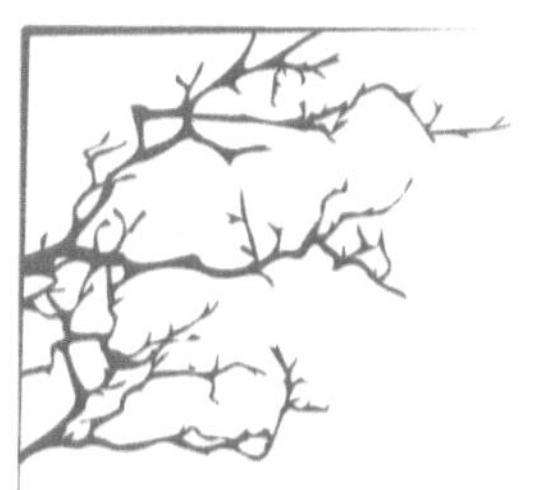

Grace

"That's impossible," I said breathlessly. My head was spinning. I'd killed him myself. I'd *watched* him die. And then it hit me.

Back in Quarter Square, I'd read about something in one of the grimoires...

But it couldn't be. That was downright evil, even for Reed.

Or was it? My disgusting excuse for a father was evil incarnate.

"What did you do to Nick?" I hissed, fighting now with all my might to break free from the restraints. The chair rocked from side to side, its legs thumping against the wooden floor. Yes, I had my powers. And now, I *finally* remembered how to use them. But I needed my hands in order to cast spells.

Reed just smirked. "You know, I was impressed when I learned it had taken Sofia two vials of powder to wipe your memories. That's my girl." He winked. "I had your memories wiped to get you out of the way. But I have to admit it's so much more enjoyable now that you're fighting back, Grace."

"What did you do to him?" I hissed.

He cocked his head to the side. "I think you already know."

"Body jumping." I shook my head in disgust. "You switched consciousnesses with Nick, didn't you? That's why you were mumbling to yourself as I killed you! You were casting a spell!"

Reed only eyed me, enjoying watching me putting the pieces together. "I did warn you about the prophecy, didn't I? Carlisle twins—one good, one evil. One destined to kill the other."

"Nick was good—in spite of you! He was good. And you... you..."

He cackled. "Who said I was talking about Nick?"

I gritted my teeth so hard they ached. "You killed him, not me. You were the one who was supposed to die that night." And then the reality that I'd spent four entire years thinking this *monster* before me was my twin set in. How had I not put the pieces together sooner? "How did you do it? How did you keep the act up for so long? And why are you giving yourself away now? Is this the part where you rattle off some ridiculous monologue before you kill me?"

"I never said anything about killing you, Grace," he said coolly. "You're the one who broke into my office. You were the one rummaging through my things. Believe me, if I wanted you dead right now, you'd be dead."

"Then what's the point of all of this?"

He laughed. "Now that you're the last of my bloodline, I have rather big plans for you. But that'll come much later." He clasped his hands behind his back and paced, smiling in amusement at my current situation. "As for why, well, it won't hurt to share that with you now. I needed to keep you from opening the portal. At least, until I was ready for it to be opened."

"Why? What difference does it make to you? You already outed the supernaturals. You already won."

He snickered at that. "You think that was the end of my plan? Oh, Grace. I'm just getting started." He stopped short and rubbed his chin. Turning toward me, he asked, "Did I ever tell you about what happened to my father?"

I shook my head. Between him making up stories about stupid prophecies, vowing to bring down the Blood Heirs and starting a war between the supernaturals and humans, it hadn't come up.

Paying no mind to the look of contempt on my face, Reed continued with his tale. "I know it might be hard for you to understand since you weren't raised within the coven—"

"Because you threw me aside like I was a piece of garbage."

"Because I was trying to protect Nick from you," he hissed. "You were stronger than him, even as a baby. The Carlisle *men* are the ones who are meant to lead." His eyes flashed, but then an eerie calm took over. "As I was saying, once, the Carlisle and Albright covens were united. But thanks to Claudia Albright casting the spell that turned the siblings, our covens became bitter rivals. Once Claudia died, her coven was overwhelmed with guilt. They created the boundary around Crescent Cape—even sent their witches to live with the Blood Heirs. Meanwhile, our coven committed ourselves to actively working against them. Centuries passed, and then my father came into power. It was his dream to reunite the covens. We'd never been able to take out the vampires and werewolves on our own. But perhaps, if we formed an alliance with our rival coven, together we could be the undoing of the prince and his siblings. Anyway, my father had arranged to meet up with Jonathan Albright, the leader at that time, at a designated spot in the woods. But when he arrived, Prince Aiden was there waiting. He *killed* your grandfather."

He said that as if that was supposed to mean something to me. I never knew my grandfather, and I already had a million other reasons why Aiden was not one of my favorite people. "And?"

"You asked me *why* I'm doing this, and I'm telling you. I was just a boy when my father was killed. It took years for me to build up my coven to the glory of what it once was. It took years of secret meetings with the Albrights to earn their trust. It took years of conspiring with witches in other realms to unleash my wrath upon that wretched family. And I'm just getting started."

I feigned a yawn, not willing to give him the satisfaction of reacting to his big reveal of what was undoubtedly a diabolical plan. "And?"

"Torturing the family was for my amusement. And I must admit, it did bring me great joy. But now, I will get the ultimate revenge. I will *undo* them."

My brow wrinkled. "Undo them?"

"I believe I have discovered a way to lift the curses of vampirism and lycanthropy. To strip the vampires and werewolves of their power. To make them human. Not just the Blood Heirs and Julian—all of them. And then," he said, flashing a bright white smile, "when they are at their weakest, when they have no choice but to beg for my mercy, I will get my revenge."

I balled my hands into fists. I could feel my blood boiling. Reed was downright psychotic. And *idiotic* if he thought for one second that I'd let him lay a hand on any of my friends. Anger swelled in my chest and spiderwebbed through my veins.

A pain-stricken cry echoed into the night, and my thoughts jumped to Ben. He'd drank Xander's blood earlier today. If he died with it in his system...

I shot daggers at Reed with my eyes and narrowed them. I unleashed a surge of power from my fingertips. I'd thought my magic wouldn't do me any good while I was tied up, but I didn't need to attack him—yet. I needed to get free.

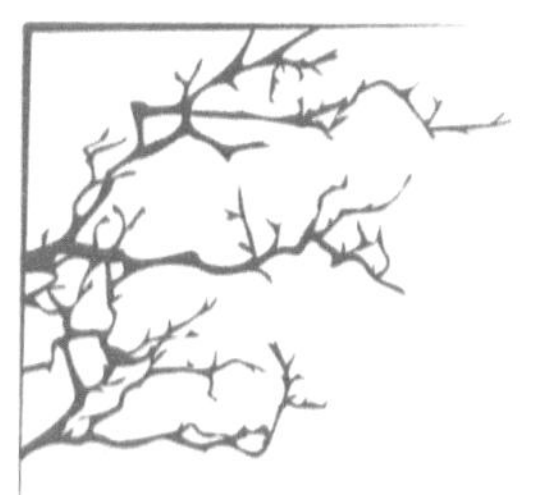

Grace

Flames singed the ropes that bound my wrists, and their ashes fell to the ground. My wrists were raw and red and oozing with blood, and I could smell my burning flesh, but I swallowed the pain. Shoving the chair back as I bolted upright, I channeled all of my anger toward my father.

I thought of how he had abandoned me as a child, all while keeping my twin as his own. I thought of how he had tormented my friends. I thought of how much death and destruction had occurred because of his supernatural war. I thought of what a coward he was to have swapped consciousnesses with Nick, making me murder *him* instead—his own son. I thought of the years he spent keeping up the charade, manipulating my emotions. I thought of how he had thwarted my quests to obtain faerie dust—the one ingredient I needed in order to unseal the portal and get Danielle back. I thought of how he had robbed me of my memories and tortured Xander. I thought of all the time he had stolen from me. And finally, I thought of how much I hated him.

Reed might be powerful, but so was I.

Letting my rage fuel me, an overwhelming surge of power coursed through me. A flash of energy escaped my palms, and Reed slammed against the door.

I thought about making a run for it, but I realized that if I had any hope of interfering with his plans, the best way to do so was to get my hands on the magical objects he stole. I didn't have time to search his whole office, but I was betting I knew where the most valuable of them was hiding.

While Reed was getting to his feet, I darted for the filing cabinet and pulled out the safe. But I felt a strong force thrash against my back, knocking the air out of me. The safe thudded on the floor as my chest caved. I struggled to breathe.

Just then, the office door burst open. Witches filed into the room, curious to see what the commotion was about. Reed told them the situation was under control, but I wasn't going to go quietly. Channeling the storm of emotions brewing within me, I swished my hands while I uttered a spell, making the air in the room swirl like a tornado. Strands of my blonde hair whipped wildly against my cheeks, and some of the other witches in the room reached for the tables and bookshelves—anything they could hold on to. One wasn't so lucky and got swept up in my windstorm. She flew through the air and hit her head on the ceiling before falling swiftly to the ground.

Two more figures emerged from the shadowy hall, the taller one covering his face with his forearm to shield himself from the wind. Thinking at first that it was more witches rushing to Reed's defense, I readied myself to blow the winds in their direction.

But then a familiar voice called out to me. "Grace!"

Xander. My heart jumped. I wanted to tell him that I had my memories back. That I knew exactly who he was now—and that I remembered how much he meant to me. I remembered our friendship, our history. And I was so sorry for how I'd spoken to him in recent days. If I'd only known…

As he stepped forward, I realized something was lodged into his chest. A wooden stake. Devastation washed over me, and I let out a shriek. The winds fell silent, and the papers, books and trinkets that had been swirling overhead came to a sudden halt and rained down upon us.

"I take it that I was right," was all that Xander said as he reached for the stake that was wedged in his chest and removed it, groaning as blood gushed from the wound. As soon as it was out, he held the scarlet-stained weapon in his hand and twirled it, aiming the sharp end toward the person he *thought* was my brother.

How was that possible? He'd said he was stronger than most vampires. But how could a vampire take a stake to the chest—and live?

The witches linked hands while Reed just stood there smiling. They began chanting, and all at once, the glass window behind me shattered. A gust a hundred times stronger than the one I'd used against them thrust Xander, Ben and me out the window. We slammed into the rough gravel and broken glass. There was blood everywhere, and it felt like I had a thousand needles piercing my skin. My head was throbbing, and my surroundings faded in and out. I knew I was losing consciousness, but there was nothing I could do to stop it.

Reed was cackling like the maniac he was. As his minions circled behind him, he stepped forward, daring Xander—who was already back on his feet—to make the first move.

My headache started to overwhelm me. I closed my eyes. Ben was shouting for Xander to stop, but Xander let out a feral sound, and I knew he wasn't just going to walk away.

I tried opening my mouth to call out his name, but I was in too much agony. I forced my eyes open, watching in anticipation and terror as the world went all wibbly-wobbly around me.

Not one to back down, Xander stumbled forward. His shirt was saturated with blood now, but his wound had started to heal.

I didn't understand—I thought wooden stakes were fatal to vampires. But he was still very much alive. Well, as alive as a vampire could be...

He charged toward Reed, his brow furrowed in such determination that I had no doubt he'd rip all of the witches' hearts out—and enjoy every second of it. But then he slammed into an invisible force so hard that it knocked him onto his back.

"Xander," I managed to call out, my voice uncharacteristically weak as I free-fell into darkness.

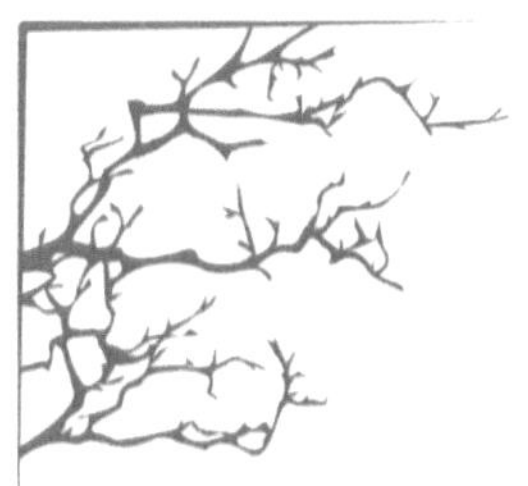

Xander

I pounded my fist against the gravel, a guttural growl exploding from my lungs. The Carlisle witches had cast a boundary spell around their compound. But this wasn't the same kind of boundary spell that once enveloped Crescent Cape, merely hiding it from the outside world. I could still see them as plain as day standing in that mess of an office with stupid satisfied grins on their faces.

Nick padded forward, shaking his head. "*Tsk Tsk Tsk.* Looks like a nasty wound," he said, gesturing with his head toward Grace, who I now realized was sprawled across the ground, passed out cold. Uncle Ben was curled into a ball on the ground, and I thanked my lucky stars he was still breathing. Since he'd ingested some of my blood earlier today, if he'd been killed, he would have begun to transition. And he'd hold that against me for the rest of his immortal life. "I suggest you tend to her before it's too late."

"Why would you let us go?" I asked, throwing my hands up in the air. "What's the point of all of this? Why not just kill us now?"

He threw his head back in laughter. Then an eerie calm came over him, and his blazing blue eyes narrowed. "Oh, Xander. Believe me, when I want you dead, you will be." He shooed me away like a fly. "Go on, now."

Everything in me wanted to beat the living daylights out of that little rat, but I'd been around long enough to know when it was time to stand down. With Grace unconscious, there would be no way to get through that boundary spell.

Ignoring the witches' snickering, I marched over to Uncle Ben and helped him to his feet. "Can you walk?" I asked.

He winced as he nodded. "I'll be okay. It's just my arm." He jerked his head to Grace. "Go get your girl."

I let out a heavy exhale as I walked toward her. It was a strange thing to see Grace unconscious—she looked so helpless. I crouched down and scooped her up in my arms. She had a nasty gash across her forehead, and shards of broken glass had scraped her cheeks and hands. Her leather jacket had shielded her from the worst of it at least. She needed help, but not here. Not where her demon-spawn brother and his henchmen could see. I didn't want to give them the satisfaction.

"Xander—" Uncle Ben started in an urging tone.

"Not here."

"Then go ahead. I'll catch up."

I hesitated, not wanting to leave him out here with these people. Who knew what they would do to him?

He motioned for me to go. "Save her."

I nodded in appreciation and told him where to meet me. It was a spot not too far from here, but far enough out of sight from the witches.

Using my supernatural speed, I fled through the forest carrying Grace in my arms. I found an opening in the trees where the silver moonlight splashed across the ground as if shining a spotlight in the place where I laid her. "Grace," I whispered, cradling her face in my palm.

Knowing what I had to do, I willed my fangs to emerge from my gums. They ripped through them, and I sank my needlelike teeth into my wrist until the blood began to flow. I pressed my finger to Grace's soft lower lip and pressed it down. My finger trailed down to her chin, and with the right amount of pressure, her mouth opened. I clenched my fist, making the blood pour faster. Vampire blood ran slower than humans' did, but it flowed all the same. "Come on, Grace," I said, even though she couldn't hear me. "Wake up. Please."

The seconds stretched on for what felt like an eternity, but then her eyes fluttered open as she gasped for air. Tears streamed down her cheeks, the salty liquid mixing with the blood. "The glass," she cried out, writhing, "it hurts."

Of course. Hurriedly, I searched her body for shards of broken glass that had been lodged into her flesh, apologizing profusely as I plucked each one out of her. Grace was as tough as nails, but broken glass hurt no matter how strong you were. She moaned, tossing and turning and flinching. I did my best to calm her, but to little effect. She was crying harder now, and I started to wonder if it was really because of the glass after all.

"Here," I said, offering her more blood. She took my wrist in her hands and pulled it to her mouth, drinking hard as she whimpered.

With my free hand, I brushed her blood-soaked hair away from her face. Using my thumb, I wiped away the blood and dirt from her cheeks while she drank.

Finally, her head fell back to the ground. She looked defeated.

"What's wrong?" I asked.

She slipped her hand into mine as her eyes turned into half-moons. Tears spilled out of them, and she sat up, now throwing her arms around my neck as she sobbed heavily.

"Grace?" I asked, unsure of what to do or say.

"My memories are back," she said, trembling. "I'm so sorry, Xander." She pulled away, and I realized her lips were quivering. I'd never seen this side of her. I'd never seen her look so broken.

I placed my palm on her cheek, hardly believing what she was saying was true. "There's nothing to be sorry for. It was Nick, wasn't it? He put the Albrights up to this."

She shook her head. "No, you don't understand. That's *not* my brother."

I looked back over my shoulder, even though the compound was far out of sight. Then, I looked back at her. "I'm not following."

"It was Reed all along," she said between sobs. And then she told me everything.

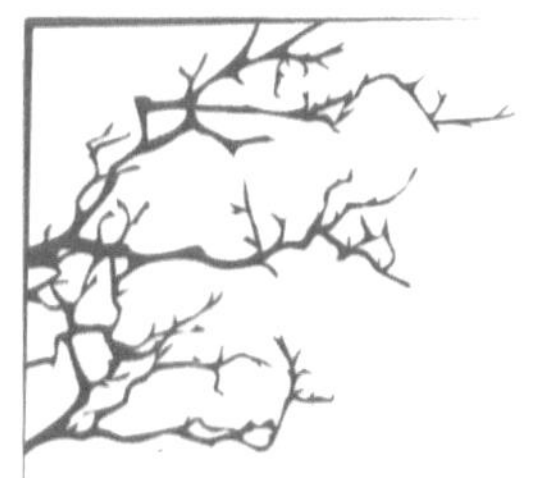

Grace

"There," I said as my arms fell to my side, the remnants of the magic I'd used still tingling my fingertips. As soon as we'd returned to Ben's house, I'd figured it'd be smart to create a boundary similar to the one the Carlisle witches had put up around his home. One that would keep any unwanted supernaturals out. "That should do it."

Ben wiped his brow, still bloodied and bruised from the events of the evening. He was sitting on the couch since his favorite La-Z-Boy recliner had been destroyed the other night. Fangs was in his lap, licking at his wounds and whining in concern. He ruffled the creamy curled fur on top of her head. "It's okay, girl." She nuzzled her face against his chest and relaxed as he continued to love on her. "Here," he said to her, rising to stand. "You deserve some fun tonight. You want to play fetch? Where's your ball?"

Fangs barked and leaped from the couch. She scrambled around the corner, sliding on the wooden floor as she did so. She quickly returned from the hall with her tennis ball in tow, and Ben led her to the backyard.

Xander finished downing his third bottle of the "red drink"—Ben always kept some handy—and crossed the room to meet me where I stood. He dropped his head to look at me.

With a tug at the corner of his lips, he said, "It's good to have you back, Grace."

I looked into his dark brown eyes, hardened after centuries of anger and loss and regret, and yet somehow gentle all at the same time. I hugged my arms around myself, feigning a chill even thought I wasn't really cold. "Can I ask you something?"

"Anything."

I drew my lower lip between my teeth, searching for the right way to phrase this. "What happened back in New York? I remember the attack now, of course. I mean before that."

His chest rose and fell, and he glanced up for a second before looking back at me. "I never should have picked that fight with you. It's just... it's hard wanting something so badly and feeling like you can never have it." He paused, and the way he was looking at me made me wonder if he was referring to the faerie dust, or me. Squaring his shoulders back, he continued, "I was being stupid and irrational. You were right all along. And now that we know what Reed's up to, we have to find a way to stop him."

I pressed my lips together and nodded. "Of course. And those magical objects..."

"We won't stop until we track down each and every one of them. We now know Reed wasn't working alone, and who's to say Sofia Albright is his only ally?"

"I can run tracking spells on the objects," I offered. "Then we can go from there."

"And then, we'll work on tracking down some faerie dust and getting Julian, Charlotte and Danielle back," Xander said, stuffing his hands in the back pockets of his dark jeans. "So, can

I get you a drink or something? I never did get to toast to your birthday, you know."

"Actually, I was thinking I'd head over to my place. I want to get cleaned up," I said, tugging at my blood-stained hair and showing it to him. "I was thinking I could pack up some things and then come back here. Even with the boundary spell, I don't feel right about leaving Ben alone again."

"You do know that wasn't your fault, right?"

"I know."

"Well, would you like a ride?"

Seeing as that the alternative was walking, I nodded. "That'd be great."

Xander headed toward the door and was getting ready to open it for me when we heard a knock from the other side. His lips twisted with suspicion, but he opened it anyway. I could see a figure of a man in the shadows. Xander cleared his throat and stepped out of the way, allowing the light from inside the house to illuminate my view.

My mouth fell open. A surge of shock, dread and guilt coursed through my veins. *"Bellamy?"*

About the Author

L . Danvers' goal as a writer is to offer readers an escape from reality—one in which they can explore new worlds, go on daring adventures, fight the bad guys and fall in love... all from the comfort of a cozy chair.

Her books are romantic, fast-paced and suitable for both teens and adults.

When she's not writing, you can find her in the kitchen trying out new recipes.

Get your FREE COPY of Blood Heirs (the prequel to Vampires of Crescent Cape) by joining her Readers' Group: www.ldanvers.com/subscribe.